WHERE THE LEAVES FALL

By: C.L. Arbo

Copyright © 2017 Kathy Oyama.

All rights reserved. No part of this book may be reproduced, stored, or transmitted by any means—whether auditory, graphic, mechanical, or electronic—without written permission of the author, except in the case of brief excerpts used in critical articles and reviews. Unauthorized reproduction of any part of this work is illegal and is punishable by law.

ISBN: 978-1-4834-7294-2 (sc)
ISBN: 978-1-4834-7293-5 (e)

Because of the dynamic nature of the Internet, any web addresses or links contained in this book may have changed since publication and may no longer be valid. The views expressed in this work are solely those of the author and do not necessarily reflect the views of the publisher, and the publisher hereby disclaims any responsibility for them.

Any people depicted in stock imagery provided by Thinkstock are models, and such images are being used for illustrative purposes only.
Certain stock imagery © Thinkstock.

Lulu Publishing Services rev. date: 09/06/2017

This book is dedicated to my loving husband Angelo and my beautiful children Dorian and Alina that I love with all my heart.

Christy

Chapter One

THIS WAS ANOTHER REALM. Imposing marble columns, ceilings high as stars, an atrium, pool house, billiard room and who knows what else this Chicagoland mansion encompassed in its mighty walls. Sleek servers carrying silver and gold trays with microscopic food and champagne flutes glided along the shiny floors. Even a pianist poured notes into a baby grand in one of the barren, beige corners.

"Rich people," I groaned under my breath, sliding my fingers down my black cocktail dress. I glanced down at my satin red pumps and let a little laugh escape. *There's no place like home,* I entertained the thought. But I refrained from clicking them together.

Seriously, I couldn't help but wonder what I was getting myself into.

Then, sensing discomfort, Gavin draped his arms around me from behind. He displayed chiseled elegance, as if he could chop wood outside a rustic cabin and then strut a Hollywood red carpet in the tux he was wearing tonight. His embrace was so sweet and warm. I remembered why I entered this world in the first place.

"You look beautiful. Relax, this is *our* party-my bride," he said.

I searched his blue-gray eyes for serenity and then gazed at the 2-carat emerald-cut diamond, which overwhelmed its host, the thin ring finger on my left hand. It glistened in the soft lights, as if feeling at home in its ritzy surroundings. I combed that and my fingers through my long, raven hair that was in thick curls for the occasion.

The diamond felt more in place than me. I decided to fake it through.

"I'm ready, my future husband."

"Future? If you don't watch out, I might marry you tonight."

Gavin squeezed me before leading us into the main room to his parents, who were greeting guests as if they were royalty. His mother, Joan, set down her champagne glass on a passing waiter's tray without asking him to stop. Then she kissed us both on cheeks without actually pressing her lips against them as not to smudge her powder-pink lipstick.

"You look darling, my dear," she complemented me between air puckers.

"Yes," Carl said with his chin naturally inclining upward. "Glad you agreed to let us throw this soiree. I know there was some reluctance, but it meant so much for us to do this for our only son."

"Only son and only child," Joan said, beaming at Gavin.

"Of course. Thank you for the engagement party." I knew I was shyly looking at the floor, fidgeting with the black clutch. I had bartered the purse down fifteen dollars at a trendy vintage store before declining the Chanel sequined version Gavin tried presenting me for the party.

These people traveled more than anyone I'd ever known and that was the main reason-along with a short courtship to their son-I had never seen their ridiculously large and embarrassingly expensive house. Previously, we'd just met over dinner at stuffy restaurants that served food I never knew existed.

"Senator, may I have a moment?" A short, thin man interrupted Carl.

"Sure," he said, winking at me before politely bowing out of the conversation as Joan chatted with another guest.

Gavin shrugged as if to say, "This happens all the time."

"When you finish law school, you're not getting into politics, right?" I wanted reassurance.

"No." He craned his neck to his father. "Hell no," he said laughing.

As the clearly talented pianist played Chopin's Waltz in E Minor, the equally fast steps of Natalia's patent leather Mary Janes could be heard on the floor. She ran to me and I quickly spun her around, relieved to see her glowing face.

"What are you doing here?" I asked in surprise of my eight-year-old sister.

"Mom let me come because I begged and begged." She paused, searching for the signs of an actual party. No cake. No clowns. Not even balloons. "But, this party is *boring.*"

"That's because it's only for adults," I winked at her. Sixteen years her senior, it was almost like I was her second mom. I changed diapers, gave bottles and even drove her to school and friend's sleepovers. It wasn't a typical age difference between siblings, but it worked well for us. I couldn't wait to return home to take her to cider mills and Halloween festivities while soaking in the ever-evolving leaf colors on the abundant maples and oak trees looming over our quiet, hard-working neighborhood just outside Detroit. It was an autumn ritual for us to pack in as many weekend daytrips in September and October as possible.

"I might be able to score some ice cream for you," Gavin said.

"No wonder you're my favorite son-in-law," Flora said as she caught up with us.

"I'll be your only son-in-law," Gavin smiled at the petite, curvy woman with the same raven hair as mine.

Her floral JCPenny dress stood out among the sea of black and white. It didn't faze her, though-if one thing never entered her mind, it was the thought of impressing others. "They're no better than you or me," she had told me as I mentioned how "different they were from us." Just because someone has money doesn't mean you need to work for their approval. Sometimes, it's the ones with the most money who have the lowest morals," she said in her schoolteacher tone. "Not Gavin, though. He's a keeper. Just look at the way he looks at you and how kind he's treated you. I'm so happy for you two."

Money was tight when I was Natalia's age, although a child rarely comprehends the extent of financial hardship. Foggy memories of walking hand-in-hand with my mother on the side of a busy road to the closest gas station because she held out paying for gas as long as possible to get home, clinging to the possibility she could putter just one more mile past the red bar pointing sharply at E. Then there were the times when I stood look-out at Kmart while she quickly switched the hangers with cheaper price tags printed on them for her garments. That was before the days of price tags attached directly on clothes and, with some creative finagling, a ten-dollar dress went for five. Of course, there were flea markets and dollar store runs, all of which seemed fun for a young unquestioning girl who merely enjoyed spending time with her fun-loving mother who never indicated the severity of her worries. And so on and so on, the examples were like sheep in a sleepy child's head. But more prosperous times followed and Natalia's upbringing mirrored nothing of the sort. It was an ongoing joke in the family with me often affectionately asking my parents: "Why did you have me when you were poor?" To which my loving mother would reply, "I had to. You're the one who made me rich." My father would crane his neck back from over the Business Section of The Detroit Chronicle and call out to the kitchen, "since when are we rich? Are you hiding a secret stash?"

"It was a metaphor...and yes, I am. My other husband won't let you have it though."

I smiled at the thought. My family was now what's considered middle class with a 1,500-square-foot home in a suburban neighborhood surrounded by shopping plazas, Starbucks and fast-food restaurants and, evidencing metro Detroit's urban sprawl over old farmlands. I had moved into a loft-style apartment within Detroit a couple years ago, but every chance I got, I was back in my parents' house, playing euchre with relatives and whisking Natalia off to somewhere fun. The Wilson Air National Guard Base was only five miles away from the home and, on any given day, powerful military jets, mainly F-16s, roared overhead. The neighborhood kids enjoyed that. For Natalia, the introductory enjoyment blossomed to a flat-out obsession, compounded by the discovery of Amelia Earhart at our recent trip to the public library. Her aviation-inspired bedroom decor décor featured pictures of the flying legend and, despite my mother and I telling her none of her friends would know whom she was dressed as, Natalia's heart was set on being Earhart for Halloween. Most girls were into the latest teen pop star, my sister was infatuated with someone who died decades before she entered this world. Damn, she was a cool kid-at least in my own biased eyes.

"I wish dad could have made it to this party," I said. My mother shook her head and said there was nothing he could do. "Work is work."

A velvet voice along the piano music entered our ears. Sierra's long, dark-red locks were tucked under themselves with a pearl clip peeking out. 'This is for my best friend and a very lucky man right over there," she noted before singing Norah Jones' "Come Away With Me." Always the entertainer, Sierra was set on becoming a bona fide star. We became fast friends in elementary school and stayed close ever since.

While I studied hard to make good grades through college and did internship after internship between bartending jobs, she envisioned herself on the fast track to fame. And she had the goods to back up the ego. Singing, dancing and acting were her life. Her agent was on her speed dial and she made monthly trips to New York and L.A. for auditions. She was even in a couple low-budget movies after Michigan declared itself the "Hollywood of the Midwest" with a tax break for films produced in the state. I tried not to indicate how dreadful the first one was to sit through. It was about people who turned into werewolves when vampires drained their blood on full-moon nights. Real original, I thought. Yet, Sierra made it tolerable with her rendition of a vampiress who stalked the town in very little clothing and commanded minions to bow to her stilettos. The other was supposedly a comedy that took place at a high school. The jokes barely got any laughs at the independent art theatre, but Sierra was fascinating as a materialistic Lolita. In reality, she mainly did catalog modeling to pay the bills--her portion of our bills, that is, since she moved in with me about a month ago when her most recent boyfriend kicked her out of his spacious house for seeing someone on the side.

The song wasn't over yet when a not-so-tuned, over-the-top '50s-lounge-singer voice beat into the microphone. "Come away with me...to the bar." Then he hollered, "Yeah, I'm talking to you, Gavin. Let's get a drink!" Best man Jeremy, clad in tux, wearing ridiculously dark and bulky sunglasses and a goofy faux rose in his pocket. Amused, Sierra graciously applauded and then playfully snapped away the mike. Jeremy bowed to her and kissed her hand.

"Bravo," Gavin said among applause and laughter from the crowd. "Okay, let's get that drink, cheese ball."

At the seemingly endless, angular bar the two pals did shots of Jack Daniel's. First one, for Gavin getting engaged two weeks before on the tour boat docking at Navy Pier, where we had met just six months prior when Sierra and I were on a mini-vacation. The second, to the last year of law school. The third, to Jeremy trying to get Sierra's number. Jeremy pressed on, but Gavin waved his hand. "No more, man. I have to be on my best behavior. This is the most important night of my life-to date."

"What's that sound?" Jeremy seemed alarmed. He cupped his hand behind his blond, spiky hair.

Gavin stared, unamused.

"It's the inexplicable and tragic noise of one's manhood going out the window."

"How exactly do you plan on having a legal career?" Gavin mused while changing the subject, knowing full well his friend earned straight As while barely glimpsing the books. A stellar brain, a late bloomer in the maturity department.

"Just plan to work my charm on the female judges."

"And the men, too?" Sierra coyly chimed in, taking a seat on the barstool next to Jeremy like a vixen in a nineteen-forties B movie.

"Oh, especially the men," I jabbed him sweetly behind her.

Jeremy sighed. "It's not too late for you to run away with me, Roni. You know this guy will never love you like I do." He clutched his heart and nearly fell off the stool as I cracked up. Sierra pretended to kick him on the floor. He fumbled a bit down there in drunken clumsiness.

"Okay Sinatra. Let's get some air," Gavin said, heading to the backdoor with him. He placed Jeremy's arm around his built frame, brushed back his gelled sandy hair and parted the crowd with a smile on his face.

Guest after guest strolled up to congratulate me. Many of them were Carl's influential friends. Some were politicians like him. Others were entrepreneurs, corporate high rollers, and social climbers.

"He couldn't ask for a more beautiful wife," one said.

"You'll have gorgeous children," another declared.

"Are you ready to be the wife of a powerful attorney?"

I felt dizzy. No one ever bothered to ask me anything about, well...me.

The whirlwind screeched to a halt when I saw Natalia's wide, blue eyes and beaming smile. Her curly, light-brown hair was taken down from her ponytail and she had removed her Mary Janes, her feet just covered with tights. Gavin made good on his promise. The ice cream was dripping down her purple-and-green dress.

"Mmmm, chocolate chip."

It wasn't until some guests began to leave that I realized I hadn't seen Gavin since he took Jeremy out for air about an hour before. I went to look for him when my mother and Natalia announced it was time for them to go.

"It's a long night for her and we need to get back to the hotel. We leave Chicago tomorrow to get home early to Detroit. I'll see you back home in a few days," Flora said, giving the place a final look-over. "Everything was nice. Real nice."

The three of us hugged interchangeably. They felt like home.

For a few minutes, I listened to Sierra's story about how an overweight politician twice her age offered to give her a ride back to the hotel-with his wife standing right there in horror. "As if," she rolled her eyes. Then, thunder roared outside. I peeked out and saw only clear skies above the upscale neighborhood of Pleasant Farms outside Chicago. That wasn't the sound of a storm rolling in, I gathered. It was the horrific mashing of steel!

Heels clicked over the floor, men cursed as we all rushed outside. Silence ensued. No one could speak for what seemed like minutes -- especially me, feeling the blood drain from my face.

At the end of the meandering driveway was the aptly named Main Street. The problem with the Remers' estate was that their unusually long driveway was nearly invisible to passersby on Main. Where the driveway merged with the street, the almost unrecognizable Dodge Charger my mom and sister were in was T-boned by a pickup truck. With Sierra sprinting behind, I rushed down the driveway. Shards of glass peppered the asphalt. Scraps from both vehicles lay nearby. The burnt smell of deployed airbags permeated the night air.

From outside the car, I didn't hear my mother make a peep. The blood seeping from her body meshed into the flowers printed on her dress.

Without moving, Natalia moaned as her eyes remained closed. A passing police officer slammed to a stop and yelled for me to stay back. Sierra had to restrain me from ignoring his orders. That's when I saw it, something in my peripheral near the pickup truck. It was moving.

"It" was a person. A man on the ground with blood covering his clothes. It was difficult to tell what the man looked like from roughly fifty feet away in the encompassing night. I could only make out the dark, maybe black, clothes and a glimpse of blond hair. Short, spiky blond hair ... belonging to Jeremy, lying outside the exploded passenger door of the pickup. My heart raced. I knew what I was about to discover with shell-shocked eyes. The driver in the strange pickup was Gavin.

All of the evening's elation, social graces, polished styling and, especially, feeling of soaring promise lay unimaginably shattered at the driveway's end. A gallery of stunned faces, alternately lit red and blue, formed a silent half-circle around the blood and wreckage.

"Roni! Get in the ambulance!" Sierra shook the frozen statue that was me. "You need to go with them! They won't let me because I'm not kin. Go and I'll meet you at the hospital."

Nearly paralyzed with fear, I stepped into the ambulance as if in a trance. The medic pulled me up by the hand while the female driver slammed the door behind us. There was Natalia strapped onto a gurney; the male medic began performing CPR as the ambulance screamed down the street.

"Talk to her," he said between chest compressions and counting.

I shook in disbelief. *This can't be happening.*

"It helps when you say something," he calmly coaxed me.

"Natalia..." I didn't know where to begin. "Breathe. Breathe. Don't go anywhere. I'm here."

Tears streamed down my face, mascara rolling like a silent avalanche indicating the crumbling of my universe.

"Breathe, Natalia!" I screamed.

The medic stopped, slid back in the ambulance and met the eyes of his distraught passenger. My throat was dry and burning.

"She's breathing. It's going to be all right."

I was trembling. I wiped tears away and clutched my scratchy throat with wet fingers. The momentary silence was broken by the driver's voice. She was radioing in.

"En route to St. John's with young female in multi-person collision. Adult male in pursuing ambulance also on way. ETA is three minutes. Fire and police at scene with other responders for two adults pronounced DOA."

I knew the abbreviation: Dead on arrival. The clear voice radioing in the tragedy in the front seat just pierced through my heart. Two people are dead? What the hell was going on? My mind slowed from mach speed for a second, eyes tracing the inside of the ambulance. I couldn't believe that in all the chaos I had not noticed the other gurney, draped with a black plastic tarp, next to my unconscious sister.

I thought the speeding ambulance was doing somersaults down the Chicago streets. Cold sweats broke from my pores and I felt like vomiting.

"Are you OK?" the kind medic asked.

Darkness enclosed me, wrapping its fingers around my paled face. I succumbed as if free falling into the night.

Another realm, indeed.

Chapter Two

WHEN I WOKE UP A FAMILIAR FACE WAS PEERING DOWN AT ME. Only, I couldn't remember whose sincere eyes they were. They were almost reddish brown and appeared to be smiling at me. Or was it pity?

"Take it easy, miss. You need to relax. Don't get up just yet. Here's some water," he said.

"Where am I?"

His concerned expression became pained.

"The breeze is good for you. Get some air and I can explain."

When I sat up, everything began to spin. I looked out at the parking lot first, then the sturdy door of the ambulance. The ambulance! Wretched feelings tumbled inside of me and, suddenly, it spilled from my mouth onto the floor. If I wasn't so horrified by what I believed happened outside of the Remer home, I would have been humiliated.

"Oh, I'm sorry," I mustered.

"Really, it's O.K. Don't feel bad. I deal with much worse, believe me."

He shuddered at his own remark upon realizing his attempt to make me feel better only hardened the blow.

"Where are they? I need to see them?"

"I can escort you in to the waiting room. Your sister is being transported to the I.C.U."

"What about my mother? Where is she?"

The silence only reaffirmed what I already knew.

"I'm sorry," he quietly said.

I never knew loss like this. It was poignantly painful and surreal. Tears weren't there when I should have them-only a stinging that pierced my rapidly beating heart.

He placed his hand on my shoulder feeling as comforting as hot chocolate after shoveling the snow on a blistering winter day. The extremities would be icicles, but liquid warmth meandered down the throat to the stomach. I turned to him and saw him for the first time. He was young, probably no more than a few years older than me.

"You saved my sister's life."

"She's going to be all right. I just know it."

"And, the others? My fiance and his friend?"

"I don't know much about that, but you will learn more when you get in there."

He helped me out of the ambulance and upon seeing me shake when the chilly wind brushed my bare arms, he cloaked me with the EMT jacket he took off before arriving at the scene. His rolled-up sleeves revealed a cross tattoo on the inside of his right, muscular arm.

The people inside the hospital waiting room were a blur as were the sounds of the ringing telephone, opening and closing of automatic doors and background television chatter of some cable news network. The paramedic brought me down a white hall with equally bright tiles and doors and, before we turned the corner, I heard the soft wailing. Joan, crying hysterically, only meant one thing: Gavin was gone. I felt my knees tremble beneath me and the kind medic instinctively held me firm.

"Thank God. Thank God," she whispered. "He's all right. He's going to be fine!"

She and Carl rode in the second ambulance, beating me inside the hospital to hear the obvious and immediate news from the E.R. staff. Carl smiled and embraced her. They looked up at me with the medic besides me.

Joan rushed to me, hugging me closely and knocking off the stranger's jacket in the process.

"He's fine! He's fine!"

Relief rushed over me.

"I'm so glad."

I bent down to pick up the jacket, but he already retrieved it.

"I have to go. Good luck to you...um?"

"Veronica. And you are?"

"Luke."

Joan took me by the shoulders and ushered me over to the chair, ending our exchange. When I looked back, he was gone. Did I even thank him? No, I forgot.

"I have to go to my sister. I have to be there. Where is she?"

"I will ask someone, Veronica," Carl said.

"Where is Jeremy? Is he all right?"

"He didn't make it, I'm afraid," he said quickly and devoid of emotion. "He was gone at the scene, so take comfort in knowing he wasn't in pain for long."

"Comfort? I can't take comfort in anything! My mother is dead. Jeremy is dead. And, my sister...Where is my sister?!" It was only by the mortified looks on their faces that I realized I had been screaming.

"Calm yourself, dear. There are people around," Carl shifted in discomfort.

The sickness inside of me boiled into pure, unfiltered rage. I sensed my cheeks reddening with anger and my fists tighten, a Tasmanian devil bracing for destruction.

"I could give a shit about people around when the earth just turned upside down!"

Stunned, Joan tried to reproach with a softer hand, "I'm truly sorry about your mother, dear."

But, it was someone else who stood by my side at that moment. Sierra's hands were frozen and she was panting out of breath.

"I got here as soon as I could," she hugged me for what seemed like hours. "I don't know what to say, Roni. How's Natalia?"

"I don't know. I don't know anything right now, really." The tears started to pour. Just then, the doors buzzed open and a short, African American doctor emerged slowly. She wasn't in a rush to deliver any news, I thought. This couldn't be good.

"I was told by your companions that you're an immediate relative of the young girl we're treating. Natalia Maye?"

"Yes, I'm her sister."

"Please, come sit with me over here."

I reluctantly followed. *Please, not Natalia. God, please don't take her from me.* I thought of our autumn trips to the cider mill, buying her pilot Halloween costume, watching the military jets fly overhead, how her face lit at the sight of ice cream, and I prayed a million prayers in one passing moment.

She sat across from me, leaning in closely like we were schoolgirls about to share a secret. She rested her hand on mine. Her short, clear-coated nails juxtaposed against my long Fire Engine Red ones.

"Your sister has been through a lot of trauma. We are fortunate she is still with us."

I sighed, "Oh, thank you God!"

"Well, I need you to understand that her body is fighting right now and she is not responding as we'd like. She is currently in a coma."

"What? For how long? When will she be out of it?"

"Well, that's not something we can readily predict. The human body is, in fact, unpredictable. We can tell you she has been stabilized. The internal bleeding has stopped and is not significantly affecting her organs. But she is in a state of unconsciousness. I can't say when-or if-she will awaken. She is a fighter though and we're doing everything we possibly can to make her better."

Her hand closed on top of mine. A healer's hand, I thought.

"I will keep you posted on when you can see her. Stay strong for your sister. She will need you, no doubt."

Then, she gently stood and swiped her badge for the computerized door to open. With that, she was gone and I was left breathless once again. Sierra embraced me and we cried through the finality of my mom and Jeremy's passing and confusion of Natalia's medical state.

A woman's deep, authoritative voice commanded my attention from the hospital television. The local news anchor cut the nightly weather segment short for a far more interesting story.

"Breaking news just in from Illinois state Sen. Carl Remer's in the upscale suburb of Pleasant Farms outside Chicago: A two-vehicle collision took place earlier tonight outside the wealthy entrepreneur and prominent politician's home while a party took place inside. Early reports from police and witnesses at the scene indicate the senator's son was involved. A fifty-year-old metro Detroit woman and a twenty-five-year-old Evanston man were fatally injured in the crash while an eight-year-old girl was transported to a nearby hospital for treatment of severe injuries. It's unclear what promoted the 1998 Ford pickup and 2009 Chevy Charger to collide outside the senator's estate. Immediate attempts to reach Senator Remer were unsuccessful."

"Shit," Carl said, staring at the screen. He turned to Joan and then to Sierra and Veronica. "Don't talk to anyone. Got it? *Anyone.*"

I vaguely recall shaking my head, but I was in such a daze from the emotional turmoil of loss.

"Got it," Sierra reassured him, understanding the importance of image in her own profession.

Carl nodded, plucked his cell phone from the inside pocket of his tuxedo jacket and briskly walked away from the waiting room. When he returned a half hour later, he seemed collected and oddly comfortable. I was in the midst of observing his disposition when a thin, small man with emaciated cheeks and a bowtie inconspicuously sat next to him. Mythical creatures flashed through my mind. Minotaurs and centaurs surfaced, but no definition transpired of what a man-weasel would be called. It seemed to me this man epitomized that very definition. It was in my withering critique of this person that I realized he was the same man who stole Carl away earlier at the party.

"Harvey," Carl sighed and patted his shoulder. "Thank goodness you're here. Are they swarming the hospital yet?"

"You got the honey, don't you? A politician. A party. A fatal accident. A family member. Shall I go on?"

"No, I get the gist and I saw the ten o'clock news."

"Let's talk positive press. You're the endearing father, concerned about his son and this was an unfortunate accident during a happy occasion. Will the girl talk at an impromptu presser?"

Carl looked over at me, my ears stinging with the casualness of the conversation.

"Leave her be. She's got enough on her plate."

"Yeah, asshole. Leave her be," I interjected.

"A spitfire, huh? This is not ideal in a future governor's family. Any chance we can get this engagement called off?" he said smugly.

"Now, now, Harv. Let's focus on the task at hand."

Sierra wisely shooed me out of the room for fresh air at a remote hospital exit away from the press. She pulled a pack of Marlboro Lights from her Prada purse, a gift from one of her admirers, and offered me one.

"I know you quit. But, I think you can make an exception tonight," she dryly surmised.

I stared at her, still shaky from my encounter with weasel man, and smirked in exhaustion.

"I can't think of one reason not to."

The smoke stung my throat on the first hit. It had been a year since my last cigarette and my body had grown accustomed to fresh air and nontoxic chemicals parading around my mouth. After some coughing, I allowed the visceral reaction to subside and let the foreign fiend back in. It felt right to feel this awful.

"What's taking so long? I need to see her," I puffed.

"You will. Just try not to attack your in-laws' friends, okay? I know how difficult it must be."

"It's difficult all right. Did you hear that guy? It's like they don't even care about human life -except their own, that is."

"Well, let's not give them credit for being human just yet."

I saw my reflection in the exterior glass of the hospital door. Mascara skid marks tracked my once-tanned face and circled my hazel eyes. The long locks that were exquisitely combed and styled were just a dark twister fallen on my crumbled dress. Then, the mess that was myself shifted away, opening up the image of a woman in maroon scrubs.

"Your fiance is asking for you. Please follow me."

My scuffed red pump defused the cigarette while Sierra stared sympathetically at me. The loss was deep for her as well, I thought as I followed the nurse. Sierra really had no family. Mine was like hers. After her parents divorced when she was only two, her dad moved to the East Coast, never to be seen again. Heartbroken, her mother turned to any vise she could retreat to, including slews of strange men. It took Sierra's maternal grandparents to intervene and raise her while her mother sought freedom elsewhere. They've had very little contact over the years; most recently was three years ago at her grandparents' funerals, which were only three months apart. Elderly spouses often follow suit when loved ones passed. I felt a blanket of sadness wrap me when I thought my mother and father would never bear the same fate.

I saw the IV. and scores of medical equipment before Gavin. He looked surprisingly well and alert. His left leg and left arm were thickly wrapped and elevated. His athletic frame seemed out of place in the tiny E.R. bed. Amazingly, his hair, face and skin were unscathed with the exception of a quarter-sized mark above his eye that apparently came from the steering wheel.

Before I knew it, I had rushed to his side, placing my head on his chest and crying like a little girl.

"I heard, Rani. I heard," he soothed me. There were so many questions to be answered, so many things left unsaid. "This is a nightmare. A real-life nightmare."

His blue-gray eyes looked at me so helplessly. I've never seen him at such a complete loss for words. Ironically, it was at a time when I needed him to speak the most.

"What happened?" The whisper seemed to shake the room.

"I don't know. I honestly don't know. Jeremy just bought some ratty old truck and he wanted me to drive it to the store so he could get some smokes and get out of there for a few minutes. I was going to pull into my parents' house from the back entrance, so I was passing the front drive when your mom, I guess, was backing out of the driveway. I didn't see her; it just happened so fast."

My head fell back in his chest.

"I'm so sorry," he kept repeating it.

"Jeremy's gone, too."

"I know," he sighed, brushing my hair with his finger. "I take it back: not even my nightmares are this bad."

Chapter Three

A KNOCK ON THE HOSPITAL ROOM DOOR ENDED OUR EMBRACE. A middle-aged husky police officer stood in the doorway. He was gruff and not interested in small talk.

"Officer Smansky of the Pleasant Farms Police Department. I'm here to interview the driver of the pickup truck. I was told by the hospital staff that's you." He looked down at his notepad. "Gavin Remer?"

"Yes, that's me." He held my arm. "You should go now, so I can answer the officer's questions."

I protested a bit, but he wouldn't budge. I knew he thought it would only upset me further. The cop barely moved out of my way when I walked through the door and then he called after me. "I'm going to need to speak with you, too." Gavin looked worried. I knew he wanted to protect me as much as possible.

I sat back in the waiting room for just minutes before the nurse in the maroon scrubs reappeared.

"Please follow me to your sister's room." She was like the gatekeeper to a magic land in which entrance is permitted only in her footsteps. I hoped this path was a fruitful as the last. But I could have hardly been more wrong. My sister seemed so small, so fragile and so distant. She lay right before me on the slightly elevated bed among a field of tubes and tape yet seemed light-years away. I heard her heart beat on the monitor and grasped for strength. *Wake up, beautiful child,* I beckoned internally.

Her hand was cold. Her hair was disheveled and her pretty party dress that had been splattered with much-enjoyed ice cream was replaced with a hospital gown she practically drowned in. I found myself kneeling to her like she was a religious shrine. The tears returned with so much forcefulness; it was an unrecognizable emotion for me. The questions I had earlier about how such atrocities could happen were replaced by horrid, unforgiving thoughts, mainly repeating to myself, "This is your fault. She was never supposed to be there tonight. Your mother, Jeremy and Natalia all would be alive if I had never agreed to this foolish party for getting a ring on my finger."

"I'm sorry to interrupt," Officer Smansky intruded again. "You see, I need to ask you some questions before I head back to the station."

His tough demeanor loosened. Maybe it was the tears. Maybe he had daughters my age. Whatever it was, he seemed more approachable than before. I forgave him for the intrusion and followed him to the cafeteria where he asked me questions over chalky black coffee.

They were standard enough: "What time did your mother and sister leave the party?" Sometime around nine o'clock. "Where were they going?" Back to Detroit. "Were there any problems with the Charger she drove?" No. "Did she have any medical conditions that would have prompted an accident?" No. "What about Gavin? How long has he had a drug habit?" *What?*

He smirked. "Come on, you had to have known if you're going to marry this guy."

I furrowed my brow and bit my lip. I thought there was some mix-up.

"Veronica, there was cocaine in that truck. Now, it's very early on to determine who had how much, but I'm willing to bet that had something to do with this crash. Your fiance is claiming it belonged to his passenger, albeit we found it opened and it spilled on the driver's seat."

He seemed genuinely surprised. "How long have you known Mr. Remer anyway? You did just get engaged to this man, right?"

"I... I... We've known each other for six months."

He looked amused.

"Well, you may want to talk to him about his extracurricular activities before you walk down the aisle. Or better yet, maybe I'll talk to him about them when he's released from the hospital. I'll be here for a bit longer while I talk to the senator, but here's my card just in case."

I stepped into the chilly night for another cigarette. As I inhaled, I thought this, smoking; is the most I've ever done. I never touched any drugs. I viewed them as a weakness, something people do when they're unable to cope with their own demons. What demons did Gavin have? Was he a social drug-user or did he have a more serious habit? Did that gray area really matter with something like that? If he hid that from me, what else was in store? How well did I actually know this person? I thought about our conversations, about anything from our favorite coffee shops to the war. Words always rolled off his tongue like butter. Perhaps his upbringing made him a bit of an unintentional snob, but he indulged me with bowling and dollar-movie dates without condescension. Through the narrow window of our long-distance relationship, had I missed something of the true nature of his persona? We always looked forward to our weekends together, planned them with excitement and put our best romantic foot forward. He never saw me with the flu or in one of my grumpy, stay-away-from-me moods, and I never saw him, I realized, at his norm, during a time he wasn't trying to impress me.

The weekend after we met on Navy Pier, he buzzed my door unexpectedly; confident I'd be there and even more so that I'd go along with the gesture. He drove five hours unannounced to prove that. He brought red roses and reservations to the finest French restaurant I never knew existed. While no one ever before went to such an extent to impress me, it was the subsequent visits that blew me away the most. He won my mother over by complimenting her dishes, my father by watching the Lions games and Natalia by playing planes with her for hours. He couldn't fathom a girl who turned down expensive jewelry or impromptu trips to the Caribbean and, without my knowing, that set me apart from all the other easily impressed girls he'd been with. Gavin was an undeniably good catch: leading-man handsome, educated and a guy who treated me like gold. "Yes," I responded when he proposed.

Everything was up for questioning now. Had it all been an act, a front to win over a woman whom he thought virtuous, who presented him with a challenge when everything else came so easy? I shuddered at the thought of being a fool. Street-smart me! I imagined a future as the unknowing wife of a charismatic lawyer who squirreled away money and drugs and women. My horrifyingly wild imagination ran amuck when someone snapped me out of it.

"I called your dad," Sierra said, taking her cigarette pack to snatch one of her own. "I didn't know what I was going to say and I'm relieved it went to voicemail. I told him there was an accident and where to go. I left him the number to the front desk. They'll give him directions if he needs them."

"We can identify the body together," I muttered.

I reiterated the story the cop told me. Sierra turned white.

"No way. It can't be. Gavin doesn't do drugs. He would never do anything to harm anyone. You can't believe it. It was probably Jeremy's. He definitely liked to party."

I reddened at the thought of slandering the dead. Jeremy partied no less than any other college student I knew. He drank with the best of them, but I never saw him do drugs. Sierra took the message harder than I thought, immediately deflecting it off Gavin. Did he have her fooled, too?

When we walked back into the waiting area, Officer Smansky's eyes seemed haggard, his hair disheveled. Carl and Harvey stood nearby with satisfied looks on their faces. Another policeman, with polished wingtips and perfectly pressed pants, was in the middle of the group. He shook the politician's hand and apologized for the inconvenience. Then Officer

Smansky gruffly stormed away, passing me on the way out. "Your fiance is lucky that some people can be bought. I hope you're not one of them."

Carl guided the other police official over to me. "Veronica, this is Pleasant Farms Police Chief Dave Cooks," Carl explained. "He's here to oversee the accident report in this matter."

"Yes, I apologize for Officer Smansky's inappropriate meddling," the chief said. "He occasionally lets his passion for police work get in the way of his objectivity."

"Isn't it his job to investigate what happened?" I offered. "And, since when does a chief of police handle accident reports directly?"

"This is a sensitive case and you're clearly upset. Please know that I'm only here to help everything run smoothly for you and your family."

He had plump, rosy cheeks and a receding hairline. He appeared in his late sixties and, by the fond exchange with Carl, it was plausible they were old friends.

"Thank you for your help," Sierra offered without invitation.

I spent the night at Natalia's side. Gavin beckoned for me by message of a floor nurse to no avail. I didn't have the words to confront him, nor the energy to spare. Sierra brought me clothes from our hotel room. She knew I couldn't bear leaving my sister's side for that long. Each flashing light or differently-beeping monitor signified terror for me.

I showered in her bathroom the next morning. The harsh heat beat down on my skin and felt strangely calming. My hair was coarse from cheap hospital shampoo, which is equivalent to liquid hand soap, and no blow dryer to straighten the natural waves. I went to retrieve some Burt's Bees lotion from my clutch when it dawned upon me that I hadn't seen it since the party. My purse was lost in the shuffle and, with it, my license, my personal information, my makeup and wallet-sized pictures of my family. If I weren't so numb, I would be hopping pissed about now. I indulged for a minute in self-pity with the lost purse as the icing on a poisonous cake. Then I set that aside for another time when my sister didn't need me. I slid into a pair of jeans and loose, long-sleeved gray T-shirt and black flats. I felt about a foot shorter stepping into the shoes after a night and early morning of wearing my BCBG Girls red heels. There were fledgling dark circles beneath my eyes, I noticed in the square hospital mirror above the sink. I located a small tube of Blistex in the bag Sierra brought and glossed it over my chapped, cracked lips when I heard my father's voice bellowing down the hall.

"Mr. Maye, please calm down. I will lead you to the room in a minute. You just need to fill out some forms," the patient woman behind the counter told him.

"Forms? Forms! I need to see my kids and find out what the hell is going on!" Calmness certainly didn't run in our family. Blame my father's predominantly Irish bloodline or my fiery mother of whom we hypothesized was a mix of American Indian and Latina but never knew for sure since she was adopted in the fifties as the only child of an infertile white couple I'd come to know as my grandparents. They passed away years ago. Either way, there are very few arguments in the Maye household that don't lead to flat-out yelling. Although, the laughter is just as loud.

"Dad, I'm here."

He rushed to me, holding me so tight I felt ready to burst. I wanted to prepare him for the burden of hearing the news. I wanted to tell him something wonderful and poetic that would bring peace to tragedy. I wanted to save him from the hurt of last night and this morning and, undoubtedly, the rest of our lives. I had none of those wise words to share. I possessed only the truth. And so, in order not to prolong the inevitable, I told him what happened: There was an accident. Mom's gone and so is Gavin's best friend. Natalia's in a coma. I didn't share the rest--about the drugs and the cop and the police chief stepping in. That seemed like fine print tucked at the end of a life-altering message.

He dropped to his knees.

I never saw him like that. He fell straight to his knees and bawled like a baby. It was like the long-loved monumental Hudson building imploding. I stood there, not knowing what to do, and then reached down to hug him. His tears, the liquid debris of the demolition, free-fell to the floor. There was so little to say, except I thought about Natalia and how we needed to be strong for her. He couldn't hear me, though. He just kept weeping. The sadness was palpable and honest and greedy, like it was searching for even more inhabitants. I steeled myself to barricade it from Natalia.

He would stay up beside her while I went downstairs to the lobby to clear my mind. It was early, maybe six in the morning, but there was some commotion in a small waiting room off to the side. I strolled to the smoking area Sierra and I went to yesterday to casually get a glimpse inside. It was Carl, clad in a navy-blue suit, and Harvey with a tape recorder held to his mouth. I could barely hear what they said, but it definitely was a practice round of questioning. I stepped closer to put my ear to the door, ducking so they couldn't see me through the elongated window panel on the door.

"This was certainly a tragedy, sparked by a freak accident at night when it was nearly impossible to see someone backing out of the driveway. My son had no means of seeing a car coming so fast and isn't even sure if the driver's lights were on in the other vehicle. While he is not responsible for the crash, we are incredibly saddened by the loss of two wonderful people and they will be with us in our prayers."

My ears burned against the door.

How dare he imply her lights were off? There were witnesses who had to say otherwise. Pretend there weren't drugs in the truck or possibly in his son's system? And, I knew too well the police chief would confirm his account. Power and money at their worst.

I burst into Gavin's hospital room. He jolted back to see me in such a mood.

"I'll give you one chance to explain again what happened last night."

He looked at me with sadness and disappointment that I would speak to him in such anger.

"I told you. I don't know what happened."

"Is there anything you're leaving out? Anything you think I should know?"

"I don't know what you're talking about. I told you already I don't know how it happened. I know you're upset, but calm down so we can talk this through."

Lies. Lies. Lies.

"And the cocaine?"

He looked at me boldly.

"What cocaine?"

He eased a bit when I walked toward him only to tense again when he saw what I was about to do. I twisted the diamond ring off my finger and set it on his nightstand.

"There's nothing left to say. Goodbye, Gavin."

"Roni, wait. Wait."

I turned around to him.

"It wasn't my fault," he said. "It was an accident, nothing more."

"That's what your father says, too. You have more in common than you think."

He was too stunned to respond. I ran out of the room so he didn't see me cry.

Chapter Four

WE WANTED TO GET OUT OF THERE AS FAST AS WE COULD. That took some logistical coordinating with a well-respected Detroit hospital in order for us to transfer Natalia. My father and I went through the painstaking process of formally identifying my mother to the local medical examiner. Dad was inconsolable and I, to my own astonishment, was the pillar of strength. I expected the worst, like a blue corpse that looked nothing like my mother. What I saw instead was her, slightly lighter, with a peaceful expression on her round, soft face. I felt an odd benediction upon leaving there. The funeral would be classy and not over-the-top religious since she was a non-practicing Catholic who attended services in Lutheran and Pentecostal churches, depending on her mood and company. From planning a wedding to planning a funeral, I thought.

"You foolish girl," Harvey hissed at me. "To think how ungrateful you are to your fiance and his family. He'd picked you out of obscurity and mediocrity to give you a promising life in a powerful family and you turn your back on him when he's in need. So what if somebody said there were some drugs in the truck? Are you so much of a Girl Scout that you can't see past someone's imperfections?"

He had cornered me in the hall on the way back from a smoke break. It was a substitution for food and he must have noticed my patterns.

"You sure have a way of toning down the facts. Someone's imperfections aren't quite as irrelevant if they caused two people to die. And, as for my background, it would do what little good is left of your soul to step away from the power you speak so highly of."

"You're no match for this family, sweetie. You should just quietly return to the dingy hole you came from."

I nearly smacked him when someone else distracted me. He was standing at the front desk, holding my clutch. It was the medic, talking to the employee as she scanned her computer for room numbers. With more clarity today, I saw him for what he was, a truly handsome man. He was slightly shorter than Gavin, with dark-brown wavy hair and reddish brown eyes and with one of those mouths that point downward at the sides as if frowning when smiling. I left Harvey standing there to revel in what he believed was the last word and approached the kind man who helped save my sister's life.

"You don't know how grateful I am to you."

He was happy to see me. I could tell by how his body language changed almost instantaneously.

"I just found it in the ambulance when my shift ended last night. I would have brought it back to you sooner, but it was really late and I figured you had more important things to deal with."

"No, I mean how grateful I am for what you did for my sister."

He got shy suddenly and at a loss for words.

"It's my job. I'm happy to have helped."

He asked me how I was holding up and I put on my best game face. I didn't want pity or prying and I had already thrown up in front of him, so I felt like I needed to hold back a bit this time.

"Luke..." He looked pleased that I remembered his name. "Thanks again for everything." I fumbled inside my purse to grab a tissue because I feared tears would roll. That's when I touched something else and a fabulous idea came to me.

"Are you O.K.?" (This apparently was the nature of our conversations.)

"I honestly don't know. I hope so."

"I really don't do this, but if you need anyone to talk to, I'm here." He almost immediately rescinded the offer when he felt he had overstepped his professional boundaries.

"That's really thoughtful of you. Although, I'm going back home to Michigan soon if all goes well. My family needs me now more than ever and I don't expect to be back here any time soon. See, I actually won't be getting married here after all."

"Here or at all?" he pressed.

"At all."

Perhaps it was the exhaustion or the emotions that ran through me. I had no idea why I was sharing so much with a stranger. The drama of last night brought us together in some weird unexplainable way. He nodded, understanding what he didn't know. We said goodbye and I even leaned in to hug him before he left. It was out of the norm for me, but hell, the whole ordeal was far from normal. He smiled slightly after the embrace and stared at my hazel eyes a second too long. He caught himself and backed away like he'd touched something breakable with slippery hands.

It was the slightest and most unexpected moment of joy through the whole traumatic night and morning. I sensed his attraction to me. It didn't take a genius to ascertain; hell, a blind bat could detect it. Surprisingly, it enraptured me although I didn't understand its origins, whether they were based on mutual chemistry or my sheer gratitude to him. Maybe I was unknowingly smiling to myself as he graciously bowed away, because I felt eyes darting through my head. Harvey was smirking at me as if implying I was trash for touching another man. Damn that weasel man. He really got my blood boiling with his smug little bow tie and sports anorexia. As he scampered off in his glory, I reached in my purse again. This time, I was the one with a cocky expression.

Sierra was back at the hotel sleeping when I phoned her to bring me my fedora and trench along with my black, heeled boots and large H & M slouch purse. She was so tired she barely cared why and I was thankful for that small favor. My dad was half-sleeping next to Natalia with the television on some awful game show. It had been years since I watched morning TV unless it the local news.

I coaxed my dad to go downstairs to the cafeteria for coffee and bagels. I noticed how haggard and thin he looked and couldn't stand thinking about how awful he cared for himself when traveling away from home. My mother fed him like a third child, knowing how he'd forgo meals to finish his sales accounts for different automotive suppliers. The man flew back and forth to so many U.S. cities he was giving Gavin and me our honeymoon air travel to Paris free with his frequent flier miles. Those would have to go to something else now.

I flipped the channel to the morning news and, as expected, the anchor announced a noon press conference outside the hospital with none other than Sen. Remer. Oh joy, I thought. Here he comes to save his credibility as a wonderful family man with a squeaky clean son and diminish my loss with his lies.

Sierra dropped off my stuff and I rushed to get everything together. Natalia would be airlifted to Children's Hospital in Detroit this evening. My father would accompany her since he flew in, while Sierra and I would drive my eight-year-old Chevy Malibu back to Detroit and I would meet them at the hospital. First, though, I needed to get my last word in.

I pulled the trench over my T-shirt and changed from jeans to dress pants. I snapped on my boots and fedora, which were perfect for this breezy fall weather. Lastly, I reached into my purse to grab my press pass.

Natalia had always wanted to be Amelia Earhart. Unfortunately for the Remers, I wanted to be Nellie Sly.

Chapter Five

MY MEDIA CREDENTIAL READ: "PRESS, VERONICA MAYE, THE DETROIT CHRONICLE, NEWS REPORTER." So what if I was outside my beat? To the public and media alike, the story had a Detroit news hook. Therefore, I doubted anyone would question my presence. I kept a low profile just in case.

I lowered my head to my notebook and pen when Carl and Harvey stepped outside the hospital. The fedora came in handy; neither of them saw me in the crowd. It was risky. Still, I knew, when put on the line, the senator wouldn't defer back to me. It would be even more dangerous for his image to cast light on an angry would-be daughter-in-law who knows too much. I was behind a few other preoccupied print people, who themselves, were standing in a row behind the TV folks. I recognized the heavily made-up man with impeccable hair from the five o'clock news, which I caught a few times during visits with Gavin.

The senator began by thanking the public for their prayers and kind words and other ramblings about what great people he serves. *Sure, you only serve yourself,* I thought. He then went into the rehearsed script I overheard early this morning, and opened it up to questions.

Among scores of inquiries one was the trombone in a sea of flutes.

"What was your family's relationship to the two deceased vehicle occupants and what was the gathering for last night?" asked an older newspaperman who strangely enough resembled Chef Boyardee.

"The young man was my son's friend from law school and the woman in the other vehicle was an acquaintance. The party was to celebrate my wife and my thirty-year anniversary next month. We would have held it later, but my schedule is quite full then."

Harvey nodded approvingly; the senator's inner circle of friends wouldn't say otherwise. I nearly broke my pen when digesting those lies.

I knew the Chicago media was good, just like us, but I wasn't aware of any leaks from police about the drugs. By the questions, I soon figured no one had heard anything and it was all on lockdown pretty well. That was, of course, until I jumped into the questioning with one of my own, Any trepidation I bore was erased by the last answer.

"Senator..."

"Yes," the ever-so-smooth senator responded before fully viewing my face. Harvey nearly choked on his chewing gum from off to the sideline. The words "live television" flashed in their heads, I'm sure.

"Please enlighten us about the reported narcotics found on your son and in the vehicle he was driving."

He stammered like a rookie politico. Harvey was powerless in the television glare, a frozen deer in the media camera lights. All Carl could muster was "no comment" and then the reporters pounced, question after unrelenting question. I felt a rush of giddy excitement powering my thin five-foot-two frame.

They had known I was a journalist. They just didn't know how far I could be pushed. I tucked my pass in my bag, pulled down my fedora and headed to the car Sierra waited in.

"You really just did that," she said in shock.

I pushed back the hat so it fell recklessly behind me and lit a cigarette. The rage was akin to charred tobacco percolating my blood.

"Yeah, I really did."

We pulled away among a parking lot full of news crews and television vans. I was leaving behind a complete future. A desirable man who could have been my husband. A senator who could have been my father-in-law. A doting mother and supportive wife, albeit a stuck-Up woman, who could have been my mother-in-law. Pangs struck most that this weekend was my mother's last. These rambling thoughts meshed into my sorrow and anger as we turned out of the lot. I did a double take as I saw him. Luke had been leaning against his ambulance about fifty feet away from where I stood at the presser. Amusement sketched the creases of his face. His head followed the car's movement and, when we were nearly out of sight, I noticed he waved ever so casually.

"Who's that?" The curiosity rolled off Sierra's tongue slyly like I'd been hiding something.

"The medic I rode with last night," I answered nonchalantly.

"Yum." This was her nature, I always told myself. I rolled my eyes.

I almost succumbed to the earlier rush of being desired. But I netted the butterflies before they fluttered too much. I couldn't just justify this as an instinctive carnal reaction based on genetic predispositions from centuries of human procreation. I was still very much in love with Gavin even though I felt more betrayed than ever. I couldn't pretend, however, I wasn't intrigued by Luke and that I wasn't storing him on a high shelf in my wildly unstable and overly exhausted mind.

As the Malibu puttered off in the non-threatening way affordable sedans do, the sky darkened in the most distinct way as though day and night were separated by a millisecond. Jumbo raindrops pummeled downward and, as I stared in silent solitude out the window, I saw my reflection in the glass. For the first time since my sideshow outside the hospital, I felt completely ashamed.

Chapter Six

"I REMEMBER WHEN WE TOOK YOU HOME FROM THE HOSPITAL. I know you love that story. Usually moms sit in the backseat with the baby on the ride home, but I insisted I do it. Mom sat in the passenger seat next to dad and I was right by you in the back and held your tiny hand in mine. Every time the car stopped at a light or stop sign, you would cry, and every time it would go again, you were quiet. I knew things would never be boring with you around and that you'd always keep me on my toes."

I laughed, eight-year-old memory as fresh as yesterday. "Think happy thoughts and tell her everyone of them" was my motto. The I.V. bag dripped to my side. I was careful not to position my chair on any cords as I inched closer to the bed to hold her hand. It was warm. Blood circulated through this child; she was far from dead. It could be only a matter of time before she woke, the doctors told me in their cautiously encouraging way. They had no guarantees, but none of us do. I had been combing her curly locks and painting her nails a shimmery purple she was always fond of. I dressed her in the blue cotton pajamas we found in the boys' department at Kohl's because none of the girls' jammies had airplanes on them like these. Fearing her skin would get dry, I applied cocoa butter lotion on her arms, hands, legs and feet. She always liked that smell. Then, I placed an avocado-based face cream on her cheeks, forehead and chin before sliding sheer lip gloss on her pouty pink mouth. There were many times she asked me for certain products or makeup, so it wasn't hard to decipher what to bring.

    I could smell the bourbon encapsulating the sterile hospital room air before he quietly inched closer. It wafted toward me the way ironing boards fall from closets onto someone's unsuspecting head. The soles of his leather loafers were whispers against the white tile. He was unshaven and unbathed and apathetic about it all. The first signs of his unkemptness flashed at the funeral a couple weeks ago. His suit was wrinkled and tie crooked. I didn't have the heart to critique his appearance in light of the occasion. I knew my mother would have been mortified at the sight of her husband like that. She wasn't interested in the finer things in life, but she certainly took pride in herself, her family and the tidiness of her house. That, too, had fallen in disarray under my father's watch. Sierra was living with me between auditions and road trips. I knew she couldn't be trusted to take out the trash or get the mail if I moved back home temporarily. And I needed some time to myself in the comfort of my own space that was quiet and clean and suited to my taste. Gavin often told me he wanted me to decorate our home since he liked the collage of contemporary furniture and traditional accents in my loft that I found at affordable prices at a variety of stores. I was actually excited to do so.

He was also at the funeral, an unwelcome guest seated in the back with an unrelenting gaze at my every move. His mouth sputtered words unspoken. His eyes failed to penetrate my soul. His presence felt abstract and meaningful like a Mondrian and I was the museum visitor who failed to pay it proper attention. I pushed the thought of him off, saving it for another time for better analysis and emotional identification. Yeah, I thought, it was that scientific-like love potion combined with whatever Dr. Jekyll ingested.

My father sat down on the vinyl chair in the back of the room and just looked at Natalia. His face was gaunt and haggard and I wondered when he last ate.

"Sit with her and I'll get you something from the cafeteria. Children's Hospital food isn't as bad as St. John's in Chicago."

He shook his head and mustered what half-smile he could.

"I'm fine. Thanks."

"Well, I'm going to run down there, so I'll see you in a few minutes." It was an excuse, I knew. I could barely sit in the same room as him. We couldn't carry a conversation if it saved our lives. I had much better ones with Natalia at this point and she wasn't conscious.

Truth was, I didn't have an appetite much either lately. I scooped up a local daily paper, The Metro Journal, before stepping on the elevator. On the National page, there was an Illinois brief with the header "Senator's son cleared in fatal wreck." There was never an arrest or even a real entertainment of the thought. "No drugs were found in Gavin Remer's possession nor in the truck he drove, despite unsubstantiated reports of them. Toxicology reports are pending on the deceased male passenger," the brief said. I was angry at the blurb, at the inability to report the truth, and yet I felt strangely relieved and protective of Gavin. I swallowed that last thought as forcefully as possible.

I never wore my ring at work. Everyone's so damn nosy. I say this with affection. After all, it's laborious to switch that reporter's instinct off outside work-related matters. In fact, they only knew I had a boyfriend in Chicago. When pressed for information by friendly colleagues, I told them he was a law student at Northwestern. That was true. Saying he was Sen. Remer's highly sought-after bachelor son would invite too many questions. I hadn't yet determined what would happen after we married except that I wouldn't change my byline. I may have been young, but I worked hard under my name to establish credibility and a reputation for solid reporting. I couldn't change that for him and I didn't want the association with his father. Gavin most likely would persuade me to move to Chicago. Without telling him, I had already submitted applications for openings at the Sun-Times, the Trib and various fashion and home-style glossies. There was no begrudging him wanting me to move to him. Detroit, as much as I loved it for all its earnest grittiness and undying hope, was a tough sell to an outsider. Plus, I loved spending days with Gavin in Millennium Park or at the Lincoln Park Zoo. We'd shop along Michigan Avenue, stopping in the Water Tower and my personal favorite, the Cheesecake Factory, and just sit on a bench along the shoreline of Lake Michigan.

"I always loved the city," he had said, staring into my eyes. His big, warm hands covering mine. His sandy brown hair waving slightly in the wind. "But, there's no doubt, Veronica, you make it more beautiful than ever." He'd slide his fingers on the back of my neck, sending shivers down my spine, and kiss me with soft, boundless passion.

I lied about the hospital food. It was every bit as bad as the other place. The only difference was this one at least cared about the façade of being a descent dining room. The female employees wore cute little checkered aprons and matching caps. The men wore white chef hats and jackets. Doctors sat together at tables, looking tired and sipping what I presumed were unhealthy amounts of caffeine. Nurses, too, were in a clan eating and chatting with each other before many stepped out for a smoke break.

I brought a bowl of chicken soup for myself and a ham sandwich for my dad back to the room. When I walked in, he was leaning down at Natalia, his graying hair falling forward because he hadn't put forth the effort to get a trim. He was weeping. Then, he retrieved a sterling silver flask from his bomber jacket pocket and took a swig. I pretended I didn't see it. He knew I did and he stammered a bit when he acknowledged my presence.

Ignoring the awkwardness, I smiled politely as if he were a passerby on the street. I placed the sandwich in front of him.

"Oh, thanks. I'm really not hungry though."

I tried to hide my disappointment. My mom would have practically shoved it down his throat.

"I actually came by to tell you that I have to go out of town for work."

"Back to Cleveland?" I asked.

"No, this time I'm going to San Diego to help assist our West Coast team with their sales launch there."

He'd never traveled to California for work before.

"How long will you be gone?"

"Can't tell at this time. I'll keep you posted though. When do you have to return to the paper?"

I squashed my annoyance as best as I could because I'd told him at least three times that my editor, Marshall Daddini-whom everyone affectionately referred to as M. Daddy like some rapper pseudonym (we even bought him gag gold chains and black sunglasses to amplify his persona)-- told me upper management approved my request for a three-month leave of absence. Of course, that meant I probably couldn't return to cops and courts and would get stuck with some cruddy beat no one wanted. But I didn't care. I needed to be with my sister and I would make due financially because I squirreled away money every paycheck. For a brief moment, I thought maybe that money would go toward our wedding. Out of pride, I had told Gavin I would chip in as much as I could. He wouldn't even entertain the thought. I was irritated yet secretly relieved. He had his own pride, too.

"Not until December. My priority is to care for Natalia."

My tone was unexpectedly bitter and his eyebrows rose when it infiltrated his ears.

"Yes," he spoke solemnly. "You've always looked out for her so well. She's almost like your own daughter. I know..."

His voice seemed distant as he stopped himself. I felt the need to reassure him that everything would be all right. My anger toward him leaving slammed the brakes on that instinct, though, and I just told him to call me when he landed tomorrow.

"Take care of yourself," I found myself saying as I hugged him with some reservations. The bourbon burned my nose.

He shuffled out of the room just in time for Sierra to enter. Her makeup was heavier than usual and enormous, shiny rubies dangled from her ears, accenting her equally dark red locks.

"Hey girl! Someone hit the bar kind of early in the day. Whew." She waved her painted pink nails before her small, pointed nose. "Damn. You need to talk to him about that. He's got more alcohol in him then the cleaning supplies in this hospital."

"Okay, you've made your point."

"Oh, come on. You know how I lighten the mood. She looks good by the way. I bet you'll bring her home soon."

Suddenly it hit me that my dad might not be there when she woke. I couldn't help but get miffed at his selfishness. Then I looked at my beautiful little sister and the anger subsided. She was worth any inconvenience he could offer. Listlessly, I traced her hairline with my fingernail; the opulent waves cascading on the blue airplane pillowcase I brought from her room. The overly feminine mane clashed with the boyish bedding. I thought if she just opened them, her big beautiful blue eyes would match so well with the pillowcase. She definitely got those baby blues from my dad.

Sierra was engaging in some elaborate tale of a "once-in-a-lifetime audition" in New York. Every opportunity was that rare and special in her mind. I was half-listening, half-intent on Natalia while she rambled that, since she didn't have the money to fly to Manhattan now, she was going with a male companion.

"Every rising star needs a benefactor of some kind," she dismissed before I began lecturing.

"So you're a call girl now? That's lovely. When you make it big, I can't wait to read all about your 'struggling days' on the cover of Us Weekly." Sure, I was known as a bit of a ball-buster, but this was my loving approach to her *artistic* ways, to put it politely.

"Stop," she waved her hand and, out of nervousness, fumbled for a cigarette before remembering her environment. "We're flying together but in separate rooms. I would never dream of it."

"You wouldn't. He's another story." I cracked a smile through my perverse cynicism.

"Well, if you need to reach me, you have my cell. But, in case she wakes up and you can't get to me, I'll be at the Mayflower. My reservation is under his name, Michael McConner, although we *will* be in different rooms."

My eyes narrowed. She darted her gaze away, fully aware of her slip of the tongue. Sierra may have been a good actress on stage, but she had no poker face in real life.

"McConner," I repeated skeptically.

She was fidgeting like crazy.

"I know that name." Then, the fuzzy recollection transpired into an actual image of this person, this round, despicable man who, with his wife standing next to him, aggressively offered to drive Sierra back to the hotel…from my engagement party.

"I guess there will never be a time I can pull one by you, Roni."

"I should only be so lucky."

Judging her would do me no good. I loved her in spite of her flaws, as she did with mine. Lord knows I have them. I'm stubborn as an ox with the temper of a pit bull. She, on the other hand, had no temper, no grudging disposition. Yet her moral compass spun quite often. And, with her unintentional admission of the ghastly McConner, I suspected there were other things she failed to tell me, probably because she didn't want my face as her mirror.

I shooed her out, saying I had a headache. I needed time to think, to stop thinking, to be alone and really not be alone at all. I longed for the earth to halt rotation, the stars to fizzle into blackness and my heart to just melt down completely from its mushy state. There was so much strength I had to muster. I forced myself to think of women, real and imaginary, who were strong, courageous and steadfast because I was feeling none of these things. I thought of Natalia's adoration for Amelia Earhart. I thought of my fascination with Nellie Sly, how that mental institution expose nearly drove her mad and how she pushed past it for the betterment of a purpose. I thought of professors and editors and fellow reporters I knew with charm and strength. And, most importantly, I thought of my mother, who was everything you could ask for in a maternal figure with strength, love and compassion. The curvy five-foot-one doting mom also had a steel backbone. I breathed deeply, deciding to be brave. I was her daughter after all.

Chapter Seven

I MUST HAVE FALLEN ASLEEP IN THE HOSPITAL LOUNGE CHAIR. My ringing cell phone didn't interrupt my slumber; it was the gentle hand of a nurse I've come to know well. Barb was a blonde plump woman in her forties with strikingly high cheekbones and warm brown eyes. I could tell she felt badly for me, but her pity wasn't offensive. It was kind of endearing in its understated approach that left me feeling cared for when I had no energy to fight off uninvited sympathy.

"Roni, I didn't want to disturb you, but your phone has been ringing off the hook."

My back was one big cramp from sleeping off to the side of the chair. I thanked her and stretched cautiously so not to embellish the pain. She checked Natalia's I.V. and monitors before leaving me to hear the messages on my phone.

M. Daddy sounded more like Marshall Daddini, a serious gruff and balding metro editor who earned his chops the same way I'd been paying my dues, which was covering every crime imaginable and hitting the pavement for every breaking news story we could find. We would affectionately verbally jab each other most days. Today was not one of them.

"Listen, Maye, you need to get your butt in here ASAP. The Corporate Suit wants to speak with you and it's not going to be pretty. You never heard that last part from me. Just get in here after the first-edition deadline," he snorted at the inconvenience of leaving a message when news copy had to be moved and this no doubt would disrupt his day.

I've heard him get angry before in pissing matches with other editors, but never so serious and forewarning to me. All things considered, it was worrisome, just not as much as losing my mother and my sister being in a coma. This was akin to tornado in the midst of the apocalypse.

The next message was from Samuel Bernett, better known as Captain Bernett of the Detroit Police Department, whose desk was right around the corner from my occasional squatting grounds in the station. Samuel was African American, standing about six-foot-four, with a shaved head and deep authoritative tone. When you got to know him, as I did, he shed his tough-guy image and chatted about his four kids and two yellow labs or that he was working on an MBA in preparation for starting his own police uniform store when his twenty-five years in were up.

"Roni, this is Sam Bernett. I know you're off on personal business and I want you to know your sister has been in my prayers. I feel like you should be aware that a man stopped by here today asking for you. Call me for more information if you see fit. Goodbye."

A man looking for me? A meeting with Corporate Suit at the newspaper? I didn't know what to think, but the messages left me with a wallowing pit in my stomach.

I had loaned Barb almost every book I finished while sitting in that unpleasant chair in Natalia's room. As I stepped out into the hallway, she was perched on a swirly stool with the latest James Patterson in her hands. I knew she was on break by the strawberry yogurt and granola bar next to her.

"Hey sweetie," she looked up. As surprising as it may seem, some people did think I was sweet. "No wonder you finished this so fast. I can't put it down if I tried and I certainly need to try soon since my break will be over in five minutes."

"Barb, I have to leave for a bit..."

She waved her hand at me like I offered money she refused. "Don't you worry about a thing; I'll keep an extra close eye on her."

She shooed me out reassuringly, but I double and triple checked she had my cell phone number.

I gave myself a once-over in the hospital lobby mirror. My raven hair was pulled back in a low ponytail, falling on the back of my scarlet sweater that hung over my dark jeans. I had on only light makeup that gave the illusion of entirely natural glow on my cheeks, and light pink lip gloss. My diet of caffeine and minimal cafeteria food only decreased my already thin waistline and the cooler weather mixed with barely any outdoor time made my olive skin uncharacteristically pale.

"That's a lucky mirror," the familiar voice said. With trepidation, I scanned up the oval mirror with a thick golden frame. His reddish brown eyes met mine and squinted like they were challenging me to flirt. I was in a rush with a heavy mind-though intrigued and secretly buoyant.

I squinted, questioning his meaning, questioning his presence. He clued me in on the first. "Lucky because you're looking at it."

He put his hands on my shoulders, spun me around slowly, and said, "Now, I'm the fortunate one."

Looking up at him, I sensed he wanted to kiss me. For a moment, I hoped he did, until I reawaked to my surroundings and realized how inappropriate that would be.

"Luke, what are you doing here?"

He shrugged as if Chicago and Detroit were a mere walk in the park from each other. He had that wonderful smell of burnt fall leaves on his thin wool jacket and loose jeans.

"I can't say I have your purse this time. So, there's no excuse. Well, no excuse except for one," he half-smiled as I tried to remain composed and attentive as if my heart wouldn't morph into Silly Putty. "I can't stop thinking about you." Putty, it is.

I didn't know what to say. Detecting that, he continued.

"I realize this is awful timing, that you're going through so much and that you don't really know me..." he reconsidered. "But, maybe this timing is all right. You need someone by your side. I'd like to be that person."

What an offer. I was mystified. I owed him so much and felt inexplicably connected to him. And, he was so good-looking. However, we were truly strangers.

"How did you know where I was?" I didn't want to sound ungrateful. Still, I needed a diversion and more information.

"It's not hard to find someone whose name appears so many times in a Google search. Damn, you write about some messed-up stuff. I thought I saw a lot of craziness." There it was again, the same amused face he made while Sierra and I rolled out of the parking lot in Chicago. "I actually figured you'd be at either Children's or Mercy because they're really your sister's only options around here. I have a couple EMT friends who work in the area who told me that. As luck would have it, I saw you on my first stop."

"I don't know what to say. How are you here, away from your job?"

"You really are a reporter aren't you?" he laughed. "I had accrued a lot of vacation time and I have this Ninja that I've been meaning to ride before winter arrives. Detroit isn't exactly what I had in mind, but like I said, I needed to see you." He couldn't read me, so he asked, "Are you not happy to see me? I was hoping maybe you'd be at least willing to let me take you to dinner."

"Oh, I am. Happy, that is." That, as odd as it was, had been true. "I guess I'm speechless." I brushed some long bangs back that didn't reach the ponytail holder. His hands were away from my shoulders now, but he reached for my hand as I brought it back down to my side.

"Dinner it is then."

"Well, I really don't leave the hospital much," I said a bit uneasy.

"Are you not leaving now?"

"Yeah, this is kind of a rarity for me." I didn't owe him more of an explanation and he didn't intrude.

"I checked in to the Marriott across the street. You can meet me for dinner there around six and still be near the hospital. Come on, I came all this way. You have to eat, look at you. And, you can order anything you want," he smiled. It was that cute upside-down frown.

"Well, in that case," I said, giving in to his charm. "I'll see you then."

I retrieved my hand from his. He took it upon himself to brush another loose bang away from my eyes.

If butterflies scrambled when I saw him before, they damn near exploded this time.

"I have to go," I meekly said. He watched me walk out the automatic door. I felt his gaze on my back as though he liked the view.

A wave of embarrassment rushed through me by the time I reached my Malibu. *I had a date of all things* when my sister is in a coma, my mother six feet under and the corpse of my would-be marriage not even cold. I didn't know Luke's last name to call the hotel and ask to be connected to his room later. So, I reasoned I couldn't cancel ahead of time. And, not showing up to dinner would be plain rude in light of him saving my sister and riding here on his crotch rocket just to see me. The date was on. But, first, I had another one, a blind one, at the paper that used to be my second home. That is, before the hospital took over that spot.

The historic building towered over the busy sidewalk. At the top a modernized sign read "The Detroit Chronicle." Over the decades in the building, as the staff was downsized, some floors were closed off. It wasn't wise anyway to give rascally reporters too much unaccounted room. Then there was a strike or two well before my time that meant more floors transformed to ghosts and, sooner or later, most everyone was on the main floor with just about thirty features folks on the second. The presses still rumbled underneath that main floor, signifying the gratification that validated every stressful moment before deadline.

It had been weeks since I left the building with such cool assurance that my life would improve in days. I had the man of my dreams-and other women's dreams, I knew-waiting for me, wanting me to be with him for the rest of his days. A gust of wind blew past me, nearly swiping a copy of today's paper out of my unsuspecting hand. It transported me to the present, feeling lovelorn and lost like the paper that eventually slid out of my hands when another gust rattled it from me. Great, I was an unintentional litterer and unversed on the news of the day. Somehow, I suspected, that wasn't the only information I was missing.

Heads discourteously bobbed upward from ongoing conversations on the phone or with each other. Prairie dogs had more tact. I gave my best yet indignant "don't pity me or stare at me" half-smile. I got a couple of waves and smiles in return, but I sensed everyone was instructed not to speak to me. Perhaps avoiding the mandate, my acquaintance/developing friend Carter, a handsome and tall man who, unfortunately for the ladies of the paper, was gay, casually walked up to me. He squeezed my hand, just like he did at the funeral. "Have you not checked my e-mails?" he whispered alongside me as if asking me for the time. "No," I gently told him while we meandered around cubicles and dingy televisions, circa 1980s, that played CNN, Fox and MSNBC until the local news pushed the cable stations aside. "Shit is hitting the fan. I only heard through the grapevine something about Chicago and you and..." His message was muffled by the uninvited appearance of Gale Babes, who was just as obnoxious as her byline although I doubted it to be her real name. Why anyone would choose that as a byline was beyond me, but there she stood in her country boots and busy blouse with poofy blonde hair to, well to boot. Someone needed to tell her Dolly Parton didn't need any more impersonators, I thought in sheer bitchiness that truly wasn't unprovoked. Almost everyone I knew from the young to the old couldn't tolerate her any more than me. She was pushy and loud and arrogant. I wish I could fetch her a favor and say her talent was unmatched. In truth, it was mediocre. Maybe that's why she needed the gimmick.

"Why you poor thing," she said, oozing sympathy that made me want to hurl. She was five years older than me but talked downward like I was a child. I was not beyond a catfight in my state and, as my family always said, I was little but scrappy. Babes wouldn't stand a chance.

"Oh Babes, there's nothing poor about me and I'm hardly an inanimate object. You did buy one of those thick books I told you about, right? It's called a dic-tion-ary," I said it slowly like she couldn't follow and there were chuckles abound, including Carter's. I had received bouquets and cards after my mother's passing and some co-workers even attended the funeral, but I hardly needed an overdrawn, melodramatic scene from Babes of all people.

She withdrew her extended arms before sashaying off to her cubicle. For a moment, I saw a flash of emotion on her face that hardly read defeat. It was more like satisfaction.

M. Daddy rose in a commanding moment from his angular desk by a bank of TV sets. His gold chain and sunglasses were off in the corner of that mess of a desk by a green lamp and a stash of AP style, grammar and almanac books. He looked pained. This was not good. I knew he was always fond of me. We had a great rapport that led to lots of 1A stories. To see him like this meant bad news and not the kind we write about that never really affects our own bubble. This was touching down. His blue button-down was crumpled, his tie loose like he yanked at it under pressure. I saw his glasses were stashed in his pocket without any protection, the way he does when he's too distracted to find somewhere safe to set them.

"Maye, come with me," his voice rough and not to be reckoned with. I sensed disappointment in his tone.

"Where to?"

He looked at me sternly. I knew to can it.

I yearned to say something familiar with him, to lighten the mood. Words, however, were remote vessels drifting farther by the minute.

We turned the corner to reach the spacious office overlooking the ground level of downtown Detroit. I had to say, it looks much better from higher floors. At this eye line, passersby and cars were really the gist of it. I scanned the room. Behind his oak desk was Publisher Randall Walker clad in his dull brown timeless business suit. A large pointed nose, small beady eyes and thin, almost nonexistent, lips punctuated his oval face. I'd only had a couple conversations with him, if you want to call it that, and they were complimentary while brief. He nodded, "Veronica, welcome." I almost slid into the cushy leather chair across from him without noticing the other person in the room, on the sofa to my right. His gaunt cheeks seemed more defined as he sucked on a mint, pursing his lips in the process. My pounding heart did an ungraceful flip.

Harvey, AKA The Weasel, scurried upward to meet my eyes. His alarmingly thin fingers grasped my sweaty hand in a firm shake. This was Disney World to him.

"I believe no introductions are needed," Randall said emotionlessly. M. Daddy reluctantly sat to my left in a matching leather seat. He didn't know Harvey, but his boss didn't seem to care. They cordially introduced themselves-Harvey with a firm shake of the head. M. Daddy with a slight nod that was nonchalant and cold at once.

"Let me start by saying Harvey is an old friend who never brought this matter to my attention. I was actually displeased to learn this from someone, a very observant someone, on staff who watches news feeds from across the country," Randall began. He turned to his plasma screen in the top corner above his desk, swirling around in his chair. I knew what was coming. I felt like the cat with the mouse in her mouth, albeit this mouse was fully devoured and rising in my throat. He clicked the remote toward the flat-screen and there was the press conference weeks before in Chicago.

"You see, the only shot of this presser is really from right in front of the lectern. So, I barely saw what Gale Babes was talking about when she indicated you were there, asking questions, of all things, outside of your beat, outside of your state even," he said with consternation. The tape did show a short shot of my face. That cameraman zoomed in quickly, catching a flash of my badge. It was undeniably me. "I had to call my friend Harv, whom I trust from our days together at Yale, to ask about who this mysterious rabble rouser was at the press conference."

Harvey shrugged as if to say "there was nothing I could do."

"Then, I was even more dismayed to learn you used your media credentials with our newspaper name on it to make an unethical-and unproven-attack on someone you were *engaged to...* Veronica, this is alarming to say the least. I understand you've suffered hardship..."

"Come on, Randall," Daddini stepped in to my defense. "Roni is nothing but one of our most promising and talented reporters."

Harvey jumped in, a bulldog waiting to attack. "The cream of the crop hardly mistakes personal relationships and work responsibilities."

It went back and forth for a bit. I sat silently, watching the events unfold. I lied to myself when I thought I could attack Babes in the newsroom. I hadn't a fighting bone left in my over-exhausted body.

Daddini tried in earnest to leap to my aid, looking at me stunned as if to beckon me to rally. I shrugged, stood and turned to Randall. "Thank you for the opportunity to work here for the past two years. I learned a lot and I am most grateful. I will turn in my things this week." He looked nothing short of stunned. Was this not what he wanted? I turned to Daddini, "You are the best editor anyone could have. I will miss working with you." He was still jawing for a fight, but hesitantly softened at my compliment and the finality of the situation. I then faced Harvey--no doubt the visitor the captain at the police station spoke of--to say, "You wanted the last word and you have it. I have nothing left to say." He couldn't resist gloating silently.

I held my head up high, walked purposefully out of the office and through the newsroom as eyes followed, and made my way out of the beautiful stone building that had been my citadel of journalistic justice. I slipped into my little Malibu, turned on the heat because I suddenly felt so painfully chilly, and cried uncontrollably.

I nearly jumped when Daddini tapped on the driver's side window. His eyebrows were arched beneath soft brown eyes. He had a Camel Light in his hand, a habit he'd deemed unscrupulous suddenly after a panic attack years ago. Still, he was enslaved to his vice-something I had a newfound understanding for.

Seeing his reaction to my tears made me cry harder. He wasn't anticipating this. The father of three teenage girls was no longer a hardened editor. He was a concerned mentor and friend.

"Let me in, Roni," he put out his smoke and walked around the car. I unlocked the door. As he plopped down next to me, he grunted a bit in discomfort. He was too tall and broad for the car's small frame. I thought he'd begin to lecture. Instead, he changed the subject.

"Look at that hobo over there. See that guy with the flannel coat, pushing the cart?" I nodded through my blurred wet vision. "Man, that guy has been trekking back and forth in front of this newsroom since I was a cub reporter. You'd think he's some crackhead, right? Maybe has schizophrenia. The truth is, he's got a freakin' MBA from U of M, had a successful career with Blue Cross. One day, his wife up and left him for another guy and he just went berserk. He stopped paying bills, jumped out of the rat race and walked away from everything." He shook his head. "Now, that's a damn shame."

So, this really wasn't changing the subject after all.

"What are you saying, Daddini? I'm going to be a homeless wanderer?" I was half-joking, half sullen.

He couldn't bear looking at my teary face. He shrugged, raised his eyebrows and lifted his palms upward. "All I'm saying is that guy, he decided circumstances would get him down. Maybe he would have met someone new; maybe he could have gotten a better job. Hell, maybe he could have moved somewhere warm and sunny where the economy isn't shit and people don't shoot each other so much," he chuckled at that strand of thought. "The point is, he opted not to fight the fight and instead took himself out of the game."

He finally looked at me, his attentive audience. "I know you'd never do that, no matter what rotten hand you've been dealt." And, with that, he picked himself out of my small car, lit up another cigarette and shot a vexed look at his lighter. "Damn smokes will be the death of me."

He started to head back when he had a change of heart. "Hey, one more thing, Maye. I'll talk to Walker about your job. It ain't over until the stuffy suit counts his beans."

I drove straight back to my apartment with a lump in my throat and sappy songs on the radio to resonate my emotions. When I pulled into the structure, adjacent from the Science Center, Detroit Institute of Arts and

Detroit Public Library-essentially the city's cultural hub-I parked in my assigned compact spot and began trudging up the concrete stairs. I lit a Marlboro Light on my way up. *Nothing like smoking and climbing stairs. Way to feel fit, Veronica,* I scolded myself. I made a stop at the keyed mailboxes in a metal box within the lobby wall. Mine was full to the max with bills and condolence cards. I had just scooped the mail a couple days ago, but it sure piled up fast. While I scampered down the narrow hallway with grey checkered carpet and beige walls, a couple tenants happily strolled by, sending me smiles in their bliss. Oh right, I recalled; they were newlyweds. "Well, la-dee-da," I felt myself mouth out of earshot from them like the truly mature person I am.

    I shook the door handle a bit for the key to take its full effect, swung open the door to my sweet gray tabby and sat dumbfounded for a few minutes on my stylish yet less-than-comfortable contemporary sofa. I scrolled down my iPod that leaned against a few framed pictures. One was of Natalia and me at Cedar Point before riding roller coasters the summer before. She had just reached the height marked by the swirly red-and-white bar, indicating she could go on whatever ride she wanted in the entire vast theme park. , threw up after the fifteenth ride. The second was of Gavin and me at Navy Pier shortly after he proposed. Gavin's sandy hair was

77

blowing a bit in the breeze and I wore my hair in a ponytail and sunglasses over my tearfully happy eyes. His arm squeezed me tightly with sheer pride and excitement that I said yes. My arms were wrapped around his stomach like a little girl would encapsulate a giant teddy bear. The third was of my mom and dad, sitting on the porch, in traditional rocking chairs with lemonade glasses in their hands. My mom's hair flowed onto her shoulders, emphasizing her dark features and casual blue blouse, khaki shorts and sandals. She was smiling brightly at my father, who was holding her free hand with the one free of his beverage. He was in jeans, sneakers and a Red Wings T-shirt. They looked serene. I cranked on every disgruntled girl singer or band I could find from old school Alanis Morissette to Fiona Apple's "When the Pawn" to Katie Perry's "Hot and Cold" song. It was silly for me to seek a theme in that tiny device, but the uprising lyrics made sense to my melancholy.

    I got careless, though, while pouring myself some cranberry juice in the kitchenette with granite countertops and stainless steel appliances because the iPod automatically went to the next artist and my would-be wedding song blared unexpectedly after No Doubt's "Just a Girl." It had been Gavin's choice and I couldn't help but agree. I felt naked standing there, utterly exposed to the moment. "When a Man Loves a Woman" by

Percy Sledge permeated my loft to deflate all my girl-power fortitude and soak up my space with indecisive emotion. I nearly began sobbing again when I decided to suck it up, shut off the song and get dressed for my date. I had the crazy idea that I would get my revenge against Gavin tonight by seeing someone else. Revenge for his lies or whatever kept him from full disclosure about that fateful night. Revenge for him having it so easy when I had it so damn tough. Revenge for him not trying to mend what was broken harder and faster, I unwillingly admitted to myself.

Enough, I told myself. I wouldn't find what I was looking for in my closet. Most of my fall and winter clothes were trendy, worn in layers with tights and boots. They'd be suitable for work and casual outings. What I needed tonight was something I could locate only in Sierra's closet, or, shall I say, my spare-room closet she'd stashed her clothes in. I opened it like a woman possessed, fingering the slinky outfits she squeeze into for verisimilitude to auditions like the vampiress role. I finally decided upon the red satin short dress with a plunging front neckline that was practically backless. Out of fear of being cold, I went to my own closet again for a black faux fur wrap and some super high heels. My makeup was not like earlier, well, what was left from earlier, that is. This time, I dabbled on darker shadow, red lipstick and spider-leg-long mascara. I replaced my usual Este Lauder Beautiful perfume with Givenchy's Very Irresistible. Emotional baggage aside, I felt like that scent's name when glancing over myself in the mirror.

This time, when I stalked out of the apartment, the happy newlyweds were returning with rented movies and Starbucks. The wife socked her man in the arm when he stared a little too long at me as they passed. She wouldn't be asking to borrow sugar from me any time soon, I presumed. If I thought his reaction was over-the-top, I certainly was surprised by Luke's.

He had traded his wool coat and jeans for black slacks, a gray button-down and leather dress shoes. The effect was a hodgepodge of sleekness and charm with a splash of his trademark mysterious demeanor and coy amusement with me. The amusement factor increased a few notches when I walked into the candle-lit elegant restaurant. He jolted up from his seat to greet me with wide eyes.

"I think I almost knocked over a candle and started a fire," he said, flustered. "Burning down a hotel is not exactly what I had in mind. Although, seeing you like this wasn't either."

"You don't like it?" My question may have sounded flirty, but I was suddenly, genuinely self-conscious. I had taken off my wrap by now.

"Like it? I do. I, uh, really do. I just don't want someone to knock me out so he can take my seat." He laughed, sort of rubbing his throat and, by doing so, unintentionally pushing down his button-down to reveal another tattoo. I pictured the cross on his arm. I tried not staring at the one on his chest, which I could make out only the top of -- a woman's head of long hair. I thought that was odd. It had me wondering about this woman-an ex-girlfriend, an ex-flame, an ex...wife? I certainly hoped it wasn't the last one. This table had only enough room for my baggage. His would have to be a carry-on or one of us would need to be excused.

"You looked beautiful earlier, too," he said genuinely.

A nervous laugh escaped. I had checked on Natalia via a long, thorough conversation with Barb, who was working a double shift thanks to the night nurse calling in with two sick kids at home. Natalia was never far from my mind, yet I had another topic on the forefront: The end of my hard-earned and hard-fallen journalism career. Luke pulled out a chair for me and scooted me back in. I was always a sucker for a gentleman. I fiddled with the menu a bit before we agreed to order a bottle of red wine with our entrees.

"You're so quiet," he said, as if he knew my typical amount of chatter. Somehow he sensed I wasn't just a quiet person. My outfit certainly wasn't the silent type. It had its own message to relay. I began feeling even more foolish for wearing it. "You must have a lot on your mind. It's okay with me if you want to talk about it."

"Oh, I'm fine. I'm just...just thinking how I didn't expect to see you again." There, I thought it was a successful change of subject. I wouldn't spill my sob story about the day's events to this man. That would constitute as entirely too confiding and borderline needy.

"Well, I'm glad that wasn't the last time I saw you." He took my hand over the table. I recalled his touch in the ambulance, how he soothed me after I got sick and walked me into the hospital with his coat over my bare arms. I squeezed back. His face, not the flickering candle, seemed to illuminate the table.

Soon, our waiter gently poured the cabernet into our oversized wine glasses, and the more the alcohol flowed, the more our conversation did. We talked for what seemed like hours about anything and everything. I was amazed by how close I felt to Luke. I learned he was twenty-nine, born in L.A. but raised in Chicago, and that he was also a part-time firefighter. Both his parents were teachers, like my mother had been. And he had two dogs, a husky and a Lab-German Shepherd mix. (See, it wasn't just flirting. I actually learned something about him.)

Since he already knew so much about my life, I reasoned finally that telling him I lost my job would be no biggie. I had finished my lemon chicken and pasta, which felt like the best meal I had eaten in weeks, when I realized how tipsy I was feeling. I disregarded my state to continue with the story of that horrid Gale Babes, Randall Walker and my entrusted editor M. Daddy. Then, as a topper to the salmonella-laced emotional cake, I told him about Harvey. By the time I finished my story, I was on the verge of tears again.

"I think I saw that guy Harvey at the hospital. Was he the one who was talking to you before you came over to me that day I brought your purse?" I shook my head, afraid that if I spoke tears would roll. He'd seen me cry before. He'd seen me puke before. I only hoped he wouldn't witness either of the two again tonight.

"He even looks like an ass. Or more like some comic book villain like an evil scientist or something," he tried lightening the mood. "You're the sexy heroine. Even your outfit could rival Wonder Woman's costume."

I was cracking up at his silliness. I liked his humor and was even more grateful to him for saving me from losing my cool again.

Luke insisted we order dessert. I got the cheesecake while he ordered an ice cream-topped brownie. We ended up casually sampling each other's desserts as if we'd been dating for months. The room was spinning when I finished the last of my wine. And, then I ordered some more. I lit up a cigarette in a move to roll with the ride. Luke, being a firefighter and all, wasn't a smoker, but he didn't give me any grief so that was a relief.

He was under the impression the date was over since our meals were finished and wine depleted. I didn't want to go home, though. I was having such a delicious time chatting with him; it was warm and welcoming and made my apartment seem barren. The wine spoke through me when I asked to see his room.

"I've never been in this hotel before. I want to raid your mini bar," I said playfully.

"You have visitor's rights, but you're cut off for the rest of the night, missy." He looked down at me, since he was about a foot taller, and brought me in close with his arm around my shoulders. I walked under his blanketing warmth, feeling his heart pound next to me and staring into his beautiful brown eyes. I envisioned him in his firefighter's uniform looking brave and even more handsome, which seemed impossible from the way he appeared tonight. We headed down the hallway toward his room when a herd of teens rushed by in homecoming attire and drunken giddiness. One girl was carrying her silver high heels down the hall, pressing her bare feet into the heavily trafficked carpet. I grimaced at the sight of that and Luke laughed. When they had all vanished, presumably toward a stretch limo, I saw someone else heading out from his room in the same direction. And, even worse, he saw us.

"Oh, hey Harvey!" I said as if we'd been best friends for years. Once it registered to him, he snarled at Luke and me in the same distasteful way he viewed us hugging in the hospital. "I just want to thank you for coming to town to destroy my career. You really outdid yourself. Is there anything else I can do for you? Maybe point you to my home for you to have it broken into or my car to have it stolen? You're such a miracle worker after all."

"Veronica, I warned you in Chicago you were no match for this family. They're high class." He scanned my skimpy outfit. "You're clearly not in Gavin's league and, as far as your career, you did that to yourself. I see you move pretty fast anyway. Well, moving fast is probably not something new to someone like you--"

His face jerked backward violently. A splash of blood shot from his nose and hit the white wall in the hallway. It took a second or two for me to gather my bearings. I was drunk, but I knew I didn't cause Harvey's rearrangement. Then I saw Luke's hand was still clenched and his mouth tight.

"You got anything else you want to say to her? Go ahead and say it," he challenged the weasel.

Shocked and shaking, Harvey stammered for probably the first time in his life. "No, no, no...I, uh, I don't want any trouble."

A bellhop ran over when he saw the aftermath of the scene. Luke raised his hands like he didn't know what happened and told the employee to ask Harvey, who quickly responded that he tripped over his own shoes and hit his face on the wall. The bellhop ran to get him some ice, but Harvey was out the door before he returned.

It was a sobering moment. Luke had punched my enemy, defending me when I never thought I wanted or needed anyone to do so. I touched his knuckles, which were starting to redden and swell.

"You need to ice them," I said, finding the nearest bin around the corner and scooping ice into a plastic cup for him. He was being tough and refusing at first, but I wouldn't relent so he went with the program.

"Your fiance, I mean ex-fiance, is really out to get you, huh?" he furrowed his brows while shaking his hand.

"Gavin?" I mimicked his hand shaking with my head. "No, that's all Harvey. He and Gavin's dad are pure evil."

Luke hardly looked convinced.

Thinking Gavin would plot against me sent razors to my heart. Couldn't he understand my irrational behavior at the news conference was grief-fueled? He had been at the funeral, after all. I couldn't imagine his presence was truly sinister. He was capable yet benevolent. Rueful, I banished the thoughts from my intoxicated mind.

We entered his room. Luke began fumbling for the light switch, located it and told me to make myself at home. "No mini bar though. You can't handle any more alcohol. I saw you staggering in here," he laughed.

"And, what are you going to do if I break into it?" I smiled.

He walked over to me with a grin. "You saw what I did to the last guy who messed with me. Trust me, you don't want any of this." He rolled up his sleeves playfully like he was gunning for a fight.

"I think I can handle you," I said with confidence. And I pulled him close to me, smelling his cologne and feeling his heart beat fast.

He swooped in to kiss me long and hard, touching the back of my neck with his warm hands. My arms were around him now and I was passionately kissing him back. When I started to think how much I wanted him to throw me on the bed, I realized how drunk I really must be. He was undeniably good-looking and easy to talk to, but I couldn't sleep with him. Not on the first date.

My body was sending different signals. Still, I figured I would have to address the extent of our intimacy in a moment-after I'd enjoyed a bit more making out with Luke. His hands glided downward from my neck to my dress just above my breasts before the plunging line that made it impossible to wear a bra. He discovered that himself when he pushed the dress to my waist to touch my chest. He wasn't just looking into my eyes when he said, "You're gorgeous." I was breathing heavily by then, moving my hand to touch him above his pants where it was his turn to moan. He picked me up so my legs were around his waist and set me down on the bed underneath him. Soon, my dress was completely off and I was lying there only in a red, laced thong. Perhaps I anticipated this ending a smidge, since these aren't my typical panties. I felt his finger slide them over so he could enter me, and in my drunkenness I was going to oblige. But he stopped, falling silent besides his short breaths.

Then he spoke. "I don't think I ever wanted something so badly," he said, almost surprised by his admission. "You're the most beautiful girl I've ever known."

I was a bit annoyed now. Talk about bad timing for a heart-to-heart.

"But we can't do this," he said.

"Why not?" I could feel a wave of hotness cascade over my face. I was thankful for the dimness.

"You'll regret it. Maybe not right away because I'm sure we'd both enjoy ourselves, but you will eventually. I didn't come all the way out here for you to hate me afterward for taking advantage of you."

"I'm a big girl. I don't need you to tell me what's best for me." I wiggled out from underneath him, but only after I got a full glimpse at the tattoo on his chest. It was of a woman with long hair and a soft, almost surreal expression on her face. I squinted at the ink on him, pondering more of its back story. He definitely caught the moment, yet offered nothing in return. That was it. I was so through with everyone at this point.

I grabbed my dress and darted for the bathroom. While I was scrambling to get back into the V-lined contraption, he knocked on the door.

"Veronica, don't be angry with me. I'm just trying to be honest with you."

I opened the door, slid out and faced him. I slapped on my nicest, politest smile and said, "I'm not angry. I'm glad you brought me back to reality. Thanks for dinner. I have to go."

And I headed for the door, inwardly fuming but outwardly gracious. He was no fool, though. He knew I was pissed.

"Okay, let me give you a ride back." I thought of straddling his motorcycle in my dress and brushed off the possibility quickly. "Well, let me call you a cab."

I couldn't tolerate the thought of him shooing me out of here. If he was doing the right thing, it sure had a funny way of making me feel like crap.

"That won't be necessary. The hospital is across the street. I have clothes there and I spend the night with Natalia almost every night." I straightened my back with pride, my voice cool and smooth. "Although, I would have made an exception tonight. Cleary, as you pointed out, that would be a mistake."

I closed the door in his face. Childish, perhaps. But it felt good shelling out some of the rejection he abundantly dished out.

Not even halfway down the hall, I sunk at the thought my wrap was back in that room. Not hell or high water could propel me backward to retrieve it, so I called it a total loss. Maybe he'd try returning, or burning it for that matter, since I slammed the door on him. Well, at least I had my purse! Nevertheless, I had to take the walk of shame through the all-too-familiar hospital path to Natalia's room. The air-conditioning was rustling in the halls, keeping bacteria at bay with Antarctica-esque temps. My pride was bruised while my body was practically blue. Barb's curiosity was overridden by sheer worry when she saw me skulk in. She gathered one of those heated, thick blankets for me and set it on my usual lounge chair that converted to a sleeper. I thanked her, kissed Natalia on the cheek and took a long hot shower. I scrubbed off every last speck of makeup, rinsed the smoky smell out of my hair and climbed into my long black cotton pajamas and matching slippers before sinking into the sleeper for what felt like my first shut-eye in months.

Chapter Eight

I NEVER HEARD SIERRA SO DISTRAUGHT, WITH THE EXCEPTION OF PERFORMANCES AT THE LOCAL THEATER. Her coarse voice spilled through the phone in despair. It took me a moment at the grocery store to shake my phone, thinking our connection from Detroit to New York was shabby. Instead, she yelped for me to listen some more. Something was terribly wrong, something I couldn't quite make out and later wished I didn't.

"Roni. Roni." Silence ensued. Then: "He's not breathing. There's no pulse. I put my makeup mirror under his nose and nothing. Nothing!"

"Who's not breathing? What is going on? I can barely understand you." I shrugged incredulously at the phone, seeking clarity with an obviously murky situation. "Are you rehearsing a play or something?"

"Oh God. It's Michael. You know..." her voice trailed away from the receiver. It was difficult to tell if she was there. Then she returned within audible reach, nearly panting.

I couldn't decipher whether she was being a drama queen or if there was a legitimate issue. My cell phone displayed the incoming call as "out of area," but it was clear she was in the Manhattan hotel, the Mayflower, on its phone or her own cell. While I heard some shuffling on the other end, I had a despicable image of McConner nude, toppled over a luxurious bed, dead of a heart attack while bedding the much younger, out-of-his-league beauty. I shuddered. Turns out my cynical supposition would be overshadowed by the actual events of his death.

"Before you say anything else," I interrupted Sierra to her exasperated dismay. "Where are you calling me from?"

"My cell phone. I'm not a total idiot."

"Coulda fooled me," was almost on my tongue when I decided to swallow it in favor of being pragmatic; plus, it would delay her story. "OK, I'm listening. Tell me what happened and we'll take it from there." Veronica Maye Crisis Specialist present. Now if only I could solve a third of my own disasters. I was ditching the cart to a far-off corner of the grocery store and heading to my Malibu for privacy.

"He was respectful the entire time. I went on my audition yesterday. The lead went to some Broadway regular, but, listen, I beat the competition to be her understudy." Then the little pride in her voice broke off like a thin sheet of ice on Lake St. Clair. "He'd been keeping his space, you know, really nice, and I thought he was totally harmless. So when he offered to take me to dinner after the audition at this really fine restaurant in Little Italy, I said 'Great.' We actually had a nice conversation and he told me how much he admired my talent." Oh boy, he played to her ego. Smooth move, McConner.

I bit my wisecracking tongue. Again, not the time for that.

"Then he dropped me off at my door and left for his own room, I think. A couple hours later, he rang my room. He said that because he was a successful businessman, he had lots of connections with people in all industries and wanted me to meet a talent scout he reconnected with while in the city. But when I got to the room, it was just him. I sat down because he said his friend was running late and would arrive any minute." She was nearly out of breath all over again. I wasn't so much on pins and needles as I was perched above nails. Her words hammered me down farther and farther into the depths of this unusual scene-leaving her lips in a bizarre way since she was relaying the story next to a corpse.

"I could tell he'd been drinking. Then he started talking about how I knew this couldn't just be an innocent arrangement. I had to pay for the trip with my 'assets' before we left town." Something in her voice told me, in her heart of hearts, she had known this would be expected. "He started to get forceful. ... He threw me on the bed. It was the scariest thing ever. So, I was struggling a bit when I grabbed a metal tray off the nightstand. It was from room service last night and the maid never took it because he had spread his prescription pills on it. I slammed the tray down on his head. The pills flew everywhere. That shook him up and gave me enough time to get away from him."

I pictured the stout, sturdy man grasping for her. My stomach churned. Sierra was crying hysterically by now.

"But he kept coming at me."

Her next words took me, crime reporter, completely off guard.

"So, I stabbed him with a butter knife."

I guessed that the silverware was still in the room if the maid never retrieved the tray. That was really beside the point, though. My hand covered my mouth, not that I would be able to speak anyway.

"You have to tell me what to do. What should I do?" she trailed off in tears.

I inhaled, pulled out a cigarette and told her to call the police.

"It was self-defense. He was trying to rape you. Tell them exactly what you told me and there's no way you can be held accountable for anything else than defending yourself."

I took a hit from my cigarette. What else could I do?

I waited for her to tell me she was going to hang up and report

McConner's untimely yet necessary death. Instead she struck me with my own figurative metal tray.

"No," she uttered, suddenly calm. "I can't do that."

My eyes widened. I almost choked over the smoke. I stared at the phone as if my bewilderment could reach her through the molecules of the modern communications device.

"I'm sorry?"

"Roni, it would be the end of me. I'd never live it down. My career is all I have, besides you, of course," I could almost sense her head shaking. "No, I never gave them my name. The reservations are under his and, as far as anyone knows, I wasn't even here."

"You're talking crazy. Are *you* drunk? You just killed someone in self-defense. Report the death. Your nonexistent fans will understand," I said through gritted teeth.

"Listen, the only thing anyone knows is that I'm in New York for an audition. He peeked into the theater for a second to see me on stage, but no one saw him, I'm sure of it. And, I highly doubt anyone in Little Italy would recognize me because I was wearing a blonde wig from the audition."

She was trying out for the stage production of "Legally Blonde, The Musical" as the lead, Elle. Now she would be the Illegal Murderous Blonde.

"You need to do the right thing, Sierra. You're not thinking clearly. Your fingerprints are in your room and he's dead in there."

"My fingerprints aren't on any criminal database. And they won't look around Michigan for a suspect in New York." She wasn't really speaking to me any longer. She was convincing herself to flee the hotel. In fact, I gathered by her movement and rustling on the other end, she had walked back to her room, collected her belongings and hailed a cab.

"You are crazy." Wasn't she my voice of reason after the crash, telling me to keep my temper in check? How did the tables turn so suddenly?

"Listen," she said in a cool voice, as if I was bothering *her* with this call. "I should never have involved you." Then, there was a click. I was left dumbfounded, completely disconnected in mind and space from my best friend-who had just killed a man and fled.

I had been praying a lot lately. In fact, I've been feeling remorseful for channeling God and Christ with such inconsistency. It seemed when things had been going well, prayers were sporadic. Now, as this unbearably tumultuous time encircled my existence, the prayers were like air to my lips.

So, needless to say, I took a long, thoughtful breath for Sierra... and my would-be slip of morality the night before.

Feeling like a battered woman, I summoned some dignity to skulk back into the grocery store, regroup my groceries and check them out at the register-clad with the emotional black eye given to me by a friend I desperately longed to protect.

I parked on the street because it was easier than carrying the groceries through the parking garage. I couldn't wait to pet my tabby, Scoop, and feel close to something warm and comforting. I also needed to shower, eat and head back to the hospital. There were inspirational books about surviving adversities I wanted to read aloud at Natalia's bedside. (The books might be too grown up, but I reasoned my soothing voice would be uplifting.) Plus, I bought some pretty new pajamas and sock set for her as well as a beautiful floral quilt from a nearby vintage store. I knew the money would dry out soon; still, I didn't possess the emotional or mental stamina to deal with it. These internal ramblings siphoned from one brain cell to the next as I approached the doorstep with heavy bags of food in hand, looking down at the pavement and series of steps. So, it was his shoes I saw first. When you love someone, you remember their shoes because, oftentimes, they appear next to your own near the door or in the closet.

If I'd been an old wise owl, I could have craned my neck every direction to heed the unexpected events of today. Instead I was akin to a heads-down possum, crossing an intersection with traffic oncoming from all directions. Gavin was the car that lumbered over my tail.

Like a klutz, I dropped a plastic bag on his brown leather Sketchers. He winced in a manly I-can-tolerate-pain kind of way. His blue-gray eyes were as beautiful as ever, except they looked surreal and sullen at once. He reached down to retrieve the ripped plastic bag for me as I gathered the cans and intact juice bottle. I stuffed them in the other bag and apologized for my clumsiness.

"It was an accident. They happen," his words were firm. Point taken, Gavin.

"Yes, but there's usually a cause. For instance, there were too many items in this bag. It ripped and that's why it fell on your foot." He encroached on my turf and decidedly took a stance with me, so I didn't feel bad for my harshness. "You see, at least I can tell you honestly what happened." My back was straighter than ever. My eyes defiant.

He shook his head. His sandy hair was an inch or two longer, a little wavier. His broad shoulders seemed a little slouched, which was abnormal for the former jock and aspiring lawyer, and they didn't exude his usual cool confidence. His brown woolen coat hung over his dark jeans. He stuck his hands in his coat pockets, since I refused his assistance.

"Can we talk?"

I peered around, shrugged my shoulders and lifted my free hand as if to say "why not?"

"I mean inside, Roni." He was growing impatient. Smartass me could hardly blame him, though.

"Okay. I need to put these away and then we can talk. Follow me."

"I remember where you live, thank you." His voice wasn't arrogant or proud. Really, I sensed hurt in it.

Scoop bypassed me to make a beeline for Gavin. He smiled at that gesture.

"At least someone is welcoming me here." He patted the purring feline. "You're a good guy, Scoopy."

I rolled my eyes as I stocked my fridge. That cat was a damn traitor.

Gavin had always been acute at reading my emotions. It was a blessing and a curse to me. "You know, not everything has to be black or white. Sometimes, it's shades of gray."

"People who do something wrong are always in favor of 'shades of gray.' I'd rather know where I stand."

He came toward me in the small kitchen. When he took my hand, it felt so familiar. It made me sad to think I was planning on seeking comfort by petting my cat when I had this gorgeous man all lined up to become my husband-or he had me lined up to be his wife.

"I missed you, Roni. Why don't you see that? Why are you so cold to me when I love you?" A wave of guilt passed over me when I thought about the press conference and how I'd been out for blood. "What's done is done. I wish I could take it back more than anything. But, we need to move forward. I hope it can be together." He urged me with his eyes. They chiseled away at the stone shell encompassing me and I fell into his arms like I did after the accident in his hospital room. I betrayed myself worse than Scoop and, even worse, I was bawling like a baby.

"It's gotten out of control. You don't know what I've been dealing with. Natalia's in a coma. Who knows if she will awake? My dad left the state for work and hasn't returned or called. He left everything to me. I got in trouble at the paper and basically lost my job. And, Sierra..." this was not my secret to tell, so I stopped short.

He wiped the tears away and shushed me like a gentle parent. His embrace was gentle yet his muscles tightened to hold me. I felt incredibly tiny pressed against his tall, athletic frame. And, of course, I felt small in other ways. I was confused, despondent and uncharacteristically emotional. Like prayers, tears were now abundant in my life regardless of the norm before.

He bent down to kiss me. It was tender and heated like his embrace. His finger tilted my chin upward so he could stare into my hazel eyes.

"Even in hysterics, you're beautiful. How is that possible?" He seemed genuinely amazed although I felt anything but. I was sure by now the mascara was tumbling down and the gloss on my ample lips was cracked and dry. My hair was mostly in place thanks to a ponytail holder that he began removing. His large fingers filtered through my hair and he began kissing my eyelids, cheeks and then lips. By the time he picked me up to take me to the bedroom, I was dizzy. Emotions poured out of me while he pulled me closer.

"I love you, Roni. It's just us. It always will be. No complications. Just you and me." He was whispering in my ear. I expected for him to undress me, but he just rested there with his arms around me. Relief swept over me. His presence was powerful and perplexing. I didn't need lovemaking in the equation. Plus, I was overwhelmingly tired from the day's shifts and turns. I sank into sleep with Gavin by my side. I dreamed of us at Navy Pier watching the Ferris wheel shrink from the distance as we chugged along the water in the little boat he proposed in. When I woke, he was gone. I looked around the room and saw a Post-it note that read, "Had to run a couple errands. Meet you at the hospital tonight." I wondered where he went and if I trusted he was actually doing as he said. I knew he would find Natalia with ease since I mentioned her room number to him in my crying frenzy. I set the note down on the nightstand when it saw it: The gleaming diamond engagement ring wrapped around my thin ring finger, as if it had never left.

Chapter Nine

CRIMSON LEAVES CRUNCHED BENEATH MY LEATHER KNEE-HIGH BOOTS. Some jolted around the late autumn air while others lay listless for a heartier breeze to propel them to their destination, before disintegration. It was that undeniably altering time of year when winter tried pushing her emergence before fall could bow quietly away.

The cemetery tucked away in my parents' neighborhood of Garden Falls was the final resting place of most people I knew. It consumed a mile-long narrow patch of land that was outlined with weeping willows. Outside the cemetery, cars zoomed by, people walked their pooches and stores invited shoppers. Inside, it was peaceful, as it should be. I wrapped my arms around my stylish plaid jacket that fell just below my waist. I felt the wind gently toy with my raven locks, but paid it no mind. There wasn't anyone in sight, to my relief. It seemed these past weeks dealt unexpected turn after unexpected turn, most recently with Gavin's and Luke's visits, and I just wanted to sit alone next to my mother's grave. The ground was cold beneath me. I mouthed psalms and set vivid red roses before the headstone that read "Flora Mayes, Wife of Robert, Mother of Veronica and Natalia and daughter of Samuel and Belinda Garrett." My grandparents had long passed away, but my mother would have wanted to pay them tribute.

    I traced the engraved words with my finger and remembered that we couldn't afford granite at the time since the funeral costs piled up and my father said he was stretched too thin. I knew his company wasn't faring well in light of the dire straits facing the Big Three auto companies, so I offered what I could. Still, I remembered that limestone fades over time. The notion that the inscription on her headstone would wear down years from now left me shaking in the wind. The dirt was still lifted and fresh around the plot.

    I rose to my feet, brushed some foliage off my jacket and passed through the cemetery gates. It wasn't until I reached the other side that I realized I had been holding in oxygen as I left the breathless behind me.

    The weeping willows loomed above and shaded me from the sliver of sunshine beaming down between the clouds. I followed the concrete path outside the cemetery to an old wooden bridge hovering over a murky creek. Occasionally, a mallard or two could be spotted in the serpentine body. Today, a beautiful swan with a fiery orange beak waded upstream alone.

    The chilly breeze swept through my hair.

When my cell phone rang, I thought it would be Gavin expecting me at the hospital. It wasn't evening yet, but he generally arrives to places early. It wasn't.

"Roni. Sam Bernett here. Hope you're all right."

"Thanks for saying so. What's up?"

"Either the Chronicle gets the story from us through you or they don't get it at all." The police captain was no stranger to firmness. "I'm not dealing with that moron Gale Baby or whatever her name is." Uh, Gale Babes. I loathed her more than Monday mornings.

"What story? I'm sort of, uh, out of the loop right now."

"Meet me at the scene on the east side. I have to go, but I'll have one of my officers shoot you a text with the address. If you want it, this will be an exclusive." I knew he didn't behold trust in any other reporter. Gosh, he was an ideal source if I ever found one. Too bad my life was tied up in a hurricane right now and I technically wasn't even a reporter any more. Then it occurred to me that this could be exactly what I needed to earn back my job. Lord knows I had to pay bills when my little nest egg dried.

"See you there," I said.

"Good to have you back." He said approvingly.

The text followed immediately: 412 Jackson, east side.

Without time to thoroughly think this through, I speed-walked back to my car, typed the address in my GPS and darted to the scene. Usually, big breaking news attracted television crews and hordes of reporters. This one was surrounded only by police cars and yellow tape. I guessed Gale only had a scent of something going on, not any concrete information. It wouldn't be surprising if she or others caught wind of it soon, so I moved quickly. My adrenaline raced.

Captain Bernett was behind the tape, directing his detectives toward the inside of the deteriorating bungalow on a street of inconsistencies. For instance, the most striking brick colonial with French doors and expensive bay windows stood disapprovingly next to a partially charred and vacant ranch. The two houses summarized this city, full of hope and despair, beauty and ugliness. It was a hodgepodge of irony, as conflicted as me.

Bernett's lean tall frame, cloaked with a tan trench, appeared almost regal as he leaned in to one officer and then the next. There was no question who was in charge.

I stood respectfully behind the tape. I wasn't one of those self-entitled reporters who acted like a cop. A line was drawn and I knew better than to cross it. That is, until he waved me over it.

I was accustomed to our small talk. His grim expression told me that was far from his mind.

"Captain, what do you have here?" My pen and notebook were in my pocket by now. Veronica Mayes, Fired Reporter at the Scene. I felt both comfortable in the routine of things and out of place for being there.

He shook his head. "Three dead of gunfire." That was pretty bad... although this is Detroit and gun-related deaths, especially relating to drugs, have been higher on a single day. I was about to inquire with some finesse why he thought this case was especially pertinent when he continued. "That's three in the house. Two more out back and one in that Escalade in the driveway."

"Holy shit."

"Yeah, that alone is a tragedy." He paused as if pondering telling me more. He looked into my eyes from his imposing height. His lips curled to one side and his face sank like a boulder in the Pacific. "The two out back are my men."

I patiently awaited more information. By the lack of it, I knew those words were like lead consuming his paper tongue.

"Are we on the record?" I wouldn't have extended that courtesy to anyone else in such circumstances. This would be a tremendous blow to his department and I wasn't even an employee at the paper. Did he want to risk releasing this so soon?

He peered over the rickety fence at hard-working detectives in rubber gloves putting mini glass covers over bullets. I couldn't see the bodies, but I doubted they were in uniforms.

"A crooked cop damages not only my force's reputation, he is a personal assault to the years I spent trying to clean these streets of thugs and their poison. Write the story. You will have full disclosure with as many facts as possible. Where there are roadblocks, I will assist you off the record the best I can."

"I'm sorry that this happened."

"Me, too." I never saw him so glum. "Me, too."

I scurried to the bodies in back first. The smell was horrid. It reeked of immediate decay. I always wondered why death rushed stench so soon. Didn't it have eternity to wreak havoc on its physical claims? I covered my mouth with my left hand while pulling my pen and pad from my pocket with the right. A tall brunette detective with a square jaw and large brown eyes sized me up suspiciously and almost ushered me away until Bernett nodded to indicate I was allowed. She glared at me and I stood expressionless until she stormed away to another task.

The first officer was lying on his back wearing jeans, Timberlands and a flannel shirt under a red hoodie. He had a full head of lofty jet-black wavy hair, olive skin and nearly red lips. I thought he looked Puerto Rican and no older than thirty. Despite the awful odor permeating the backyard, he was serene. I soon realized the color of his hoodie nearly camouflaged the bloodstains on his chest. His gun not more than a foot away on the grass. The second officer, who was a younger light-skinned black man, still clutched his handgun. He wore khakis, a bomber and Nike sneakers. His body was contorted and I could tell he died in pain. A trail of their own blood, smeared by their injured bodies, connected their path from the house. Who knew how long it took for someone to discover him while he bled out from gunshot wounds to each leg and his back. Crooked or not, I just felt awful for him. No one should die like that.

    I didn't dare encroach on their space. I did, however, head into the bungalow where my nose burned with the contained rank of death. Before reaching inside, I saw a short, stocky dark-skinned black man outside the doorway, his body curled and gun in his hand. No doubt, this was the cops' shooter, whom they fired upon as well.

The stench wafted around outside, but in the house there was nowhere for it to turn. I jotted down the gruesome scene: A heavy white man and a thin, emaciated blonde woman to his side, covered in blood and bullets. The wooden coffee table in the middle of the small room contained what I would later learn were packs of heroin, crack and pot from the police department evidence room.

I spoke to neighbor after neighbor who slammed the door in my face. They had a reason to be scared. Criminals in this neighborhood would not appreciate a snitch. Finally, as the chill seeped into my bones and I felt the urge to surrender to defeat, an elderly black man opened the door to his incredibly well-kempt home.

"I surmise you would like to hear about the scum of this neighborhood. The delinquents who belong behind bars instead of imprisoning these good people." His bushy gray eyebrows rose for my response.

"Yes sir."

"Well then, come in dear."

His home was as pleasant and tidy as his yard. I could tell it had been decorated by an older woman by the affinity for pastel flower wall borders and curtains. I wondered if his wife was there.

"I understand, sir, if you are not comfortable using your name because of the violence on your block."

His face scrunched and his shoulders rose proudly. "Young lady, do I look like I'm afraid of little boys with baggy pants that don't cover their behinds? That's all these thugs are-little boys who never became real men. Real men make honest livings, provide for their families and are upstanding citizens of their communities. I am a retired educator, a high school principal, and I have five grown sons who earn honest livings."

"That's wonderful. You must be proud of all your accomplishments." I was sincere and he knew it.

"Yes, I am proud. But, pride does not change the fact that gunfire rings near my home on a regular basis and my grandchildren cannot visit because it's too dangerous for them to play outside or even walk up my front steps."

I nodded for him to continue.

"My name is Roland Whitikar. I'm seventy-nine and I've lived on this street early enough to witness its prosperity and long enough to see its demise.

"The man who 'owns' that house is Jerome Unine, a heavy white guy who lives with his crack-fiend girlfriend and his best friend. I don't know the girlfriend or his friend's name, but they are nothing but trouble as well. They get visitors at all hours, as most drug dens do. They're fond of yelling and hollering in the streets when they've injected too much of that junk in their arms. Lately, a couple guys have been going in and out of there a lot. It's kind of hard not to notice them because they don't seem like the usual trash that Jerome brings in." He paused, and then spelled out his and Unine's names for me.

I described the officers lying in the backyard. Could these be the recent visitors? He concurred.

"So they met their maker today?" He didn't seem sad at all. "It was only a matter of time."

"They were actually police officers who were allegedly doing illegal activity on the side."

"Wouldn't be the first time. Won't be the last time," he said with an air of infinite knowledge. I thanked the first-hand historian of Jackson Street for his time and frankness. He said to think nothing of it. He stood as I stood and showed me out.

Bernett confirmed the identity of Jerome Unine for me as a well-known street hustler with a reputation for brutality and tendency to dip into his own stashes. His girlfriend, Star Thomas, was an Eight Mile Road prostitute and crackhead whom Unine had known since she was a teenage customer. The curled body was that of was Marcus Jones, who was

Unine's good pal since they served time in state prison on felony drug charges and a rough-and-tumble enforcer. Officers Manny Perez and Donell Michael were on the Narcotics Team once upon a time, before they were transferred to the Gang Unit. It was impossible to say whether they met Unine and posse during their narcotics work since even Bernett wouldn't disclose their background, or lack there of, in a criminal investigation. I figured too many of the other players were still out there, along with upstanding undercover guys whose lives would be in jeopardy if too much got out.

As far as investigators could tell, the unpredictable Unine pulled his AK47 out on the cops during the botched drug deal. Maybe the cops skimmed some off the top before selling him a stash. Maybe Unine got paranoid they were legit. Only God could tell. No one in that bloody bungalow would now.

One of the cops fired first, killing Unine and his girl. His muscle followed the pair and none of them made it out alive.

I rushed to my car, headed to the newsroom and bypassed any bumps in the road to my writing. M. Daddy darted up with a grin, strolled over to me with his gold chain hanging from his neck. He was in a playfully good mood.

"Yo, yo, yo," he sounded absurdly hilarious. "Check out my fave cub reporter comin' back to the beat." I couldn't help but muster a laugh for his effort. He leaned in, speaking in a serious low tone. "You're ready to fight the good fight? It was my compelling story about that homeless guy, right? I can squeeze you into the Suit's office and make a case if you can remember your ability to speak this time."

"No verbal fighting today, M. Daddy." He glanced down in disappointment. "I've got it in writing. Make room on 1A will ya?" Astonishment swept his face.

"Oh," I continued with confidence. "Better make room on the payroll for me, too. Once this story runs, I want my job back *and* a raise."

He rubbed his balding head. "It better be damn good, kid."

"That it is."

I jogged to my desk, high-fiving my friend Carter, who had overheard the conversation.

"You go, girl!" He yelled with a beaming smile.

I saw Gale staring our way. Curiosity was gnawing her nylon-clad leg. She had tried desperately to listen to M. Daddy and me with as much tact as she could assemble, to no avail. Tempting as it was to rub it into her phony face, I decided that the moment she picked up the paper in the morning was enough sweet revenge for my liking.

If it hadn't been so close to deadline, I could have looked up the deceased folks' families and knocked on their doors. Instead, time crunched me to phone calls. It was actually call after call of the most dreadful opening conversations you could have. The officers' wives declined comment through barrels of tears. On the Perez call young children were audible in the background. I feared them seeing their mother in hysterics would be damaging, but then again, they lost their father today. That was life-altering in a more severe way.

I got caught up in the writing, in having things just so, that I forgot about time and everything else. M. Daddy, smelling of smoke, edited it at his angular desk while I watched carefully over his shoulder in case he had questions. His silence was killing me.

Then, he inhaled, scooted his chair back and turned to me with a wide grin.

"It *was* damn good, kid. Welcome back."

For the moment, I reveled in his praise. Nothing could bring me down from that second-when he gleamed at me with pride.

Wired from the events of the day and working like a dog on deadline, I grabbed my belongings and headed for the door. By the time I lit a cigarette and turned on my iPod hooked up to the car stereo, I recalled two crucial things: Gavin's sly slip of the sparkly engagement ring on my unknowing finger and our scheduled meeting at the hospital... hours ago.

My pace picked up to compensate for my inconsideration and also because the air was well overdue for clearing. I needed answers from Gavin about what led up to the accident, why he couldn't be forthright and how we were to proceed from here. I nearly started rehearsing my speech t when I accidentally slid past Luke, who was leaning on the cushioned hospital bench in the lobby.

He grabbed my hand while I scampered by, still pumped from filing my story.

"Sit by me, will ya?" He patted the bench. His brown eyes were as gentle as his touch. He wore jeans and his leather coat with his helmet next to him on the bench.

"I didn't know you were still in town," I obliged, but didn't sit too close.

"A couple of my firefighter friends out this way and I hung out for a bit." He glanced at me. "I figured I'd swing by here to see you before I leave."

"Oh, Okay. Well, drive safely."

"Veronica. I didn't imagine it to be this way. I didn't mean to offend you."

Embarrassment flushed over me.

"We don't need to have this conversation. Really." I said politely. His downward lips unmistakably frowned. "Look, I'm a total mess right now. I know it. Maybe when things calm down, I can take a step back and think clearly."

"Well, when that happens, call me and we'll try this again. Promise?" He handed me his number in chicken scratch on the hotel stationery. Then, we stood and he wrapped his arms around me and, to my astonishment, kissed my lips. I pulled back gracefully, as not to hurt his feelings, but the damage was done. Gavin was on the lobby's side of the closing elevator, looking exhausted. Well, as tired as you can appear through seeping anger.

Luke was oblivious to his presence. *Thank Heaven for small favors,* I thought. He released me, strolled out the automatic doors and, presumably, hopped on his bike for a chilly drive back to Chicago. I braced myself for the oncoming storm. Flashes of a yelling match ensued in my mind. In hindsight, I would have found that favorable to what he did next. His sunken shoulders raised and lowered with each deep breath. I was the possum in his path again. Ever so still, I stood with bated breath for his reaction.

Anguish was the most noticeable feature laid in those grayish-blue eyes. For the first time, I feared a life without him, devoid of those loving glances, warm embraces and his pillar of strength. Had I been lying to myself all along? And here he was, back in my life, willing to slide the ring back on my finger despite me humiliating him, attempting to slander his good name. I didn't invite Luke here, nor had I slept with him...Well, that was actually credited to his restraint. Regardless, words were elusive beings in the universe of my mouth and mind. I had no good explanation.

His exasperated tone was low, almost a whisper.

"For the past few weeks you've been thinking that you don't know me. I thought it was confusion and loss that muddled your mind.» He stepped closer with too much hurt in his eyes to bear. "Turns out, it's I who doesn't know you."

Fishing for the first words that came to my mouth, I started to say something, but he shushed me. "Your wish is true, Veronica. You are free of me. I won't pursue you any longer. Goodbye."

I felt a flood of sorrow and wished unspoken words to rise and reverse his decision.

And I hadn't forgotten that I was still determined to get answers... before he stormed off. I needed to know what happened before the crash, how he could live with his father's blatant attempt to cover up what happened, whether he knew Harvey had been following me and... if he wanted this beautiful diamond ring back forever.

Clutching my unbuttoned coat to keep it closed, I sprinted after him. He was much taller and covered an impressive amount of ground with me trailing along in heels.

"Gavin. Gavin," I called his name, but he refused to turn around. Since he never stopped walking and I was running like it was Field Day in fourth grade, I finally got in front of him. Forced to stare at me with wild raven hair blowing behind me, I saw the tears in the corners of his eyes.

"You don't understand," I mustered. "Let me explain."

I figured if I offered my situation, it would open the door to his explanation.

He waved his hand, "No thanks. It's unnecessary at this point."

He began to tread away when I found myself screaming in indignation.

"Well, it's necessary for me. You owe me a damn explanation. You can't just pretend you didn't kill my mother and put Natalia in a coma. *You owe me!*"

He spun incredulously, a devilish grin upon his face that I never saw before.

"Ask your friend, Sierra."

My head jerked back in confusion, but when I was about to question him, he'd already darted to his BMW and began speeding off.

I peered down at my watch. Exactly one hour since I left the newsroom, reveling in my high.

Chapter Ten

NATALIA'S HOSPITAL ROOM HADN'T BEEN EMPTY DURING THE HOURS I SPENT WORKING. Gavin's law schoolbooks were spread across the portable bedside tray, which stationed itself in front of the cushy chair-slash-makeshift bed I used so often. His ballpoint pen lay next to paper scratched with his tight, cramped writing. A Vernor's bottle from the vending machine was half consumed and still fizzing from his touch. He could have left when I wasn't there. Instead, he stayed.

The scene revealed he had no plans for an anger-fused rushed exit and I knew he would need those books. "Why can't anyone storm out with no strings attached?" I moaned to myself. Then, I realized that Luke never returned my wrap, although his visit to the hospital lobby would have been as good a time as any to do it. "I wonder if I can hold these books for ransom until Gavin tells me what I need to know..." I let the immature thought roll off me before kissing Natalia on her cheek and holding her hand for the rest of the night.

I recognized the smell of his Camel cigarettes on his rumpled clothes before I saw his face. Daddini was gently shaking me. Sympathy filled his eyes at the sight of me slumped over the chair onto the bed, clutching

Natalia's fragile hand. When I turned to him with sunken eyes, he immediately wiped the pity-riddled look off his face. He knew me well.

"I'm not going to lie, it wasn't the easiest pitch, but you landed your job back...with a slight raise. Randall says 'take it or leave it.' I say you take it, kid." He smiled softly and placed his large hand on my shoulder. "I got your leave of absence reinstated. Come back in a couple months. Carter is going to follow your 1A, but we may call you in if absolutely needed." He paused. "Babes wanted the story."

I felt my stomach tighten. *Of course she did.*

"I put her on something else. She's not pleased. Then again, neither am I. She caused me a lot of unnecessary trouble by meddling with that press conference footage and going above me to the Suit. Besides, I thought you looked pretty inconspicuous when I first saw the live presser."

"You saw me?"

"Right away, kiddo. Cool trench." He winked.

Moving past my surprise, I switched to say, "That was pretty low even for Babes. What did you put her on?" I wondered aloud.

"Weather stories for the remainder of the calendar year." He flashed a scoundrel's smile. Reporting on the freezing Michigan temperatures, often from varied places across the region, was no one's dream assignment. Bypassing Daddini to mess with me had been a mistake indeed.

I felt my cheeks raise and lips widen.

"Now, that smile says it all," he said. "Take care of your sister and come back ready to work in two months."

He trekked out of the room. "Daddini," I sleepily called after him.

"Yeah, Maye?"

"Thanks for everything."

Usually one for witty responses, he just let this gratitude roll off him paternally. He beamed at me before ducking out of the room.

I was consumed by gratefulness for Daddini at that moment. The feeling filtered through me, undulating waves of longing for my own father's presence, some reassurance, someone who could look out for me when times were tough. And, Lord knew these were the toughest times I'd ever encountered. Days had passed, weeks, at a snail's pace. At first his cell phone rang the obligatory four times before directing me to voicemail. Now it didn't ring at all. In the beginning I wondered if he was drowning himself with work and job-related travel. That worry soured to exasperation.

Barb was beginning her shift. She raved about the latest novel I loaned her and asked if I needed anything. She was a saint of a woman.

My sole request was that she help me finagle around Natalia's cords and IV so I could give her a sponge bath and put fresh pajamas on her. She could be a surprisingly shy child and I knew the thought of her receiving baths from someone she didn't know, even as kind and professional as Barb, would freak her out. I didn't know how much of her mind was tuned into the activity around her sleeping body, but I tried to make it as pleasant as possible. Her curls appeared even longer than days before. The nail polish I previously brushed on was chipping. Yesterday, with Gavin's visit and the hours-long multiple-deaths story, was the longest I'd been away from her.

When all was finished, I rubbed off the nail polish, repainted her nails with a bright pink and combed her hair. Being that she was fed intravenously; her typically rosy cheeks were concave and pale. I'd been making a long list of restaurants to take her to when she recovered. Milkshakes and burgers from Red Robin, her favorite, were at the top. I tried not to think about the heaviness of her body or the lack of muscle movement or facial expressions through the entire process. It would have been too much to endure. I sat to read aloud to her. Each sentence vocalized was a distant dream, far from my inner thoughts of the night before. I was in a daze, yet continuing to read, when I saw a twitch to my side. I almost dismissed it as imagination, but my excitement at its very possibility cued me to perk up and stare at Natalia with intensity.

Her hand twitched again. I waited for what seemed like hours for another twitch, which came with three more. Then, she was as still as ever. I paged Barb, practically yelling when she reached the doorway. "She moved! Barb, she really moved!"

My heart fluttered lightly like hummingbird's wings.

"I'll page the doctor," Barb couldn't hide her excitement. "I'll let you know when he's coming."

My gaze didn't stray from Natalia's hand.

I kept waiting for movement to occur, but it didn't. Anxiously, Barb checked her vitals over and over until one of the doctors on call entered the room. There were five of them who did rounds in this particular unit. I knew them all. This one, Dr. Schwartz, happened to be the oldest, with a full head of gray hair, an outdated Magnum PI mustache and trim waistline. Dr. Schwartz's bedside manner couldn't be described as poor because he simply did nothing wrong. He just wasn't what you'd call a "people person" and his all-too-self-aware intelligence led to little patience with questions.

"Good morning, Ms. Maye. Barb has informed me that Natalia's hand twitched a bit. Did you witness this?" He questioned without peering up from the chart.

"Yes, her hand twitched several times. Does that mean she will be waking soon?" I asked hopefully.

My eagerness didn't rush him from his chart reading and page-turning.

"I mean, she's never done that before and I thought..." suddenly I felt unsure of myself, inferiorly inarticulate and uninformed. Funny how fragile we really are.

"Well, I think it's safe to assume she had involuntary muscle spasms that were either a sign of stepping out of a coma or harmful internal activity. Her heart rate is normal, her vitals are good and there's really nothing to worry about," he said in a dry tone devoid of emotion.

"Oh, I see," I said, noticing Barb's disappointment radiate the room with my own. "I wasn't so much worried, as I was hopeful about her coming around."

"Yes," he nodded. "When she wakes, you will know it."

"So, there's no way of knowing when that will be? I mean, could it be soon like days? Or, longer?"

"It's unpredictable. Just keep doing what you're doing and we will keep on with our treatment. She is young and strong. I suspect it may not be long."

Suddenly, his words felt like stardust.

"Thank you!" I nearly hugged him, but knew the affection would be unwelcomed. He had never been so promising; in fact, squeezing optimism from him was pulling teeth, the wisdom teeth, that is. He mustered a professional smile and excused himself. Barb walked over to me, hugged me and simultaneously patted my back.

That night, I added another ten minutes to Natalia's usual "exercise" routines in which I lifted her limbs to benefit flexibility and circulation. There was no true way to gauge the impact of my little aerobics-yoga class, but it just seemed to make sense and help prevent clots.

My preoccupation with the possibilities drove me away from mourning, men trouble, work woes, fears for Sierra, and frustration with my father. I had a serious task stowed down a narrow tunnel that required unequivocal concentration. She had to wake up. I talked to her nonstop, prayed for her aloud, sang to her silly songs from when she was a small child and began reading her a new biography of Amelia Earhart. Once a day, I would go home, retrieve mail, feed Scoop, shower, change and return to the hospital. This was the tensest time of the day. I tried to force the pace, and it got to the point of catching myself running once. Twice a week, I would swing by the cemetery during this outing.

Perhaps, if I hadn't been always rushing, I might have noticed, a few days after Natalia's hand movement put me in high hopes, that Sierra's luggage was in the hallway outside my former home office that she had converted to her bedroom. We might have bumped into each other had she not begun singing "So Much Better" from her new role with enough projection for Madison Square Garden. *Never one to consider my neighbors,* I thought.

As ridiculous as it seemed, I was genuinely happy to see her. Startled, she jerked back in the middle of her rendition. "Roni, I didn't hear you come in," she said pleasantly as if she had no cares in the world.

"I don't think you could have heard a freight train coming in here." I smiled somewhat sheepishly. What is one to say when her best friend spills a confession only to dismiss your advice and then returns to your home where you could be considered an accomplice?

"I have so much to tell you about the audition. I start rehearsing next week. We have to go out and celebrate tonight." She had compartmentalized her life, placing the pretty patchwork face-up and the sinister side down. I wasn't mystified by this pattern, considering it was her lifelong defense mechanism for the skid marks her parents left on her heart, but now it seemed extreme.

129

"Listen, I'm real excited you landed that part..."

"I know, right? It's just what I needed. This is it—my big break!"

"Right," I nodded. I hated to rain on her parade. "But, you know we have to talk about what happened."

Her enthusiasm darkened to stern intensity. She leaned into me, red hair dangling in the line of serious green eyes, her expensive-looking gray wrap over her thin shoulders, nearly brushing her long, dangly gold earrings. "Nothing happened. I traveled to New York on a separate flight, his from Illinois, mine from Michigan. He reserved two rooms under his name. I didn't come to the desk to check in and I most certainly didn't check out. So what if someone saw a tall redhead at some point on security cameras? There couldn't have been a close enough shot and no one would recognize me in Little Italy dining with him." She shook a drugstore hair-coloring box with her painted red nails with chagrin. "Besides, I'm Legally Blonde now."

Her crafty coolness triggered an itch deep under my skin.

"This is craziness." It was merely a whisper, but I knew she heard. Yet, it was dismissed before the words completely vacated my mouth. "And is it really necessary to dye your hair if you're the understudy?" I asked to blankness.

"We are going out tonight to celebrate my big break. Don't make me force you," she said sweetly, completely switching off the fervor from a minute before.

"I should get back to the hospital. You know I sleep there."

"Oh, Roni. Give yourself a break sometime. You need to sleep in a bed, an actual bed and, preferably, with a handsome man in it," she smiled coyly while picking up her luggage and carting it to her rented room.

That stung a bit, especially because she didn't know about my drunken rendezvous-that-never-was with Luke or even that he had visited. She was, however, aware of the broken engagement with Gavin, albeit not his foray into Detroit post-breakup. That reminded me of his bizarre response outside the hospital. I decided to go along with her plans for a night out because I could approach the more sensitive issues in our lives later when her guard was down. I didn't expect anything useful to come from bringing up any of the recent events now.

"All right, I'll go with you. Just let me get some things done, run back to the hospital and come back to get ready. Say we leave around ten?"

"It will be just like old times," she said giddily. As she assessed her room, she noticed the skimpy outfit from her B-movie cleaned and placed on a hook near her closet. Amusement caused her eyebrows to rise. "Did you borrow this while I was gone?"

I sighed, grabbed a towel for what I anticipated would be a long, hot shower, and called, "long story."

When I started renting the apartment-style loft a while back, I was drawn to the granite countertops in the one-and-a-half bath and kitchen and the open floor plan that still had bedrooms off to the side. Thankfully, the place was in my price range due to the heightened effort to lure people back to the revitalized residential section of the city. Sierra's inconsistent occupancy brought in some extra money here and there, but it would be more practical in these times to have a steady roommate and additional income. I didn't know whether she expected the door to be open when she returned from her theatrical run in New York, if she planned to come back at all. It was yet another unpleasant subject to approach tonight. Were there delicate ways to craft these questions? Yes. It would require as much concentration as I could squeeze into my overstuffed, overworked brain, but I would do it because, in the end, she was my best friend, and I definitely wanted to avoid hurting her feelings. I dared to dream for a second of taking Natalia, looking healthy and bright, to Manhattan to see Sierra perform. The three of us would ice skate in Rockefeller Center near the towering Christmas tree and stop at a nearby coffee shop for hot chocolate. We'd even indulge ourselves in a silly horse-and-buggy ride around Central Park while huddling close for warmth. I smiled at the thought while washing myself in the shower.

After throwing knee-high leather boots over my skinny jeans, long knit top and matching knit hat, I called goodbye to Sierra over the boisterous music accompanying her singing voice. Inside my slouch purse, Gavin's law schoolbooks were neatly placed along with the address to his Chicago apartment. Fed Ex it was. This may have been the coward's way out, but stomaching a phone confrontation wasn't in my itinerary. I dropped the books off, sans a note, and had them shipped off along with my broken heart-twice shattered that is. The first time, I think I was too numb to feel it; this time, pain paid homage to every joyous memory we shared in a meticulously slow and dreadful way. I thought enough harm had been done the night of our engagement party. Whether this was my fault or not, the last encounter was almost as painful. Perhaps that's because he was ripping off the Band-Aid that time. Images of his longer sandy hair recklessly blowing in the wind while he turned to look at me with such malice pierced my vulnerable heart. His face had never contorted with such disdain-ever--especially not when I was on the receiving end of the gaze.

I shook the thought from my mind as I exited the store, heading back into the crisp autumn air. The sun was beaming through Natalia's hospital window. I opened the blinds to let the rays cascade onto her pale face. Like me, she possessed our mother's high cheekbones and generous lips. Her much-lighter hair outlined her angelic face. As I stared at her, she appeared different, older, and it made me uneasy to think she could be aging into oblivion.

I glanced down to the scores of people leaving and entering the hospital, which was somewhat distanced from the hustle and bustle of the city streets because the campus was fairly large and set back from the main road. From my bird's-eye view, none of the ant-sized humans were familiar. No Daddini, gruff and gallant, pacing to the hospital entrance because free time is terse away from the paper. No Gavin, athletic and gently confident, strolling up to snuggle close to me and kiss my sister's soft, sweet cheek. No Sierra, statuesque and steadfast, rushing to my side to comfort me while ranting about her dreams of stardom. Instead, she was back at my place, no doubt leaving a mess behind her as she readied herself for the night. No dad, gaunt and broken, reeking of bourbon and unreliable, yet still my father. And, finally not even Luke who mystified and miffed me.

Knowing there were no visits under way, I sighed, sat back in my usual vinyl convertor chair that now was getting my personal butt cheek indentation and closed my eyes. Well, they remained shut for a whole three seconds before I opened just one eye to ensure I wasn't missing any spontaneous movement from Natalia. Nothing. Add it to the list of emptiness for the moment. But, if history taught me anything, I knew it wouldn't be uneventful for long.

Back home, my squeaky door was in need of grease. It was a simple task that would take no more than a minute to complete, but was last on my lengthy laundry list of things to do. It did annoy a bit every time I opened the door. That irritation took a backseat to more pressing chores like laundry and washing dishes. At this moment, though, the creak of the wooden door was apparent because Sierra's raucous stage music was missing as well as her thunderous voice. Scoop crept up to me, purring and rubbing his whiskers on my calves. I bent down with mail in one hand and a tote bag of random belongings like books and toiletries in the other. I set the bag on the floor and gave Scoop his proper dose of affection. Amid the humming of his contentment, I heard a low, male voice in Sierra's room. I couldn't make out whose it was or what it was saying, but I heard Sierra's serious tone in the exchange. It was my place, but it wasn't my figurative place to impede on the conversation, no matter how intense my curiosity.

I shuffled through the mail in a lame attempt to seem occupied in the clean, small kitchen, which held some promise of seeing this mystery guest leave. I brewed some Colombian coffee in my single-cup pot and ate a chocolate chip granola bar. Nearly ten minutes had passed since I came home and not a single muffled word traveled the air with clarity. Nor did a name pass through my friend's lips. I was deduced to glancing over Macy's and Bed, Bath and Beyond ads just to have something to do when she emerged from the room with a strangely stark expression on her makeup-free face. Following her was a tall, lean man with short, light-brown hair and green eyes. His eerily familiar face wasn't the only impression made. Rather, in my experience with covering crime, I thought he undeniably looked like a cop. Granted, he wasn't in uniform and I didn't notice a gun in plain sight, but he possessed a rough authority that could not be confused with a politician or other non-law-enforcement occupation of influence. I tried my best, nonchalant peer up from the ads as if I wasn't dying from the unknown. A half-smile that said, "Oh, someone is here? I didn't even notice" stretched my face. As Sierra filed to the door, I noticed she had been crying, which explained her lack of eyeliner and eye shadow. With all her faults, she had always been nothing but cordial. An introduction was not only polite, it was expected. This moment, however, set a discourteous precedent. As her guest approached the counter where I leaned, to extend his hand, Sierra cleared her throat and opened the squeaky door. He obliged, walked through the doorway and whispered something inaudible under his breath. She shook her head and closed the door. She pressed the back of her head on the interior side of the door, closed her eyes and let a tear roll down her fair face.

"Who was that?" I asked gently.

She lifted her head from the door. "A detective sergeant from the New York Police Department. He knows about the incident with McConner."

"Oh shit. Is he going to arrest you?"

"No," she said solemnly.

"Really? That's great. But, why not?"

She paused and stared at me blankly with tears flowing down her cheeks. "Because he's my father."

Chapter Eleven

THE FAMILIARITY MADE SENSE NOW. He had the same piercing green eyes as his daughter, same slender physique, same magnetism that drew people to him. Since he left when she was a toddler, I had never met her father. But I did see a picture of him once when Sierra was about twelve. She hid it in her locker. The photo was of her as a baby with her young, handsome dad outside in the snow. They were bundled up and she sat between his legs against his chest on a sled. They looked so happy.

I hugged her. The absence of a father scarred a child for life, whether she realized it or not.

"He has a family," she wept. "A wife and two teenagers. It's as if I never existed. He moved on like I never was born."

"How did he find you? What did he say?"

"He said one of his detectives brought surveillance tape from the hotel to him along with accounts from hotel staff like maids and room service that a redheaded woman in her twenties was with McConner. This detective is very thorough, one of his best, and he checked airport security tapes the day we arrived. Since we were on different flights, nothing seemed to match up. But then, he came across one tape by the baggage claim where I was standing and waiting for my luggage. That's when

McConner approached me and took my bags to the cab. I guess knowing I was on that flight from Detroit and matching the other accounts led him to identify me.

"So then, he brought his report to his boss, who is, uh, my father. He oversees criminal cases in that section of the city and saw my first name and Blake as the last name, along with my date of birth and hometown. It wasn't rocket science for him to know it was me. He told his detective that it was a simple case of self-defense and, even though I fled, it was probably out of fear and humiliation. He said that since the stab wound was underhanded from a butter knife it helped prove that theory. He told him that he had roots in Detroit and planned on visiting soon anyway, which was a lie but a good cover. He told him he would interview me himself and determine whether charges should be sought. It didn't take long for them to find out it was me or for him to come here, as you see. I guess you were right all along."

"Who cares about who is right. Are you okay?" This was a life-altering moment and we both knew it. No one ever really believed her father would come back into her world, especially not me.

"I had this crazy plan in my mind. Don't laugh, but I always dreamed of being this big star with so much success everyone would have to know who I was. And, if everyone knew who I was, then he would have to recognize me as well. He would regret leaving someone so special, so famous and important. He would realize what a terrible mistake it was. But now he knows me for something much worse."

"Sierra, you are special now. You were special as a baby and a child. His actions are no reflection on you. You are innocent in all of this." I was patting her back now.

She eased up on the crying a bit.

"He explained to me that things were so bad between mom and him that all they did was fight. He said he wanted to take me with him to New York, where he has family and had work opportunity, when they got divorced, but she wouldn't let him. She told him he wouldn't abandon her and get to keep me -- he would have to suffer. She thought that her keeping me would mean he would stay with her. But he left. Soon after, she checked out, too."

I thought about her grandparents and what saving graces they were for her. They always tried to make her feel loved and cherished. They always told her how smart and sweet she was. Their love was not in vain. Although recovering from the wounds of physical and emotional abandonment is a long and painful journey.

"Neither of them did the right thing. Neither of them put you first."

"Now, he's not seeing me on stage where I feel strong and in charge. He saw me weak and vulnerable and in need of his help!" That was a big gulp of pride to wash down. "The saddest part of all is I just wanted to hug him and for him to tell me how much he missed me all these years."

"Did he?

"No. He said he would protect me from getting in trouble with the law. He said it was putting his job and reputation on the line if anyone were to find out what he was doing and whom he was doing it for. He said he was sorry for the time he missed and that he'd like to get to know me if I was willing. He didn't seem sad or remorseful. Then again, he is saving my ass."

"I don't know what to say."

"Me either. Let's go get that drink."

The bar we chose was walking distance from my apartment, a bar with a mixed crowd of young hipsters and older professionals unwinding after work. It was called Starry Nights Bar. The walls were dark blue with glow-in-the-dark stars spattered on top of them. The focal point of the room was a well-lit stage that hosted blues singers, rock bands and poets, depending on the night. Tonight, a thin man in his twenties with unkempt hair and tattoo sleeves commanded the audience with a band of equally straggly musicians behind him. Screamed lyrics hardly passed for entertainment, but the bar was right around the block and booze is booze.

"Dry martini with three olives," Sierra ordered while waving her dollar bills at the male bartender. "What do you want?"

"I'll have a glass of red wine."

"A dry martini and red wine for the loveliest ladies in the house," he said before fixing our drinks.

Sierra handed over the money despite my protests.

"Relax, I have a real job now. Besides, you've been letting me rent that room for next to nothing. Let me get this at least."

Truth was, I really didn't have the extra money to be out drinking, so I was relieved when she insisted. I was trying to stretch my savings as far as possible in light of my leave of absence. It felt nice knowing that my return to work would come with a cushy little raise, though.

"Thanks. Let's sit. How's over here?"

She grudgingly agreed to my suggestion of the small table in the corner, away from the bar's activity and patrons' gaze. Sierra's style was never low key, but she concurred to appease me, a person way more comfortable in the background.

The blaring music relented as the band, billed as Death Valley, took five.

"At least we can talk now with some peace," I said sweetly, keeping in mind to be considerate of her father's bizarre visit and my own agenda to ask her what Gavin implied.

"I was actually looking forward to hearing their set. That lead singer looks familiar. I wonder if we've met before..."

"Okay, sure." I reluctantly sipped my wine.

Sierra guzzled her martini. When Death Valley resumed their hair-raising ruckus, she began banging her head to the sounds and then ordered another martini. There were words on my tongue that dreamed of escaping, but it was one disadvantageous moment after another.

"Loosen up, Roni," she turned to me amid chair dancing. "She'll have another one," she hollered to the waitress while holding up my half-filled glass of wine to indicate the order.

The music was not my cup of tea. I preferred pop and R & B over heavy metal rock. But the wine was more up my alley. I caught a buzz from the second glass and the sounds were so blaringly loud, I had given up on a serious conversation.

The lanky waitress with a black bob approached our table with oatmeal cookie shots.

"From those gentlemen over there," she said disinterestedly as she pointed to a table of frat boys.

"You can send it back. We're not really into shots," I called to her over the music. In the corner of my eye, I saw Sierra jerk back her head to consume the shot.

"Yeah right," the waitress said before apathetically walking off.

"Have yours, Roni."

"No thanks. You go ahead." And she did. From there, I lost track of her alcohol consumption. The frat boys continued to send over shots, but not without strings. A couple of them, clad in checkered button-downs and baseball caps, came to the table to introduce themselves. The rules of the bar were in full effect: They sent the drinks. We accepted. Now, through Sierra's negligence, they had the go signal.

"Hi. I'm Kevin and this is my friend, Bobby," the taller of the two said. "You girls look like you know how to party."

"We do. Thanks for the shots. We're celebrating my engagement. I'm so excited!" I said in my best sorority girl cheer. Perhaps it was pathetic I was still wearing Gavin's ring, but it made for an ideal flea collar at the moment. I thought Sierra could get stuck with them at this point for all I cared.

Kevin's face fell. Apparently he was interested in me and had been the shot buyer all along. He turned his attention to Sierra. It was too late though. She was out of her seat, swaying Violently to the music at the edge of the stage. Her seductive sashay garnered the attention of Death Valley's lead singer, who extended his hand for her to join him on stage. Never one to shy from the limelight, she capitalized on the moment by tossing her red hair back and forth to keep in sync with her hips. Death Valley's groupie was now stealing the show, not that the tattooed singer seemed to mind.

"Come on, Bobby. These chicks are a waste of time," Kevin said to his friend just loud enough so I could hear.

I shrugged. I truly would be a waste of their time, considering my emotions were wrapped up in Gavin while I couldn't shake thoughts of Luke. *"No, you definitely don't want to be on the conveyor belt with this baggage,"* I thought as they huffed away.

The band wrapped their set for the night and Sierra, sweaty from dancing, strolled up to the table to grab her drink. It was finally relatively quiet enough to speak without shouting.

"Hey, I need to ask you something. It's kind of important."

She peered at me from behind the funnel-shaped glass, recognizing my seriousness. "What's up, Roni?"

"You know, when you were out of town for the... audition, I got a visit from Gavin."

"What? You're just now mentioning that now? What's it you newspaper people say? Oh, that's right, you buried the lead."

"Right, well it's not like we've had much time to talk. Anyway, we kind of got into it about the night of the engagement party and the accident. He said something kind of strange when I was asking him for information about what exactly happened."

"What did he say?" Her look was intense.

"He said I should ask you."

Her eyebrows raised and spine straightened. This was a sobering moment indeed.

"Me? Why would you ask me? What do I have to do with it?"

"I don't know. I just figured I'd run it by you," I said, feeling awkward and foolish for even bringing it up.

"Sounds like Gavin's using some sort of deflection technique. Maybe he picked that up in law school. I can't really blame him though. If I caused two people to die and another person to be in a coma, I'd have trouble confronting that as well. I guess he just wanted to bring me into the mix."

"Thanks for not taking offense. I guess I'm still confused over everything."

"No problem, Roni. You've been through a lot in such a short time. It's not going to pass overnight."

I felt like reaching over to hug her, but the Death Valley front man toddled up.

"Bunch of us are going to my friend Victor's house for an after party. You girls want to join us?" he mumbled lazily.

"No, thanks," I smiled politely.

"Sure. I'd love to go. Mind if I ride along?" Sierra asked.

"It's all good," he said, not to risk his laid-back image.

She had her own agenda and there was no stopping it. Still, I was less than thrilled with her lack of courtesy. That feeling amplified when I realized I'd have to trek back to my apartment at two in the morning by myself. My pride wouldn't allow me to say anything to her about it. I didn't want to admit to her or anyone that I was afraid to head back one block; it seemed ludicrous. By the time my internal monologue was complete, she had blown me a kiss and darted toward the door with the unkempt singer's arm over her shoulder. I threw my black fall jacket on, grabbed my clutch and headed home. I was only a few paces from the bar door when I realized there were footsteps behind me. Figuring they belonged to other patrons on their way out, I made nothing of it, although a nervous feeling tightened my stomach and I knew the culprit wasn't alcohol. I held my clutch tight at my waist.

Suddenly, the footsteps sped up as if a sprinter were on my heel.

"She doesn't look like thuch a waste of time now, does thee, Kev?" The frat boy's words slurred in drunkenness.

"Nah, she's ripe for the pickin'," Kevin replied in an awfully low and sinister voice.

I turned, determined to find the upper hand in a situation that was likely to spiral out of the bounds of acceptable behavior.

"Listen guys, I think you maybe had a few too many. My fiance is actually meeting me halfway and should be walking up any minute. I'd hate for this to be uncomfortable, given that he's with some friends who don't have the best tempers, if you know what I mean. So, why don't you call it a night?" My voice was cool and even, not indicating anger or fear, to my knowledge. Internally, my heart was pounding against my chest like a hammer on nails.

Kevin, whose button-down was now untucked and hosting a beer stain, menacingly stepped closer to me. "Hey Bob, you believe this bitch?"

"Not for a thecond," Bobby called behind him.

"Neither do I," he snarled, stepping closer and closer until his mouth was near the crown of my hairline. I smelled the beer on his breath.

"Well you're making a mistake," I said. This time, my voice quaked and they smirked at audible anxiety.

"I don't think so. You know, you're just my type actually, with your long black hair and light eyes. Why don't I show you to my car," he growled as he placed his hot, large hands on my shoulders.

Movements to follow happened quickly and almost confusingly. He screamed horrifically as Bobby stood in clumsy silence. Thankfully, the breeze was minimal so that all the pepper spray I directed didn't stray from his face. They hadn't notice me slip it from my clutch to my jacket pocket when I first sensed their presence behind me. I made sure the actions were quick and small and in front of me.

"Ah, that bitch! My eyes are stinging!" Kevin cowered into his hands in a vain attempt to ease the pain. Bobby fumbled around him, not knowing how to help.

"You know," I said cooly. "You're just my type, too. You know when to shut the hell up. Granted it might take some coaxing." And, to even my own shock, I kicked him as hard as I could in the groin. He yelped some more and continued to call me disparaging things, but they were lost on the early morning air. I stormed away as fast as I could without turning my stride into a full sprint.

When I reached my steps, I looked back a few times to ensure they weren't there. I locked the deadbolt and the regular knob, changed into my pajamas and fell asleep with the television and lights on and the phone next to me. In the morning, I entered Sierra's room, packed up everything she had and boxed it up.

Chapter Twelve

THAT MORNING I SHOWERED, THREW ON JEANS AND A LOOSE SWEATER AND WENT TO THE HOSPITAL. I sat there for hours, watching Natalia sleep serenely with no movements or noise, then treaded back to get the mail and make lunch at home. I needed a break from hospital food.

The narrow metal box was full of the usual contents: bills and junk mail. However, as I shut the little door, a small envelope fell onto the carpet. I opened the ivory envelope to find a small letter about the size of a thank you card. The letter had one line: *Only you could make Detroit the best vacation I've had. -Luke.*

I pictured his face, his smile, his kiss. The note was the best pick me up I could have asked for.

Sierra was in her walk-of-shame clothes, thanks to me packing her belongings the night before. She was sipping coffee quietly at the table.

"You're kicking me out, I take it?"

"Yes, I am." I was about to explain my anger over her leaving me last night for her own selfish reasons, reasons that could have got me attacked by idiots at the bar. But she spoke first.

"Okay, you always know when something isn't right, when a story doesn't add up. That's why you're so good at what you do." She was crying now. "Let me first tell you that I had no idea everything that happened would happen. I would never have..."

"Never have what?" I asked on the edge of my seat.

"Gave Gavin and Jeremy the cocaine," she spit the words out so fast my mind had to race to catch up.

"You did what?"

"I got it from a friend at a catalog shoot. Models do that stuff all the time to stay thin. I hadn't mustered the gall to take it and Jeremy was rambling about celebrating with more than Jack Daniel's. He said 'an occasion like this deserved more.' I thought he was serious, so I slipped him the coke before he and Gavin left the party that night. I doubted they would do it because, by the look on Jeremy's face, he seemed pretty surprised about the whole thing. I guess he just meant more booze or something.

"I've gone over this in my head many times. The final conclusion is that maybe Jeremy had a change of heart and wanted to do some. I think there might have been a little bit of a struggle between them, which would have distracted Gavin as he drove."

My mouth was agape.

"You've gone over this in your mind? Did you ever think for one minute of telling me on your own accord? Or was this something you'd rather keep inside to make you feel better about yourself? Or was it to protect your *image* for when you get famous?" I said, rolling my eyes.

She was silent momentarily, insulted and intimidated, but she spoke soon after.

"You have to understand how something can spiral out of control. There was nothing malicious in my actions, I swear. I kept quiet at the hospital because you weren't thinking clearly and then the story took on a life of its own and there was never an opportune moment to kill it. Look, I murdered a man in New York and, believe it or not, this weighs heavier on me than that. Because, at least with that, he did something wrong to me. You, on the other hand, have been nothing but good to me my whole dysfunctional life. I couldn't bear the thought of us not being friends.

"And I need you now more than ever. You need me, too. You just bottle things up, Roni, and stay strong for everyone else. I'll be leaving for New York in a couple days and I should be there for at least a couple months. Let me sleep here until I go? I promise to stay out of your hair while things cool down." She spoke with the softest expression on her face, like a child pleading for candy for being good.

I stared incredulously at her. In the sequence of a few minutes, she dropped a bombshell about the single most important night of my life and then presumed I would get over it. Perhaps my constant habit of balancing both sides transformed me into a softy because I was buying stock in her point that we needed each other for support, she with her father's return and trauma in New York and me with my slew of problems. I thought about Gavin and why he wouldn't have just told me what she said and I wondered if Sierra theorized the chain of events correctly. If so, why would I begrudge him? I had a sudden, animalist even, urge to see him, to bury my head in his chest and make everything right that had turned so wrong. I felt disloyal and cruel when I should have had patience to listen and understand. And, I was most of all hurt that neither my best friend nor former fiance instilled enough trust in my temperament to have told me the truth. I sighed; so many thoughts toppled my head.

"Stay until you have to go," I said shaking my head in exhaustion.

"Thanks, Roni! You know I love you," she stepped forward to hug me but the action was premature and she reluctantly backed off when she saw my face.

I rose early to sit at Natalia's bedside, make phone calls and avoid encountering Sierra in my apartment the next morning. Brushing Natalia's wavy hair was soothing to me. I read her excerpts from an Amelia Earhart biography and sang some of the songs my mom would always hum or sway to. She especially liked *Can't Take My Eyes Off of You,* which I tried mimicking from memories. I could care less about sounding silly; pleasing her was at the forefront of my mind. The rest of the world fizzled to the bottom of my full cup.

In a futile effort, I dialed my father's cell phone number. As expected, it went straight to voicemail. "Hello, you have reached Robert Maye, sales manager for Motor City Wheels auto supplier. Please leave me a message and I will return your call promptly." Promptly my...

His voice was pleasant and professional. The outgoing message was recorded before the accident sucked the life from his sound... or soul, I thought darkly.

"Dad, it's me. I don't know where you are or what's going on, but you need to call me back on my cell. It's been weeks with no word from you. Don't you want to know how Natalia's condition is progressing?" I nearly spat the words in disgust. How could a parent leave a child in need and not even think to check in? I reconsidered, wallowing in self-pity for a second -- make that two children in need.

By the time I trudged downstairs for an unsatisfying bowl of chicken noodle soup, I was hotter than the broth before me. I left word with the nurse on shift, a tall brunette in her early thirties with a soft voice and good work ethic, that I would be returning later that evening. I double-checked she had my cell phone number in case anything happened. She assured me she already had the number, but was kind enough to jot it down again.

Leaves swayed in an adagio dance on my windshield. Their colors so vibrant and breathtaking, it was like a theatrical performance in the middle of the city for my own amusement. The sun was shining between cotton candy clouds and the October weather was warm enough to allow some fresh air to sink into my lungs through the car window. With Sierra's confession, Gavin weighed on my mind. Chicago streets in the fall would be beautiful, especially if we strolled them hand-in-hand.

Reality set in as I pulled into the visitor parking lot outside Motor City Wheels, auto supplier, in northwest Detroit. The secured parking lot was adjacent to a staff lot. From my limited view, I couldn't see my father's car. Beyond the gates of the beige factory-like setting, graffiti splotched the overpass that possessed a few transients descending to its bowels with sleeping bags. I had been there only a handful of times. It was a less-than-pleasant workplace. I swept my hair back into a low ponytail, buttoned my brown fitted coat and straightened my khakis. Visitors willing to check in must come as a surprise to the front desk employee; the staff probably couldn't leave soon enough.

"Can I help you?" the man with gray hair and glasses asked.

"Hello, my name is Veronica Maye. I'm here to surprise my father for lunch. Do you happen to know if he's in his office today?" I tried sounding innocently sweet, a good daughter springing up a casual meal on her pops.

His brows furrowed. "Well, let me check. Hold on please."

He lifted the receiver, pressed a couple of digits and asked someone on the other end of the phone, I presumed, about my father. "Uh huh.... Right. ... Okay.... All right, thank you." He hung up and looked at me with confusion.

"Ma'am, I regret to tell you this, but your father no longer works here."

"What? That must be some kind of mistake. It's Robert M-a-y-e."

"No mistake here."

I regained my thoughts and composure. "I was not aware of that. How long ago was he let go?"

"He wasn't let go. I was told he stopped showing up for work last month." His polite nature stopped him from asking why I didn't know that.

A month ago, I thought, meant he had not gone to work after the accident. That meant there was no business trip after all. A surge of feelings from anger to abandonment subsided when I felt a genuine wave of worry. Had I dismissed all the signs of his depression and despair with my own concern about Natalia's well-being? I guess I didn't know the appropriate reaction for someone who lost their spouse, and still don't. After all, I had lost a mother and would be barely hanging on if it weren't for the purpose of seeing my sister pull through. Flashes of his gaunt face, bourbon breath and sunken presence rotated to the front of my mind.

Mustering coolness, I casually thanked the front desk employee for his time and was on my way.

The sun disappeared behind the clouds and rain seemed imminent. I practically kicked myself for leaving my umbrella behind, along with failing to check the forecast at home. The drive to Garden Falls would be a little more than a half hour given it was three o'clock by now and workers from the auto factories on my route would be getting off their shifts and heading in the same direction. The last time I was at my parents' house was directly before and after the funeral. I had cleaned and packed Natalia's things before we laid my mother to rest and then hosted a small gathering of close friends and our very limited family (my father's estranged brother, Charles, who lives in Arizona, and my mother's adopted parents' close friend, Estelle, whom we referred to as Great Aunt Estelle). Knowing that didn't prepare me any better for what I was about to see. The normally well-kept yard was blanketed with weeds and long, uncut grass. I imagined the neighbors' horror at the sight of it and then a worse thought entered my mind. If the outside was this unsightly, what was the inside like? By the time I parked in the driveway, the rain was falling from a darkened sky. I rushed to the door, pulled out my trusty key and pushed it back.

I flipped the light switch to see my mother's tidy house turned to complete chaos. Newspaper accounts of the crash, clipped from Chicago dailies, were scattered illogically across the carpet. My mother's clothes, shoes and jewelry were piled carelessly on tables and chairs. Dishes sat in murky water in the sink, pervading the once spotless kitchen with a rank aroma, compounded by the fact an overstuffed garbage can wasn't emptied. The angle of the roof wouldn't permit rain to seep in from the kitchen windows, so I darted to open them. I tried not thinking, just doing the tasks at hand. The garbage was the first to go in a Hefty bag outside. Dishes were washed next. Newspaper articles were stacked neatly and put off to the side. My mother's belongings were folded and tucked away in her closet, well they were after I nuzzled them to me to intake her citrus and floral perfume scent.

I was making progress nicely when I heard a thump from the basement that I couldn't ignore. I wondered if, all along, my father had been sleeping in his leather lounger by the old television set in the partially finished basement. Eagerness led me noisily down the stairs. I found the lounger vacant, TV off. I thought maybe I had imagined the sound, like I sometimes do when I'm home alone with Scoop in the apartment. Usually, the building just stretches or rustles with no other explanation. The house was built about fifteen years ago, so maybe it was having some growing pains, I reasoned.

Not to mention the fact that the F-16s boomed overhead more than normal today. Upon hearing their roaring, I wondered if they were rumbling on to Iraq or Afghanistan, or maybe both. This seemingly never-ending war weighed on us like oil-drenched pelicans in the Gulf following the BP spill. We weren't close enough to see the full scope of the damage, but our world was muddled with its filth. I had no personal connection to any of the servicemen or servicewomen. Yet I admired them for their commitment to the cause, their bravery and selflessness. I even thought more than once that if, for some dreaded and unimaginable reason Natalia didn't pull through, I would request assignment to cover the war for our newspaper chain. People with little to live for can afford such danger.

I turned to go upstairs, close the windows and leave when it felt as if a migraine struck me from nowhere and I fell hard on the linoleum bottom step.

My head throbbed with the force of a million white-knuckled fists clenched around it. Instinctively, I dabbed my nose with my fingers to see blood blotches on them. I had fallen face forward on the step. Horrified and fearful, I strained to see around me. The first thing I saw were the darkest, most bottomless pair of eyes I've ever seen. I struggled to speak, but semi-coherent thoughts funneled into incoherent moans.

"You don't need to say anything, sweetheart. In fact, it's best you don't," the words slithered around me. "The only thing you need to do is listen. Can you do that?"

I nodded to the best of my ability, which was minimal.

"I know you're Bob's daughter, the reporter, right? Like I said, you don't need to answer. You tell your scumbag of a father that his little gambling problem doesn't pay for itself. Tell him he can't run forever.

People want their money returned. And if he doesn't hand it over soon, money will be the least of his worries," he hissed.

The pain segregated emotions from thoughts and, through the basic necessity of survival, I didn't waste any time on this newly discovered gambling addiction. My only goal was to obtain one piece of information from my attacker: "How much?"

He contorted his square-jawed and unshaven face with amusement. "Now, that's a good girl. Ten thousand dollars."

"Where does it go?" Short questions were all I could muster, but brevity is always wise in compromising positions.

"Bob knows where."

"Tell me."

Before he spoke, I saw a flash of metal. It was the crowbar he struck me with. Upon seeing it, my head pounded harder. I clumsily felt around the back of my head for blood, but to no avail. Ah, what a pleasant surprise, it was a *gentle* strike to the head with a crowbar.

"Johnnie's Sports Bar at 225 Green Street, Detroit. Ask the bartender for Zambi."

"Okay."

"He's got until Saturday night and make no mistake about it, reporter, we will find him." He ducked down closer to me for sheer emphasis of his next threat. He was a burly broad man who seemed to possess no remorse for hitting a young, unsuspecting woman. "And if we don't, we'll just go looking for you."

I heard his thumping footsteps lumber up the linoleum stairs, cross over the family room and exit out the front door. He must have parked farther away from the house, and maybe he came through a window. I didn't know, but it crossed my mind to call 911, to report the entire incident. Then, common sense made her harsh presence known. The troubles would just be enhanced for my father if this man were arrested.

The urge to sleep was powerful. I fought it like a warrior on her last leg, knowing a concussion could eradicate critical information from my attacker. Coming to my feet had never been so hard. I felt the rush of blood to my body ripple over me like a cactus shower. My bloodied nose made for a disgusting display all over my shirt. There was nothing around, not even a stray paper towel, to intercept the bleeding. So I trudged upward, dripping with blood and covered in pain. A damp washcloth felt comforting on my nose while the plastic bag of ice eased the oncoming swelling on my head. I sat on the portion of the comfy leather couch my mother would say was "her spot" for reading and knitting with one of her robes draped over my lap. And, for the first time in a long time, I didn't summon the strength to stop feeling sorry for myself.

Chapter Thirteen

WHEN DARKNESS FELL OVER THE HOUSE, I SHUDDERED WITH FEAR. I hadn't gotten up to leave yet. There was still something I needed to do. I walked slowly, with less pain than before, to my parents' bedroom. I stood before the solid oak dresser my mother bought when they married and peered into her black-and-gold jewelry box. The miniature doors opened, setting off the sweetest, most feminine classical tune. It was one I knew well, since my mother would allow me to see her prized possession when I asked, from the time I was a small child. My breath held with anticipation and hope. The diamond studs she had in the first compartment were gone. The gold necklace that draped over the ridged portions of velvet was missing, too. But, to my relief, the white gold bracelet inset with rubies was perched in its normal resting place. He had raped the box of its riches, not its worth. I scooped it up with anxiety, as if someone would appear to yank it from my hands, and closed the box, ending the music. As I made my way to the door, I noticed her prayer book sitting out on the nightstand. Though never a religious woman, my mother was a person of untainted faith and she highlighted passages from the Bible that she then transcribed to her prayer book for retention. I tucked the hard-covered journal into my purse, turned off the lights and locked the front door.

It wasn't my intention to see Sierra tonight. Yet I longed for a shower in my own bathroom, sleep in my own bed. When I got home, she was sitting on the couch, studying her lines. She half-smiled as she peered up at me, an expression which then disintegrated in shock.

"Oh my God. What happened to you?"

Dried blood must have stained under my nose. I was sure my hair was disheveled and makeup smeared.

"I don't want to talk about it." First a near attack from a drunken frat boy and now a real attack by a loan shark enforcer. What was happening? Through her own careless ignorance, she knew of neither incident and I was intent on keeping it that way. The sooner she left, the less complicated my life would be. I needed to focus on Natalia, make amends with Gavin and find my father before someone else did.

"Oh, all right." She was clearly disappointed that my anger with her had sustained the day. "Well, I'll be leaving for New York on Tuesday. My, uh, dad, geez it sounds weird saying that, wants to visit before he leaves. I thought maybe you could join us for lunch and get to know him. It would really mean a lot."

Ordinarily, I would jump at the chance to support her during such a sensitive meeting, especially since I knew she was co-dependent in tough situations. My heart hung too heavy to agree to that tonight, though. I just couldn't bring myself to say "yes."

"I'm sorry, I can't do it."

Her face fell before turning back to her lines. "I understand."

"Good night," I mumbled before escaping to the shower.

I lay in bed that night wondering what would become of my own father, where he was and how he got in so deep. I tried his phone again, which went straight to voicemail, and left another pressing message without telling of the encounter in his basement. I worried that telling him what I knew would only make him skulk away even more out of shame.

In the morning, I drove to the county offices, parked by the Land Records Department, and positioned myself at one of the public computers. I was fortunate enough that no one was nearby in the fluorescent-lit mundane space. I typed in the address of Johnnie's Sports Bar. The deed came up to Gabe B. Varney.

Everybody in the city knew who Gabe B. Varney was, for one shady reason or another. The story that stuck out the most in my mind was the one about his embezzlement arrest several years ago. It became a newsroom tale for rookie cop reporters. At the time, Varney owned a popular nightclub in the bustling city of Victoria that was jam-packed on the weekends with twenty-somethings looking for a good time. Club Aquatic was lined with gigantic aquariums filled with small, toothy sharks. Besides the dancing, the fish were the main attraction and a frequent talking point for club-goers. Around then, Varney was known more as a businessman with a sleek appearance and sly tongue. When his criminal activities surfaced and an arrest was under way, it was clear to Varney he'd lose the club he had worked so hard to establish. That's when he took bleach to the shark tanks, meanly killing every one of them.

Not much was known about him since his release from prison a few years back. He generally kept a low profile. Johnnie's Sports Bar couldn't be called a "hot spot" if its liquor license depended on it. But there he was on the deed and apparently a sense of humor to boot-the man who now goes by Zambi, the name for a bull shark, one of most aggressive and dangerous of sharks and one that can adapt to fresh or salt water.

Any uneasiness I was experiencing before didn't disappear with that knowledge.

I was grateful to see Barb at the hospital, which was humming with activity. It was almost Halloween. The weather was cooling off and the colds season was starting early. That could lead to a slew of trouble for the weakened patients in her ward who could catch something from well-meaning visitors.

"Roni, she's looking good today. Nice, full cheeks with a rosy color," she chirped. Barb was always trying to put a positive spin on Natalia's condition, God love her.

"Thanks, Barb. I'm going to sit by her now."

She was right. Natalia's color looked rosier, cheeks plumper and even her wavy hair looked fuller. She appeared better nourished and healthier. I didn't know why or how, but I took the blessing as it came with complete gratitude. I spent the day with her, reading from the Amelia book, singing silly songs and even repainting her nails. By the time evening fell, I had my mind made up about where I needed to go. I packed up a change of clothes, socks, underwear, toothbrush, shampoo, conditioner and makeup before stopping to chat with Barb, who was on her second consecutive shift.

"Here's another one for ya," and I told her about the latest James Patterson thriller. "I'm sure you won't be able put it down, like me."

"Thanks, Roni. Heading home?"

"I need to go somewhere, but I'll be back tomorrow afternoon. Can you just make sure they call me if anything changes?"

"Of course, sweetie. Don't you worry about a thing."

"I appreciate that. I'll see you soon."

I had made the drive to Chicago countless times. Never once was that trip unannounced or spontaneous. A phone call didn't seem adequate though, given the note Gavin and I left on-or should I say the note *he* left on. After four-and-a-half hours of shuffling between NPR and my iPod, I finally approached his place overlooking Lake Michigan. Feeling foolish, my heart pounded nervously. I had given myself a once-over in the visor mirror before stepping onto the pavement. I dressed for comfort because of the drive, but still looked stylish in dark jeans tucked into gray boots and a form-fitting sweater under my plaid jacket. It was around ten o'clock, a little late for an unexpected visit. However, this was my fiance; we have gotten together at less decent hours.

I tapped lightly on the door, almost afraid to mimic an actual knock. For a minute, no noise could be heard and I began to turn away. Hearing the door open, I turned around expecting to see Gavin in his pajama bottoms with messy bed hair. Instead, I turned to a pretty blonde with thin lips and a narrow nose, wearing a preppy cardigan, dress slacks and loafers.

"Hi, can I help you?" she said as if she had opened the door to her own apartment.

I pressed down hard on my mouth so it wouldn't fall open in unbecoming surprise. "No, I must have gone to the wrong door. Sorry." I turned, hoping to vanish, click my heels and reappear in Detroit. Then his voice rang out.

"Veronica, is that you?" He saw the back of my head moving away rapidly. I knew there was no running from this awkwardness. As I spun to see Gavin, I was expecting the worst: him shirtless, clad only in crumpled pants, indicating my interruption of something starting between him and Miss Preppy. I felt my cheeks flush just for being there, unexpected and foolish. Instead of my seedy image of him, he was wearing khakis and a Calvin Klein black sweater. His sandy hair had been cut since our confrontation at the hospital and he looked even more toned and tan than before. It made me think of his parents' vacation house in St. Croix and how he said he couldn't wait to take me. I wondered if he took my little blonde door greeter.

"It's me all right," I said, wishing I could disappear into the architectural landscape. Glancing over to his guest, I muttered "Don't worry, I won't be staying" and turned away to leave.

Always the gentleman, he looked over at his guest and said, "Excuse me, please." She nodded with filtered envy.

I realized how tired I was from the drive in, the humiliation and disappointment of this moment and the soap opera of my family life. I thought of checking into a hotel, resting on fresh linens and turning off the lights for hours on end.

"We need to talk," he said. "Let's go to the coffee shop downstairs."

Exasperated, I began to protest. He would have none of it.

Java Bar was one of those twenty-four/seven trendy coffee spots with WiFi, upscale décor and ridiculously overpriced lattes. I knew Gavin often paid it visits after late classes or, in better days, to stay up when I was coming in late on Friday nights after my shift. I always felt bad about my tardiness, but he never got upset or even seemed inconvenienced.

He pulled out a chair for me, ordered our usual drinks (me, a chai tea latte, him, a cappuccino) and sat down heavily. A break-up talk? I wondered and was about to spew something to that effect to break the ice. But then I decided the best approach was to stay silent, hear him out, even though he didn't extend the same courtesy to me after seeing Luke.

"Her name is Sarah."

Nausea sunk in. Did I really need to know her name?

"I have to say, Veronica, it brings me a bit of joy to see you this jealous, especially after what I saw back in Michigan." This was more painful than I could have imagined. "But, in all honesty, Sarah is my assigned partner for a class project. We're not dating, which is obviously the conclusion you jumped to. Jumping to conclusions seems to be your forté lately." Hurt blanketed his face and I knew the wounds of my impromptu appearance at the presser were not healed.

"You jumped to your own conclusions not too long ago." Deflection was my best defense at this point.

"Did I really?" He stared incredulously. "Was that not the medic who's been coming on to you since the night of the crash? The same person who punched Harvey while you two were walking to his hotel room? Tell me, please, how I have jumped to conclusions?"

Never underestimate the grudge someone carries for you. Obviously Harvey wasn't going to keep that information to himself. I don't know why I hadn't considered that. The revelation left me defenseless and shameful.

"So, you knew Harvey came to the Chronicle to tear me down?" It was off-subject but I needed to know.

"No, but when I found out I wasn't happy about it," he replied. "Please don't change the subject."

"Gavin, nothing happened." More articulate, convincing words were lost on the air. My mind was cloudy and exhausted.

"You expect me to believe you went to his hotel room and nothing happened?" He looked down at my finger, perhaps giving me some credit. "Yet, you sit here wearing the ring I gave you.... A ring you returned at one point...." He was clearly conflicted. "Although, I understand you weren't thinking straight, given what happened...."

He was nothing but pragmatic. I knew he'd make a great attorney. However, the jury was still out on me. Suddenly fearful of solitary confinement, I decided to plead my case at the eleventh hour.

"I expect you to trust me. Trust me enough to tell me that Sierra gave Jeremy drugs, that you two were fighting over them in the truck, that you hid that from me to protect me, for some strange reason. I expect you to know that I wanted the truth from the beginning, to hear it from you and to know that you will always be honest, even when you think you know best. And I expect you to believe me when I say that nothing happened in that hotel room - even though at the time I wanted it to because I thought we were broken up and I was angry at you and very alone."

I never saw Gavin so flabbergasted. He took a sip of his cappuccino and gathered his thoughts before speaking.

"Is that what you heard from Sierra?"

"Yes, she told me the other day."

"What else did she tell you?"

"That she got the drugs from her agent. Did you and Jeremy really struggle in the truck?"

"He wanted to try it and I said no. He was so drunk; he was horsing around and grabbing the wheel when I told him to give me the cocaine. I could have stopped if I wasn't so distracted with all that was going on. It's really my fault. I lost control."

"You couldn't have helped it. Someone was taking the wheel from you."

His head was cradled in his hands now. It finally dawned on me the real reason he never talked about what had happened was not to protect me from knowing there were drugs in the truck. It was because he was riddled with guilt. He couldn't talk about the accident at all.

I stood, walked over to his side of the table and placed my arms around him.

"It's over. It's over. You need to let it go. It's not your fault."

"Your mom is dead because of me. Jeremy is gone. I should have let him do the drugs, no way would fate be worse than it is. And, I saw how Natalia is. It's more than I can live with," he croaked. Melancholy mingled with guilt; he appeared smaller for the first time.

"Let's get out of here," I told him because people were starting to stare.

We walked back upstairs, arm in arm.

"Oh, there you are," Sarah slyly said as she opened his door. "I was starting to miss you."

"Sarah, if you don't mind, I'm just going to call it a night. I'll finish my portion of things tomorrow before everything is due."

She glared at me, then eased up for his sake. "Sure, see you tomorrow."

I gave her my best "good riddance" look. It was less than appreciated. Sarah was working on more than a law degree. She was hoping to land a husband, a fellow attorney, by the time she took the bar exam.

When the door closed behind her, Gavin pulled me near. His warm lips felt firm against mine, his large hand cusped the back of my neck, bringing me even closer than before. The familiarity of each other was far from stagnant in its comfort. It was right. He scooped me up in his muscular arms, kissing me along the way before entering the bedroom.

"Does this threshold count for now?" he asked quietly.

"It will do," I whispered.

"Then let me pretend you're already my wife."

Chapter Fourteen

I HEARD THE COFFEE BREWING THE NEXT MORNING. Sunshine seeped through his panoramic windows to warm the entire bedroom. For a second, I indulged in the notion it was mid-summer, before the engagement party, and allowed myself to smile in the delirium. In the spirit of comfort, I threw on Gavin's Northwestern Law T-shirt that fell a couple inches above my knees. I stopped in his bathroom to wash my face. As I opened his medicine cabinet in search for the mouthwash, I found my trusty purple toothbrush in the place I last remember stowing it. Had I been too harsh to think he had tossed it?

This morning, he was wearing only pajama pants with disheveled hair. He stood over a pan, making omelets. The sun hit his serene blue-gray eyes long enough for me to admire them without him knowing. When he saw me standing there, he smiled.

"There's my girl. I hope you're hungry." He pulled out a kitchen table chair.

Scrounging on hospital food or quick bites here or there for weeks could have altered my taste buds, but memory served correctly as well.

Gavin's cooking was one of the many reasons I fell in love. I was no stranger to making meals, as my mother and father worked and I would often feed Natalia dinner when they were gone late. What I cooked was pretty standard, decent tasting, not very creative. Culinary arts had never been my forte.

"Aren't you going to have any?" I asked when his eyes continued to press on me.

"I enjoy watching you."

"Stop," I said, throwing my napkin across his small glass table.

His laughter was deep and gentle as he got up to playfully mess my hair. It happened so fast, I didn't get a chance to distract him with something else, or pretend I didn't want my hair unkempt. The back of my head throbbed with soreness from his innocent gesture.

"You're hurt? I'm sorry, was that too rough?" He muttered as he stepped away from my crouched position over the table.

I raised my hand to symbolize everything was fine.

"I don't understand, Veronica. What happened to your head?" His stance was firm, his look grim.

I felt the ice cascade over his brilliant blue eyes and knew he wouldn't tolerate half-truths. I quickly weighed my options. If Gavin knew, he'd want to intervene, which no doubt meant asking his father for money and continuing to perpetuate the notion my family is scum, therefore, he'd be marrying scum. He then would insist on moving me out to Chicago to keep an eye on me, ensure my safety. And that would mean transferring my sister's already weakened body to another hospital, maybe even the one she initially was treated in. Lastly, it would propel me to break a promise to Daddini that after the leave of absence I'd return to the grind. Randall the Suit possessed none of my loyalty, but Daddini, on the other hand, worked hard to secure my job when I had nearly damned it to hell. I owed him a return.

"Come to think of it, did you also hurt your nose? It's a little red and scabbed. I didn't notice it last night."

I resented answering to him, mainly because it was requiring me to lie. In my mind, there was no way around this.

"Sierra and I went out drinking the other night. I was so stupid. I was wearing these really high heels and fell down a half flight of stairs at the club. It was really embarrassing."

"What club?"

"This new one on Ford Street. It's called Nitro."

He squint his eyes. "That's not like you.... Oh, well be careful, babe."

"Trust me, I don't want to relive that again." At least that part was true.

He hugged me gently. "Sorry I hurt you."

"It's nothing. Really."

"I have to go to the library to finish that project I'm working on with Sarah. I have class in the afternoon. Can you stay today and I'll take you to dinner tonight?"

"I can't. I need to be back at the hospital. I don't like being away for long. Can you come up for the weekend?"

He looked down. I knew the answer was no.

"My dad is having a fundraiser. He's actually putting his hat in the ring for the governor's race. I'd invite you to come but..."

"I've been blacklisted?"

An uneasy laugh escaped him. "No, nothing like that. I just know you have more important things to do and I don't think Harvey would be too accepting of your presence in light of your last meeting."

I was about to agree with him before an unsettling larger thought entered my mind. "Where will I fit in your world, Gavin?"

His expression was devoid of surprise, as though he'd considered this himself but hadn't dredged up an answer that aligned with his heart.

"You don't fit in my father's world. But you fit in mine."

"Tell me they're not one and the same."

"They're not, Veronica."

"Tell me you still don't want to follow in his footsteps." This was more of a statement than a question.

"I don't."

"You're not entirely convincing."

"You're not conducting an interview."

"If I were, I'd press harder. But since it's you, I'm afraid of the answer I would find."

He sighed. "He is not without flaws, true. He has handlers like Harvey, who are obviously ruthless, and he's always whisked away from one place to the next. Hell, he was barely around when I was a kid. Yet he's accomplished a lot in regard to improving public schools, transportation and opportunities for the underprivileged. If he becomes governor, which is not a sure thing, he wants me to work on his team. It would be sort of a training ground for me, in case I decided to run for office, like say, contend for his state Senate one day. Voters would recognize the name and hopefully want to continue to see an impact on our behalf."

"I knew it." I shook my sore head.

He stepped closer. "You have to stop seeing my father as the devil reincarnated and see him for what he is. Is it so bad for me to walk in his shoes?"

"I thought you wanted to carve your own path. Whatever became of setting up your own practice? How could a reporter be married to a politician in the same city she would work in? A city in a state your father could be governor of? Did you consider the conflicts? Or was I supposed to relinquish my career once we got married?"

His face twitched.

"You're kidding me," I said. "You want a Stepford wife?

"No, Veronica, you're over-analyzing this. I just would like you all to myself and, when we start a family, I figured you'd be home with the kids."

"I'm glad you have a game plan, Gavin. Thanks for sharing it with me."

His arms were around my petite frame. "Let's calm down. We'll work this out somehow."

"I need to go now. I have a lot to think about and I have to get back to Natalia."

"Don't leave angry. We've had enough of those exits as it is. I had a wonderful time with you. It felt like it should. Let me be there for you. I'll come up in a couple weekends and help you keep Natalia company. You need a break, too." His voice was soft as his down pillows.

I nodded and returned his embrace.

"You have no idea," I responded without looking up into his eyes.

I called the hospital as soon as I entered my chilled car. Halloween was approaching and I held out hope Natalia would somehow waken by then. The medical assistant who answered the phone told me there was no progress. I blasted the pop hits station on my way out of Chicago and angled my Marlboro Light out the slightly lowered window. As I passed Wrigley Field, an ambulance zoomed by. The odds of Luke being behind the wheel in a city that size were minuscule. Yet, it made me think of him.

My cell phone rang just minutes after I put it down on the passenger seat. By the fringe of chatter and commotion in the not-so-distant background, I deciphered Daddini was on the other end until Carter's slightly high, effeminate voice came to the forefront.

"Have you been reading the follows?"

"Of course. Good work."

"Don't patronize me. A high school apprentice could do this. It's been all status quo, nothing new since what you reported, except some tidbits of info on the cops' personal lives. It's not your fault or anything. The story is just exhausted."

"I understand."

"So, Daddini wanted me to tell you it's pretty much going on a shelf from here. If you want to pick it up when you return, given there's something else to report, then it's all yours. I'm getting back to my expose on shabby water systems throughout the region."

"Gotcha. Thanks for the heads-up."

"How are things on your end?"

"Besides my life careening down a cliff? Oh, it's grand."

"Well, look at the bright side, at least you don't have to sit next to Gale five days a week," he chuckled over the morning television news in the background.

"You know, you definitely have a way of putting things in perspective."

"Talk to you soon, Roni. Call me if you need me."

"Thanks." Whether that was a genuine offer or not, I appreciated the sentiment.

There wasn't time to shower at Gavin's apartment. Even if there were, I couldn't have left soon enough following our conversation of his sudden change of life plans. My squeaky apartment door opened to reveal

Scoop, who needed a clean litter box, soft food and some fresh water. I was hoping he'd be my only greeter. When I pushed the door open completely, I realized there was no such luck. Sierra and her estranged father sat at my little table with coffee in front of them. A discomfort between them shifted around the apartment like a child in need of the bathroom. I resented feeling this uncomfortable in my own home.

"Roni, you're just in time to join us for lunch." Sierra rushed out of her chair to hug me. I stood there, unable to return the gesture. Clearly our talk got muddled between her ears.

"Oh, I can't. I'm on my way to the hospital."

Her father stood, his tall frame overpowering my small contemporary chair, and extended his hand toward me.

"Nice to meet you, Veronica. I've heard many good things about you. I'm..."

"I know who you are, Mr. Blake."

"Actually, I hate to be a stickler, but it's Detective Sergeant and I'm here officially for work, so I need to request your presence for some questions." He said this pleasantly enough, as if he wasn't asserting his authority over me.

"I wasn't in New York recently and I have no direct involvement in anything you may be investigating."

"Your cell phone records indicate you were called by Sierra minutes after Mr. McConner's death. That's deemed involvement."

"Are you seriously going to arrest your own daughter?" I stared at him in disbelief.

"The purpose of my visit is quite the opposite. I need to thoroughly understand the events of what took place in order to protect her should someone else get their hands on this case. I'm already told his wife is demanding answers and she is aware he had a certain affection for other women, especially those who were years his junior."

I sighed. Once again, Sierra the Wrecking Ball was swinging in full force. Why couldn't she just leave? I wondered.

"Let me change real quick and I'll come with you two," I muttered.

"I appreciate it," he responded with a smile.

My long, hot shower would have to take a rain check. For the moment, I was only able to switch clothes to a loose pair of black pants, a baggy knitted grey sweater and black flats. The drive made me tired and longing for comfort, regardless of fashion today. We arrived at Bev's Diner three blocks from my place. It wasn't The Ritz, but it had good breakfast and lunch food. Our timing was somewhere in between those, so the location made sense. I ordered a coffee with cream to get my energy going.

"So, Sgt. Blake, how do you like New York?" I was trying to mind my manners and keep in mind that a lot was riding on this, mainly Sierra's freedom. No matter how pissed she made me, I still wanted her to be free.

"It's nice, thank you." Not exactly Mr. Conversationalist, this one. I sipped my coffee, thinking, let's get on with this.

Sierra chimed in. "Roni is a journalist. She's a very talented writer."

"You don't say. What publication?"

"The Detroit Chronicle," Sierra nervously continued.

"How nice. What is your beat?"

"Cops and courts," I told him.

"Oh, so this is not new territory for you," he said, amused.

"I beg to differ. I've never had any conversations like this before and I don't intend to have any like this again."

"Well, then let's proceed," he pulled out a handheld notebook. "What was the nature of your cell phone call from Sierra?"

"She told me that Mr. McConner tried to sexually assault her and she fended off his attack."

"With what object?"

"At first, I think she hit him with a room service tray and then, when he pursued her further, she picked up a butter knife."

"And did what with it?"

I thought I had resented his presence at my apartment. He already knew all of this yet he was making me go through these motions again.

"Pierced him with it."

"By 'piercing' you mean stabbed him with it?"

"Yes. That is my understanding."

"And then what happened?"

"Is that a tape recorder in your pocket?"

"Yes, pay that no mind, it's just for me to help make sense of my chicken scratch later. So, then what happened?"

"Well, Why didn't you just tell me you were going to record this conversation? I mean, it seems unnecessary to me if you're just going to keep that information to yourself."

"You're getting distracted and for that, I apologize. Please continue."

"Roni," Sierra interrupted. "It's fine. He did the same thing when he got my account."

I looked from her to him. Their resemblance was uncanny. Her green eyes pleaded with me.

"She left the room, hailed a cab and ended up coming back to Detroit."

"Is it your understanding she left the scene of a crime?"

"It is my understanding that it wasn't a crime. That she acted in self-defense, fled out of fear and came home."

"Thank you," he shut his notepad and clicked his recorder off.

"May I leave now?"

"Please stay and order a meal."

"I'd rather not," I said, not caring if I sounded rude.

"Roni, why don't you order the pancakes you like here," Sierra offered.

"No, you two have a lot of catching up to do and I'm late for a visit at the hospital. Goodbye," I said as I pulled myself up from the vinyl booth cushion.

I left the awkwardness behind me for the people who earned it. Their uneasiness became more distant with each step of my beeline for the door.

The tables had turned, I thought. All these years Sierra's father was nowhere to be seen, a ghost of a person she once knew and loved. While at the same time, my father was a constant force in my life, as trusty as the morning paper on my doorstep. Now, he was an apparition.

His life was in danger and, without delivering the money to Zambi, so was mine. I feared Natalia's would be as well. Her fragile existence already clinging to earth, I couldn't imagine fears heightened even more by looming threats of a loan shark enforcer. Yet, I reasoned, if they knew who I was, they may well know who she is. I felt my jaw tighten and fists clench at the sheer thought of my father's concave face and sunken shoulders. I pictured our last conversation in the hospital, his restrained "you've always looked after her so well." I realized now that he knew all along he would be leaving me to fend for her, perhaps indefinitely. Unforgivable as that was, he left me with a headache of problems to solve. I fingered the back of my head where Eyes of Darkness gashed me good. Yes, I thought, a true headache.

My body, worn down and dirty from travels, begged for that shower. My mind longed for peace. I needed to be alone, truly alone, to strategize my next move. I returned to my apartment, along with the squeaking door that remained neglected, poured Purina catfood into Scoop's dish and refilled his water bowl. Then, I escaped to a long, hot shower that pulsated down on my exhausted body. When I was through washing, I cloaked myself in a robe and wrapped a towel around my head and laid down on my soft down comforter. I didn't even summon the strength to dress in pajamas before I let my two-ton eyelids fall to form darkness all around.

When I woke, it was dusk. The phone was ringing on my nightstand.

"Hello." There's no masking my resting voice.

"You do exist."

"I'm sorry?"

"Well, since I never heard from you, I thought I'd check to make sure you still exist. Okay, I can go now." I could almost hear his smile forming.

"Wait. I'm glad you called." It was true and for that, I felt incredibly guilty.

"Oh, you are? That is surprising. May I remind you that I drove a painstaking four hours on my bike to see you, only to never hear from you again." Luke laughed softly on the other end.

"That's not true... you're hearing from me now."

"Well, even though I called you, I'll still accept that." I smiled. "So, how is Veronica?"

"All right, thanks."

"Liar. You really are not a good liar at all. And, were you sleeping? I know there's an hour time difference for us, but that's a bit extreme."

"Luke, you have no idea." No idea I was just in the city you live in, I thought. No idea I got bashed in the head by a thug soon after a frat boy nearly attacked me. No idea I have to find some way to payoff my father's outrageous debt, for an addiction I didn't even know he had. Suddenly I felt very tired all over again.

"I would if you told me," his voice gentle and sweet.

And, for some reason or no reason at all, I did. I spilled it all to a man I barely knew. I was able to share with him the atrocities of my world in shambles because he had no direct connection to my everyday life. There was no fear of Luke insisting I move, quit my job or rearrange my plans for him. He pulled no weight in that department and that felt pretty damn good. There was one thing I left out--the emerald cut elephant in my room. It may have been selfish to lean on Luke emotionally while keeping my engagement to Gavin from him, but the closest things I'd had to therapeutic conversations were the one-way ones I had with Natalia. I wanted to hear a voice on the other end. Rather, I *needed* to hear a voice on the other end. His ears cushioned my fall beautifully; his voice the comforting drip-drop of rain on the windowpane. I was grateful his handsome face wasn't before me to distract or intimidate me from sharing with him. Staying isolated in my room was not only safe, it was fitting. But, even as I reveled in the distance, Luke's tenderness spanned miles and I could sense his warm heart pounding. This time, it wasn't lust. It was beating for compassion.

"You're a very strong person. I could tell that from the moment I met you. You've been given more than most people could handle, and yet I know you'll persevere," he coaxed. The tears from my eyes felt hot like jalapenos streaking my face.

"How do you know?" My voice quiet and weak.

"Because I have great instincts. The gut feeling that tells me you will be fine is the same feeling I have about you and me."

"Which is?"

"That we'll be together." Luke's voice was neither squeamish nor arrogant. It was matter-of-fact confident.

With me remaining quiet, he pledged to be there for me whenever I needed him. It was an overwhelmingly sweet offer that I didn't know I would feel right cashing in on. I wanted to ask him about the tattoo on his chest, who the person was and if she still meant something to him. Doing so, however, would be turning our talk into a tit-for-tat information exchange and that didn't seem fair.

Although, at the moment, I had to be honest with myself, I had been enraptured and flattered at the thought of this man seeing a future with me. But I didn't know why he would say that about me, whom he barely knew. Perhaps that's what drew him to me, that despite my exterior of strength, inside I was more vulnerable than ever. Or, despite having looks others praise, I was far from seeing myself as a beauty queen. Then again, he could have succumbed to the same feelings that stirred inside me when we saw each other....

It didn't matter that evening had fallen over Detroit, I trudged to the hospital to see my sister in her usual unresponsive state. I gave her a sponge bath, washed her wavy hair, painted her nails magenta, lifted and stretched her legs and arms to keep the circulation flowing and read her mother's prayer book in a soft voice. Barb peeked in and beamed with approval.

Inside my knapsack was a leather pilot's hat, aviator glasses and a white thin scarf I found piecemeal at three different vintage stores. Was it wishful thinking she'd wake by Halloween? I dreamt that, if she did, I'd set up candy stations throughout this level of the hospital, wheeling her to and from until she had the strength to rise from the chair on her own. In this fantasy, I wouldn't have to deliver the tragic news about our mother because she would have visited her as an angel in her dreams and explained the whole thing to her in a serenely acceptable way. I looked down at Natalia's long black lashes over her closed eyes and, for a second, was almost relieved she was asleep. It was a heavy-handed thought that waded in every guilty crevice of my brain, but it was accompanied like a violin to the orchestra, striking an absent note in the abyss of my sorrow. The money was due in four days. Halloween was in four days. Not only had I not scrounged up the ten grand, I hadn't the slightest idea how to do it, especially when my father remained elusive. A chill rushed over me, ice-cold steel over a boxer's puffy eye, but I felt oddly steady with the blow. After all, there wasn't much control in my bloodied hands at this point. I relinquished the worries to the universe. What else could I do?

I nearly jumped when Sierra walked into the room. Her eyes timid, she reluctantly closed the door, devoid of her usual sway of the hips.

"I didn't mean to scare you. Sorry for the intrusion." She whispered as if speaking normally would wake The Sleeping Child.

"It's nothing. Please sit." My voice sounded strange from a lack of speaking for so long.

I stood to offer her my lounger chair and sunk in on the edge of Natalia's bed. The move was part polite, part protective, as I didn't want her sitting that close to my sister. Problem was, our positions put us in a stare-down sitting stance that could readily allow a honest-to-goodness war of words. The anger boiling inside me had not lessened with time or burden of her father's presence. I still bore ill will stemming from her drug supply to

Jeremy to overall shadiness for shafting me that night at the bar. Seeing her leave for New York, along with her ever-absent father, couldn't come too soon. But I tried, as best as I possibly could, to play nice. And *she's* the actress.

"I just wanted to say goodbye."

Good riddance, I thought. Although I opted for "oh, are you going now?"

"Well, I'm all packed and ready to go. I have a flight early in the morning, so I am going to stay at a hotel by the airport. My, uh, dad is already on his way back."

"Will you two stay in touch?"

"Yeah, I think it will be nice that we can finally reestablish some kind of relationship. It will be slow-moving and there's still a lot to work out, yet I'm looking forward to it."

Nothing with Sierra is "slow-moving," so I wondered how this would pan out for her.

"That's nice," I said.

She inhaled a deep breath like she was prepping to project into an audience. Her face fell when I halted her would-be speech with a quick, "have a safe flight." I had known her long enough to tell when an apology was under way. In better, more patient times, I would have let the cameras roll. Today, I called scene.

"Okay, thanks," she muttered, coupled with a half-hearted hug.

A few days passed with little excitement, except for the happiness that exuded from me as I walked into a clean, empty apartment with only Scoop sprawled regally on the sofa every night. Hospital coffee was no treat, so I brewed a fresh pot of a Colombian blend and sunk into the couch next to my feline friend and pored over the mail. I threw the utility bills onto the side table, tossed junk mail in a pile on the floor and thumbed over a white envelope with no return address. As I opened it, I sensed the outline of a picture inside. A silly elation swept me as I thought of Great Aunt Estelle and how she liked sending family pictures. That would be a welcome reprieve from the daily events.

Instead, what greeted me was a snapshot of Gavin, clad in tux and smile, with his arm draped around Miss Preppy herself. Sarah in a pink lace cocktail dress grinned from ear to ear as she gazed up adoringly at my fiance. I could have almost credited her with sending the picture herself, but she wasn't nearly as cunning as my prime suspect, Harvey. I cringed at the thought of him having my home address and shuddered with anger that, despite hearing from Gavin the morning of the fundraiser, he never once mentioned bringing a *date* to the event. I'm sure he knew that would go over like a metal rod in a thunderstorm. I'd be the storm, of course. My wrath felt pretty epic about now.

I decided not to call him, not to send a nasty e-mail, not to say anything. Instead, I squeezed my damn bruised lemons into lemonade, albeit tart and bitter. I remembered a feature in the paper a while back about a high-end pawnshop, if there is such a thing, that did rather well in this economy. Since people were losing their jobs and houses, many of them needed to cash in whatever valuables they owned. My limited experience with pawnshops was quick ins and outs. Once I hawked a camera someone gave me, and another time I needed to grab a couple comments from storeowners about a proposed property tax on small businesses.

The next morning, I pulled up to The Pawn Palace, with a sign resembling the Taj Mahal, and entered the spacious store with faux confidence. A middle-aged Middle Eastern man sat behind the counter with a Coke in his hand. The twelve-inch television set before him displayed a fuzzy picture of the Pistons' game. It was hardly a palace, but slightly larger and better decorated than the average pawnshop, I surmised.

"Yes, honey. How'd you like me to help you? Have something to unload today?" he asked with thick accent. "Well, come on, don't be shy. What it is? A gold chain? A camcorder? We take everything and offer best return out there."

I realized I wasn't talking or moving when I should have been.

"Come on, dear. Show me."

I stepped closer to the counter, slid off my exquisite engagement ring and leaned forward.

"How much for this?"

The smile turned into displeasure. "Are you sure 'bout this? Once something pawned, it gone forever. Such a pretty girl should not take these matters lightly."

"Yes, I'm sure. How much?"

He handled it gently, placed his glasses at the edge of his nose and then called for someone in the back in his foreign tongue. A younger man, I presumed to be his son, stepped beside him with a jeweler's loupe. His chubby fingers clad in gold encircled the magnifying glass that he stared through for three minutes. He peered up at me with furrowed brows.

"It didn't work out, huh? Too bad, that's a beauty," he said in a voice devoid of his father's accent.

"Could you just tell me how much, please?"

"Nine grand."

"It's Tiffany's."

"Okay, ten. You won't find a better price than that."

"There's no need to look."

Chapter Fifteen

IT SMELLED OF BURNT LEAVES WHEN I LEFT FOR THE HOSPITAL. Evening had fallen and, with it, all the wonders of Halloween, the magical time of year when kids and adults alike indulge in fantasy and sweets. Last year, Natalia and I dressed as hobos, begging from door to door for goodies until my mom's cell phone call that it was "too late for normal people to stay out." That was one way she'd put it. Another was to say "rarely do good things happen after dark." I would be testing that theory tonight, as my father's debt was due.

There wasn't an abundance of time before my dreaded visit to Johnnie's Sports Bar, so I mainly came in to check on Natalia, kiss her and set the costume beside her. Barb was working three-twelves this week and always kept close tabs on my sister. My dream of her awakening had been dashed. I held out hope for tomorrow.

Green Street ran east and west through a seedy section of the east side. It was the kind of route you'd take as a novice to the city or, in my case, if I covered a shooting or two. The collection of random men loitering outside the barred-windowed liquor store was no comfort to a girl carrying ten big ones, cash. Their bagged bottles and half-smoked cigarettes, which were left on the sidewalk from passersby, hardly eased a white, native suburbanite's fears. Admittedly, these apprehensions brewed inside me on assignments as well. But this time I had no cloak of professionalism, no deadline adrenaline. It was just me wading in vulnerability and discomfort.

I parked directly in front of Johnnie's, a stone's throw from the seedy crew congregating at the party store. Their hoots and hollers rolled off the wind like some werewolf bellowing at the full moon. The heavy red door that had been repainted more than a few times resisted my pull with the wind. I yanked it harder in a nervous jerk that nearly sent me to the pavement when it slid from my grip. My audience found this comedy routine quite pleasurable in their drunkenness.

The urgency I felt to take shelter inside dissipated in the darkness within. A row of round middle-aged men puffed cigars and cupped beer bottles along the mahogany bar. Their expressions were just as perplexed at seeing me as the men outside. I inhaled, straightened my back and clutched my slouch bag. The bartender was a tall, slender man with a receding hairline. He didn't stop polishing cognac glasses as I approached in trepidation.

"Excuse me, I'm here to see..."

The bartender set down his glass and white cloth and walked away.

"Excuse me," I called in vain.

He disappeared to a back room as I stood there clumsily. The patrons watched my awkwardness in amusement. One of them, in a windbreaker jumpsuit and Nikes, said through a cloud of smoke, "I think you're in the wrong place, sweetie, but let me buy you a cold one anyway."

Before I could politely decline, the antisocial bartender (isn't that an oxymoron?) skulked back over to me.

"He's expecting you in the back." He sounded like Lurch from "The Addams Family."

I leaned my head to the side of him, in order to peer at the red vinyl booth beside a pool table. In the dim light I could make out his gray newsboy cap, white button-down and cigar and his medium-sized frame. He didn't seem so frightening, I told myself. But then a flash of metal to my skull served as a much-needed reminder that this person was morally myopic. I realized that categorizing someone as wholeheartedly sinister flew in the face of my journalistic training that everyone is three-dimensional and news stories can be as complex as their characters. In this case, though, my bias mentality against Zambi kept his potential danger at the forefront of my mind and, I hoped, would keep me alive.

Upon closer view, it was easy to see how the word charisma was a common description for him. He hadn't spoken yet, although his dark hair and eyes appeared to gleam in the dark. It was both mesmerizing and chilling.

"Sit, please," his voice deep and rich like imported chocolate. A Rolex dangled from his wrist.

"Perhaps it would have been wise for us to search you. After all, you probably own a recorder or two in your profession."

"I can assure you, there's nothing like that on me." I tried to sound cool, in charge.

He leaned forward, cigar in one hand and a Grey Goose on the rocks in the other.

"I thought you were a smart girl. That's what my associate said, too."

I bit my lip. Associate, that's one way to put it.

"And you're a loyal daughter. That's endearing to me, as I myself am a loyal man to my family. In fact, the gentleman working behind the bar is my brother. Sure, he's not much for chit-chat, but no one's family is perfect-as you well know." A grin waltzed onto his face.

"Yes," I said, knowing that keeping my chatter to a minimum was key.

"You know, your father is a fortunate man to have such beautiful and smart daughter. It's too bad he's a degenerate gambler. I have to say, I'm not too pleased that he just up and left on his debt like that." He shrugged and puffed his cigar. "That's not to say it would be difficult to find him, if I really wanted to."

He raised his eyebrows and tilted his newsboy cap back to reveal a full head of curly black hair tinged with gray. "Tell me, do I really want to find him?"

"That won't be necessary," I mustered. "I have your money."

"Ah, a good daughter indeed."

I handed him the thickest envelope I ever possessed. He passed it to his brother, who showed up out of nowhere, to haul it off into privacy.

The uneasiness beckoned for me to leave, but Zambi seemed comfortable with the conversation. When I stirred, he protested by raising his hand.

"Please, have a drink on me. It's the least I can do."

"You mean after having me bashed in the head and taking thousands of dollars from me?" I felt like saying. Instead, I went with the ebbs and flow of this sit-down, as I doubted he would take rejection with a smooth temperament.

"OK, I'll have a glass of red wine; cabernet or merlot would be fine."

He smiled. "Great." He subtly waved his brother over from the bar to tell him my order. It returned a couple minutes later. Those minutes were disguised as hours. I lit a Marlboro Light when my wine arrived. Drinking and smoking were the troublesome duo that thrived on each other's misbehavior.

So, there I was, sitting with a morally amiss man. A person who invoked fear and danger to practically all he encountered. And I had no one to thank for this menacing meeting other than my very own father.

"Veronica."

The sound of my name off his sly tongue seemed foreign as this environment to me. Goose bumps popped up along my arms.

"Yes, ah..." Mr. Zambi? Sharky? No, that probably wasn't appropriate.

"Just call me Gabe," he smiled.

"Okay, yes, Gabe."

"The good and bad news about gamblers is they don't stay away for long. There's always a lure to return. Like your father, for instance, he's big on these underground card games we so happen to organize. Sure, the casinos might fill a void for a while, but they don't quench the thirst like the games he enjoys so much."

"What is it you're saying?"

"Well-hey, I said you're a smart girl, right? So, let me cut to the chase," he leaned in, puffing his cigar. "It's only a matter of time before your pops shows up again, racks up his debt again and can't pay it again."

"I can't say I understand why he'd do such a thing, but I hear your point."

"So, what I suggest is maybe you and I work out some sort of arrangement." He traced his fingers along my arm, the goose bumps ready to explode.

I yanked my arm away. The wine and cigarette were gone by then.

"I hate to disappoint you, Gabe. But this will be the only time I pay my father's debt. You have my assurance of that."

"Pity for that," he shrugged. "By that I mean, pity for me," he said as his eyes scanned me up and down indecently. "Even more so, pity for your dad."

His words haunted me for days, a true Halloween scare. A man like that found no solace in wasted threats. Although my anger with my father hardly depleted with the passing of the envelope, I still held the memories of a loving man who pushed me on swings, kissed scraped knees and spent hours doing homework with me at the dinner table. Couple those recollections with the sobering fact he was my sole living parent, the message was like a rock in the bottom of my stomach. Had he found peace in recklessness after my mother's passing? Did his depression morph differently within him, in a way I could not relate to? I was sad he was sad, hurt he was hurt, but also angry that he borrowed my time to wallow in his melancholy. We could have been a team, taking shifts by Natalia's side, placing flowers on my mother's grave, grocery shopping, working, and all the things required for survival and sanity. Instead, he abandoned me-and Natalia-when needed the most. Ironic, how the man I love saved my father with his betrayal. Had Gavin not rendezvoused with Sarah, his ring would have never covered my father's debt.

 I sat on my couch, drinking green tea and listening to smooth jazz on much of my downtime from the hospital. Gavin's voice, perplexed and questioning, went unanswered on my machine. His messages usually alternated with Sierra's, ranting about her rehearsals, asking me to pick up to chat. My father's voice never accompanied theirs.

 I asked God to give my mother to me as an angel. I needed her so badly it hurt my heart.

 When I had had enough of feeling sorry for myself, I peeled myself off the couch one sunny, brisk afternoon to see a movie at the Eaden Independent Theatre a few blocks from my apartment. The lines may have been cheesy and the actors laid it on a little thick, but the romantic comedy-drama lifted my spirits for nearly two hours, namely because it was sheer escapism. If sitting in the audience transported me for a short time away from my troubles, I got a hint of how Sierra felt on the other side. I sincerely wondered how she was doing. It sounded like she needed a friend. For a minute, I entertained the thought of returning her calls. But the idea lost in a psychological tug of war with my stubbornness.

By the end of the month, I was due back at the paper. In advance, Daddini requested to meet for coffee to discuss my return. When I pulled my Malibu up to the curb of a downtown café, I saw him standing outside with a Camel Light in one hand and the morning edition in the other. He appeared neater, more put-together than usual. When I stared, unintentionally, at his outfit, he shook his head laughing. "You spend years dressing your kids and then, all of a sudden, they become teenagers and they think they should be dressing you."

"You look good, Daddini. Maybe too good for the paper."

""How ya doing, kiddo?" He patted my shoulder and ushered me through the door to the counter. "Coffee's on me today. Hey Gill, I'll have the usual and my friend here will have a mocha jocha latte or whatever liquid sugar drinks these kids drink nowadays," he said laughingly to the thin, middle-aged owner with sandy hair and glasses.

"I'll just have an espresso. Thanks."

"Sit down, Roni."

My best face was painted on. I strived for professionalism, pure business, no pity party. Perhaps, I tried too hard. Daddini sipped his coffee, fiddled his thumbs and half smiled at me across the circular wooden table. I pressed my lips upward as much as possible in return.

"How is your sister doing?"

"She's the same, but the doctors say she could wake up any day."

"Well, here's hoping. I'm sure it will happen soon. Kids are resilient."

"Yeah."

"How are you? Are you taking care of yourself, too?"

"I'm fine. Thanks." I smiled as convincingly as I could.

Daddini sat back in his chair. A sigh escaped him. Confliction consumed his face.

"What is it?" I asked.

"I want to be sure you're ready to come back next month. You have a lot on your plate and I don't want to push you too hard."

"You're not pushing me, Daddini. I want to get back to work. Not only will I need the money by then, I *need* to do this."

He nodded, slowly, the wheels in his overworked mind grinding tirelessly.

"All right, kid. If you can handle it. But don't internalize any problems. You come and talk to me if you need anything. You may feel alone in this, but you're not. There are people at the paper who care about you and are rooting for your success."

"Like Randall?" I chimed in smugly.

"You know what they say about inept managers, they have to rise to your level of incompetence. Well, the Suit has gotten as high up as he can and he'll be happy as long as the paper is in the black. Amazingly, in these times, it actually is. So, let me handle him and you focus on kicking butt like you always do."

I wanted to hug him. Instead, I just agreed.

"Now, let's go outside and have a smoke before I start convulsing," he said.

As we stepped outside, the homeless man with scraggly hair Daddini had pointed out before shuffled along across the street-to my smoking buddy's masked elation.

Chapter Sixteen

THE BUZZER TO MY APARTMENT SERVED AS MY ALARM CLOCK THE FOLLOWING MORNING. It was a crude, unwelcomed awakening that unavoidably set the tone for the day. My spirits were usually much higher when Scoop rubbed his whiskers against my arm for his morning feed. I stumbled out of bed and fished for my Victoria's Secret black robe for warmth over my long nightshirt and pulled on some furry slippers. My eyes were half-closed when I pushed the intercom button.

"Who is it?" My voice was muffled with sleep.

"Your fiance-you know, the one you can't get enough *of.*"

Oh boy, the sarcasm was almost too thick to infiltrate the intercom.

"Come up," I said unenthused, unlocking my door and heading for the coffee pot.

His impatience was far from masqueraded; I could feel the frustration percolating in succession with the coffee. Any other man might enter bellowing, but Gavin was accustomed to social suppression, given his upbringing. Yet another way we're different, I thought.

He stood just adjacent to my kitchen, staring as I casually offered him a mug of joe. (The well-mannered politician's son accepted it.) Even in my apathetic state, I couldn't help but feel inadequate in my robe and slippers, disheveled hair and no makeup. He looked as handsome as ever in dark-blue jeans, a black Calvin Klein sweater and Prada sneakers. I longed to pause time to run to the bathroom and ready myself for this confrontation. An ordinary breakfast with the man you were going to marry would be one thing, but ending a relationship looking like the bottom of a dirty dish is another. I brushed vanity aside for time's sake, sat at the table and gestured toward a chair for him. He obliged.

"What time is it?" I said groggily.

"Seven."

"Geez, Gavin. What time did you leave Chicago?"

"Around midnight."

"Well then, what have you been doing since you got here hours ago?

"Sitting on your stoop," he said in a quiet, controlled voice.

"Why?"

"What choice do I have, Veronica? You won't even answer my calls."

I sipped my coffee. The hazelnut creamer tasted as good as it smelled. I wanted to escape in it, as silly as that seemed. I buried my nose in the scent, sliding more and more down my throat.

"Are you going to say anything or did I drive all this way to be ignored in person?" he asked across the table.

I lifted my tired body from the chair, walked to the bedroom and returned.

"Some things don't require any words," I said, placing the picture of Gavin and Sarah on the table before him.

I could have slapped Gavin and he would have looked less stunned. His brows raised and jaw dropped. While I found this all amusing, I cared not to beat a dead horse. I escaped out the sliding door onto my cramped balcony for a smoke in the chilly November air. A brisk breeze swept under my robe, leaving me shivering for a minute. The city noise was a hodgepodge of rush hour traffic, end-of-season construction and stray passersby chatting on their cell phones. The morning activity would become a ghost of itself at night, as most daytime dwellers would be tucked in their suburban beds by then.

I felt him cloak me with a woolen blanket that had been folded half-heartedly on my couch. His touch was warm, familiar at first-before I reminded myself those same hands could have been on Sarah not long ago. I shuddered.

"It's a little too cold for sitting out here. Don't you think?"

"It's a little too late to care for my well-being. Don't you think?" There was no anger in my voice, just sorrow.

He leaned against the black metal railing. Pain overcame his face.

"Sometimes, a picture is worth a thousand misleading words," he said gently.

"And other times?"

"This isn't one of those times."

"Well, even if I gave you the benefit of the doubt, do you ever think that we're against the odds? I mean, haven't we been through hell in the short time we've been engaged? Don't you think it's a sign?"

The surprise returned to his face.

"Wow, Veronica. I didn't know you blamed all of life's obstacles on our engagement."

"No, I don't. It's just that I can barely pick myself up out of bed and muster the strength to be there for my sister. I don't feel I have the stamina for the challenges I know we'd face."

"Such as?"

"For starters, your family's disdain of me."

"Irrelevant," he said, shaking his head in dismissal.

"Then there's the issue of our careers, me uprooting Natalia to Illinois..."

"What about your father? I had assumed he would take care of her on a full-time basis."

For a minute, I forgot about how much I had left him in the dark about my family situation.

"Well, yeah. I don't know; I guess my thoughts are cloudy right now. Either way, though, I'd want to be near her. And then there's the Sarah factor." My voice trailed off as if sampling rotten food.

"There is no Sarah factor. I didn't invite her. I don't know who did, but Harvey asked me to pose with her..." He paused. "So, I guess we have our answer right there."

"Nevertheless, the distance between us is palpable." I nodded, forgetting whether I was trying to convince him or myself. My mind had been made up from the minute I stepped into the pawnshop to barter my love life for my father's physical one. As far as I was concerned, there was no turning back. The absence of the ring was not lost on Gavin; he gazed at my bare finger more than once, but said nothing.

A narrow ray of sun meandered through the buildings to grace my face for a mere second. I relished its warmth like a stray dog in the cold.

"I can't convince you to be with me. It's something you'd have to want," he said. Then, he looked at me in the most alarming way. I realized the expression on his face was sheer pity and loathed every inch of him at that moment. "Perhaps you no longer want things for yourself anymore."

The brief cascade of warmth abruptly parted, leaving me shivering in its absence. I turned to him with venom on my tongue. "There are plenty of things I want. The main one being my mother back."

He was gobsmacked with guilt, an unfair blow.

"Well then, you are right by saying there are some challenges we could not overcome. I came here to work things out, but it's clear you had other plans. I won't be bothering you again."

With that, he slid open the glass door to embark on his life without me. I closed my eyes that night to find myself lying in a meadow of grass and sunflowers with the brightest, most comforting sun shining on my long locks and on the creases of a purple sundress that made me feel girly and sweet. My bare feet rubbed against a patch of dirt where sunflower seeds had just been planted; the grains sifted between my toes. When I heard the cries of seagulls, I picked myself up, reveling in my lightness, and followed them to the still waters of a vast lake. It clearness enlightened me and I just gazed at the even, slow movement of the water. I dipped my dirt-covered toes in it, seeing the brown spots part outward. The water was incredibly warm and I couldn't deny myself a dip. With my pretty dress, I dove into the lake. I swam for what seemed like hours, just relishing in its liquid embrace. When I had enough, I brought myself to the lake's shore and spread out on the most beautiful, vivid array of flowers. I had never seen anything like them. Their colors were brighter than any in my frame of reference. They accepted me with open petals, a sort of mosh pit in a concert of silence. Stunningly, my hair dried instantly into floral-smelling waves that trickled down my back. My dress, once a sopping mess, was perfectly smooth and sweet again. My smile couldn't leave as, if it had always been a permanent fixture on my face. Peace encompassed my body; I felt the presence of God. Then, a familiar touch sent shivers down my arm. Yet, I wasn't afraid. I knew whose gentle hand embraced mine. I turned to see for myself. She smiled warmly in return.

"Mom!" She was leaning on one elbow, facing me with her right hand stretched over her gleaming body to reach me. Her dark hair shined in the sun, falling magnificently on her floral dress, absent of blood.

"Roni, my love," she whispered as we stood to embrace.

"But how?" I asked incredulously, to which she simply responded with a "shh" and lead me to the most decadent display of fruits, chocolates, pastries and wines.

"You must be hungry," she said, pointing to the gold-encrusted table. "Please, eat."

When she saw me glance back at her with hesitation, she nodded reassuringly, "I'll still be here when you're done."

I collected the largest, juiciest strawberries, melon slices and oranges on a bronze saucer along with chunks of dark chocolate and frosted pastries with jelly inside. Then, I filled a goblet with red wine. Not enough to get drunk, but enough to enjoy nonetheless. Suddenly, as if a cloud appeared beneath me, a soft encompassing chair held me while I nibbled on the best food I'd ever tasted and washed it down with the delightful wine. Hummingbirds vibrated nearby. When the clouds drifted above, each one appeared to be an angel.

Pleasantly full, I turned to my mother. She looked radiant as ever, a glow brightened her cheeks and her skin was like the crescent moon. Her fingertips ran upward on my face, wiping away tears I hadn't noticed fall.

"Mom, I'm so alone," I said as the crying took force of me. Immediately, the richness of the food and drink became a distant memory. An emptiness started to creep in to my stomach.

"No, my beautiful child, you are never alone," she smiled and kissed my cheeks. That vacant emotion faded with her affection.

The warmth blanketed me even as I awoke. All along, I had sensed it was merely a dream. A certain melancholy came in with the morning light. And still, I knew it was more than a dream. Much more.

When I snuggled next to Natalia, as I sometimes did on her small hospital bed, I stroked her hair and told her all about it, how amazing the lake, flowers and food was. But, more importantly, I described our mother and how incredibly gorgeous and radiant she appeared to be.

"You look so much like her," I told my sleeping sister, kissing her cheeks as my mother did to me in my dream and reading excerpts from the little prayer book.

The last visit I made to my parents' house had been frightening and painful. Like a little child quivering under the bed during a thunderstorm, I had yet to muster the courage to face the monster. I knew the lawn would be a jungle, an embarrassment to my mother if she were alive, that the mail would have been piled into the mailbox until the postman discontinued it out of exasperation, and the house would need to be aired out to shuffle away the dust and staleness. Now that Zambi's debt was settled, I had no reason to believe an enforcer would be waiting in the house to attack. That, however, wasn't enough to ease my shaky stomach. I told myself to grow up and face the music. No white knight could stampede into this situation for me, with a broomstick and a lawn mower nonetheless.

It was Saturday morning. I arrived in a Detroit Pistons' sweatshirt and leggings with sneakers and my hair pulled back in a ponytail. This would be the last lawn mow of the season from the looks of the November weather, so there was some comfort in that. I figured getting the hardest part over first would be best. I opened the garage with the remote code on the side panel to push out the mower, which I double-checked had gas, and started it up. About forty minutes later, the modest backyard and much smaller front were done. Of course, I didn't create any of those fancy mowing patterns that others in the subdivision did, but I was pleased to finish.

I left the mower under the back overhang to cool off and headed straight for the sink to fill a glass of water - and then I heard jazz streaming from the bedroom. I became paralyzed with fear, reliving the emotions of the last visit to a house I had previously found so much comfort in. When he bopped up and down to the sounds from down the hallway into the kitchen, I dropped my glass on the floor. It shattered at my sneakers and still I couldn't tear my eyes away from him.

"Are you all right? You look like you saw a ghost," my father said as if the last time I had seen him was five minutes ago.

"I think I just did," I said, feeling clammy and weak.

Chapter Seventeen

HE WALKED OVER TO ME IN A SORT OF HALF-STEP SHUFFLE. I couldn't pry my eyes away from his gleeful expression, despite his sunken face and alarmingly thin frame. Holding the sides of my upper arms, he kissed my cheek. I could smell once again the bourbon on his breath, albeit fainter than the last time he was near.

"Come on, get the cat off your tongue. What, are you hungry?"

"No, no, I ate not too long ago," I said, still frozen.

"Yes! You must be hungry. Let's go to this great place I like. I know you'll like it, too. They have the best lunches-shrimp, pasta, fish, steak, salads-you name it, they have it. And don't worry about the desserts. They're just as delicious."

Before I could begin to protest, he grabbed my purse off the counter and whisked me to the garage, where his Jeep was nestled inside.

"Dad, I don't understand..." I began, but he cranked the knob of his radio to full blast. Another bebop song permeated the space. His hands wildly motioned to the music while finessing the wheel as he backed out of the driveway, turned on side streets and onto the expressway heading west to Detroit. I thought of the bourbon, slightly aged on his breath, and reasoned by the fading scent that he was sober.

"Cigar my dear?" he asked, pointing to the glove box.

"No, I'm good." *Like I smoked cigars in the first place,* I thought.

"How about getting one for your pops then?"

I lifted the latch to locate the pack of cigars, which was propped on top of some random papers along with his registration and proof of insurance. When I grasped the pack, I realized the papers were uneven because of an item underneath them. That's when I noticed the glimmer of a handgun.

"Thanks. I have a lighter around here somewhere." He was nearly shouting over the music. I had never witnessed his taste for such loudness. Then again, I never knew he owned a gun either. I closed the glove box. My mind was trying to keep pace with the moment, which changed quicker than I could process.

When we passed the downtown exit, I began to get even antsy.

"Where is this place?"

"Oh, have a sense of adventure. It's worth the wait."

He curved with the expressway exit leading to the tunnel to Canada.

"Dad, they require passports now. I don't have that on me. Why didn't you say where we were going in the first place?"

"You worry too much. We'll get through. It's not like we're terrorists."

He was chuckling over the music at my protest as if logic was just a notion in the far corners of his mind.

"Maybe you don't worry enough." I spit the words like poison yet he kept smiling, driving and bopping to the music.

We waited in the relatively brief line to the booth allowing access from one country to the next.

"Citizenship?" A heavy, elderly black man with a bald head asked.

"U.S." We both said.

"Identification, please."

My father handed him our driver's licenses, which seemed to appease him, and he told us to proceed.

"We have to get past these formalities, Chuck," my father said with a smile.

"Just doing my job, Robert. You catch a break more than most. Have a good one."

"You, too," he said before turning to me. "See, no sweat."

As the Jeep meandered along the two-way streets and approached the banks of the Detroit River, I quickly saw the bright lights of the Windsor Casino.

"I thought we were going to eat," I said.

"We are. There's a great restaurant here."

"Must be pretty good for us to come all the way to Canada," I said dryly, but he ignored my sarcasm.

"It is. You'll love it."

Walking into the casino was like stepping into some tacky sixties movie in which smoke formed a translucent wall, big-haired women with faux fingernails cupped whisky sours and old men sat solemnly at blackjack tables. The carpet was a dizzy array of red and orange patterns that clearly were designed by someone with attention deficit disorder. The constant clicking and ringing of the slot machines was enough for me to want to cover my ears like a child.

While I loathed every crevice of this place, my father was in his glory.

"Want to sit down and try our luck first?" His question exuded sheer hope.

"No, I'm ready to check out the restaurant you've been telling me so much about."

Disappointment ran across his face; I could tell he needed a fix.

"Sure, it's this way."

He led me through the wide aisles amid the clinging and clanging of slots and rustle of cards over green felt. For a second, a flashback came to me of following my father through the mall, a crowded store, church, you name it. He led me to our destination and I safely trailed behind. Only, this time, I was as lost as ever.

The sign above the doorway arch was inscribed with gold cursive letters scrawling "Casino Chophouse." Cherrywood tables were closely placed throughout the dark restaurant. Waiters performed tableside service of créme brûlée and bananas foster. The repressed hunger inside me subsided momentarily with the meek embarrassment of my appearance. Mowing-the-lawn attire isn't exactly conducive to fine dining. I was surprised by the maitre d's nonchalant reaction to my wardrobe. But I soon discovered the influence of my father's regular visits extended beyond the tunnel tollbooth.

"Robert, how nice to see you. Whom might this be?" A slender man in his late fifties pondered before showing us our table.

"This is my daughter, Veronica," he said.

"Nice to meet you, Veronica. Your father is one of our best customers. Let me seat you this way."

Best customers? I scoffed to myself. This was becoming an informative field study into my father's life. A life that apparently entailed not working, not caring for his daughters, racking up debt he had no means to pay while eating expensive cuisine and indulging in leisurely gambling in Canada. Who was this person? My questions were consuming me, but I decided to put them off. I was dumbfounded. I knew anything I said now would be murky, inarticulate and anger-induced. I tried my best to be ladylike, to listen and enjoy a good meal.

No sooner was our water served than my father excused himself to "run to the restroom." Minutes, in which I sipped water and tapped the table with my unmanicured fingernails, passed. I grew restless. The waiter politely told me he would be back to take our orders when the other member of my party returned. Since I never once had been in a casino that had a clock, I guesstimated ten minutes had passed. Then, when the waiter finally offered a bread basket, I figured it had been fifteen. By the time I scarfed down two buttered bread rolls, I was past the whole ladylike notion.

Informing the waiter I would be back shortly, I stepped outside the restaurant and back into the main area of the casino. To my complete shock, I saw him. He was laughing and smoking a cigar at a poker table. I felt my fists clench, the blood in my veins boil. I don't remember storming over to him or swatting at the chips on the table, which flew into the air and onto the hideous carpet, although I do recall the mask of utter disbelief across his face. A husky, short security guard rushed over to escort me out, but I had beaten him to the punch. Running away to the parking structure, I left the physical commotion behind. I had yet to address the rage inside me.

Grateful my general mistrust of people led me to bring my purse with me when I got up from the table, I pulled out a cigarette to ease my nerves. Sure, I had been panting a bit from my impromptu temper tantrum followed by my impromptu sprint across the casino like a madwoman. Still, it was nice to have a vice when a vice was warranted.

So there I was standing alone in a casino parking structure. At least my grubby outfit would mean no one would mistake me for a hooker, I thought-since I, believe it or not, try to look on the bright side sometimes. At one point, I casually leaned on a stranger's Escalade because I was exhausted and in desperate need of regrouping. I dialed the trusty old 4-1-1 for a cab company willing to transport me from Windsor to Detroit. I was intent on going home, climbing into bed with Scoop and delaying the inevitable-making sense of what happened.

I began walking toward the structure exit to make my way to the casino's front entrance. It would be easier for a cabbie to find me there and for me to find my cabbie amid the local ones that typically didn't leave the country. That's when I saw him approach, half sulking, half perplexed. The cigar was a stump by now, dangling like a forgotten price tag on his shirt. His hands motioned slightly upward, as if to say, "what gives?" I crossed my arms, turning my back to him to shield the tears I knew were stubbornly intent on falling.

"I was going to come back in a second. I promise," he said.

"Sure you were," I muttered under my breath like I did when I was a rebellious teen.

He placed his hand on my shoulder. "Turn around, please."

I obeyed. Silently, I cursed the tears that had betrayed me.

"Roni, I was going to come right back." His eyes pleaded with me.

"Is that what you said to yourself when you left the hospital and told me you had to go away for business?"

"I just got back from my work trip," he said quietly.

"Lies. Lies. Lies!" An avalanche of anger cascaded inside me. "You've been gone all this time, but you never went away. You checked out when your daughter-no, let me correct *myself-daughters* needed you most. I know you left your job. I know you've been gambling. And I know about Zambi."

"How...how do you know about him?" He was taken aback.

"How do I know about him? Well, let me tell you how I know about him. One of his cronies came to your house while I was there and hit me in the head with a damn crowbar, threatened me and told me they were going to kill you if you didn't pay your debt!"

Now he was the one crying. Passersby entering the casino couldn't help but gawk, the way onlookers politely yet indiscreetly stare when something's too arresting to turn from.

"They hurt you?" He asked in disbelief.

I shook my head. "Not as much as you hurt me."

"I promise, you have nothing to worry about because I'm going to pay them back every cent."

"Really? When do you plan on doing that? After you gambled some more tonight?"

"Soon. It will be soon."

"Did you ever wonder why you're still alive right now?" I asked like I was the parent reprimanding a child.

"Because... because they know I'm good for it," he said unconvincingly.

"No. That's definitely not it," I said, nearly laughing at his naivety. "It's because I paid it off."

"You?"

"Yes me, the daughter you left to take care of everything after mom died. The one you lied to, forgot about and left to be alone with Nat. You have no idea what you've done and yet you have the audacity to casually take me out to the casino-oh, and leave me in the restaurant so you can play poker?"

He was quiet for a while. He was digesting my words that were hurled at him with nowhere to run and no way to ignore.

"Roni, I'm sorry. I love you. I'm just so lost without your mother. She was my rock all these years."

"Make that two of us," I said. "Only, I know she wouldn't be ashamed of me."

He let his cigar roll from his pointer and thumb down to the concrete.

"When it comes to my presence with you and Natalia, you should know that sometimes the thing your life misses helps more than the thing which it gets." His gaze shifted to the passing cars and stayed there, completely transfixed as if in a trance.

"Dad, snap out of it," I said, growing more impatient with his silence.

Suddenly he shook his head like a dog rids the water from his fur after a bath.

"Your cab is here," he gestured. "Better go now."

I experienced such a rapid, heavy pang in my heart at that moment. *He wasn't even willing to drive me home.*

He opened the door for me. The smell of leather rested on the seats. The driver asked me for my exact destination. Before I had finished telling him, the door was closed and my father had turned to walk back into the casino.

By the time I had reached my apartment, I was out of tears and money.

Sleeping on the lounger-turned-lumpy bed at the hospital for the next few nights was killing my back. When Yolanda, a sweet Guatemalan nurse who often worked the night shift, inquired about my comfort, I almost joked that sleeping on the floor would have been less painful. Then I glanced over to Natalia and told her it was fine. In the beginning, the doctors and their teams would frequently swing by her room to check on Natalia as well as give me updates or answer questions. Now, it had become a routine brief check in the long hallway of patients. I wondered if they viewed her as a lost cause. The mere suggestion of that, albeit to myself, boggled me. I didn't know whether paranoia had set in. Then again, I didn't know much at all these days. I did, however, make a mental note to track down physicians more frequently to remind them my sister would wake from her coma. I didn't believe this because of anything they were doing. I just wanted to let them know it would happen. My faith in God would make it happen - because it had to.

We did all the usual leg and arm exercises, excerpts from my mother's prayer book and nail painting before I cranked my neck, cracked my back and trudged downstairs to the coffee stand for a pick-me-up.

As I ordered a regular coffee with sugar and cream, I couldn't help but feel someone's heavy glare on me. Turning to my side, I saw the woman with hate in her eyes. Shivers ran down my sore back. I hadn't known why this person would look at me with such disdain until it registered. I've seen her before. But where?

She wore dark-blue jeans, heavy brown boots and a green sweater. Her short hair fell just beneath her chin. I couldn't place her, and Lord knows I was trying. I uncomfortably accepted my coffee from the pick-up counter and began to head back to the room. That's when she spoke and it all came back to me.

"Maye, right?" she asked although, judging by her tone, it was more of an accusation than a question. She stood about a foot taller than me.

Her shoulders were broad. I had to admit to myself that I was intimidated. Although I managed to seem casual, cool as can be.

"Yes, I'm Veronica Maye."

She snorted at my response as if my name were an epithet.

"I bet you think you did well, probably even congratulated yourself on your big story, maybe even got a promotion," spewed the female cop who had shot me a dirty look at the drug den-turned crime scene.

"What would you like me to think?" I asked without pride or defensiveness.

"That you stumbled on two slices of rotten cheese, but couldn't sniff out the mouse."

"I don't know what you're talking about," I genuinely told her.

She shook her head. "Figure it out."

"What's your name?" I called as she thumped away without answering.

The idea that I missed the bigger picture in that story tugged on me for days. A flush of embarrassment rode the waves of my skin. Had I made a fool of myself without even knowing? There would be more digging required when I returned to the beat. I didn't even have a clue where to begin. Maybe Captain Bernett or some other police sources could point me in the right direction. Those nagging notions were banished to the far corners of my brain that had been reserved for Natalia, my father, Sierra, Gavin and, as I had to admit, Luke.

Later, an envelope with two front-row tickets to that weekend's premiere of "Legally Blonde" came to me by mail with a handwritten note from Sierra that read, "Hope to see you opening night." Even if she was an understudy, I figured it was still a big night for her and I couldn't brush the nagging feeling that I needed to be there. Leaving Detroit was less than ideal at this time, though. I knew Barb could be entrusted to notify me of any changes in Natalia's state. I also knew that it wouldn't be too difficult to hop a relatively short flight back to Michigan if need be. What I didn't know was whether I felt up for a trip alone. Before I had the chance to logically process anything, I found myself dialing Luke's number.

"Hey beautiful," he said in a sleepy voice.

"I'm sorry, were you sleeping?"

"I just crammed in some downtime after a long shift, but I'm up now. Glad you called. What's up?"

"Are you working this weekend?" I asked a bit nervously. This was new territory for me.

"Not after the hours I clocked in over the last few days. Why do you ask? Are you coming to Chicago to finally see me?"

"No, more like New York to see a friend."

"Okay," he sounded confused.

"The reason why I mention this to you is because I'd like to know if you want to join me. I mean, if you don't have any plans and you're up for it."

Luke was quiet for a moment, which made me regret asking him and even more insecure for such a bold move.

"You mean go to the most exciting city in the world with the most exciting girl I know? I'm in."

I couldn't help but smile from cheek to cheek.

"Okay, great. So, I'll book the flights and hotel rooms." I didn't want to share a room at this point. We weren't a couple after all and I figured I would charge the trip on my credit card since I invited him to go. While Luke was more than gentleman-like about the separate rooms, he was not all right with me paying for the trip and insisted on using his card for the arrangement.

"Well, then, how would I be paying my share?" It was a slightly awkward conversation.

"You won't. Just consider this my chance at finally taking you on a proper date." He came across as more kind than proud. "And, if you don't let me, I just won't go."

"You're such a shit. All right," I relented. "But, I get to buy you dinner."

"Deal," he said.

He promised to drive into Detroit so we could fly there together, which would prevent any traveling snafus.

"On your bike? It's not exactly nice out," I stated the obvious.

"No," he laughed a bit. "I do have a car for the ten months out of the year when the weather just sucks in the Midwest."

"Okay, well I'll see you Friday morning? Should I meet you at the airport?"

"I'll come in a little earlier in order for me to pick you up and we can drive to the airport together. Let's keep the logistics uncomplicated. I don't want to lose you in the shuffle. I'll e-mail you the flight and hotel confirmations once I get that all together. What time is the play Friday night?"

"Eight o'clock. I think we'll be allowed backstage afterward to see Sierra. Anyway, we should have plenty of time to check into our rooms and get freshened up for the show." I wondered if I emphasized the plural form of "rooms" too much but he didn't seem fazed. After my slutty dress and too-much-to-drink incident last time we were together in a hotel, I was trying to redeem myself in his, and my own, eyes. I hoped he didn't think that was a norm for me.

"Just check your inbox for the confirmations later today and be sure to rest a bit when you're not caring for your sister," he said.

"Thanks, Luke. Don't work too hard."

And, with that, I was eagerly awaiting a mini vacation with a dashing man. So what if I was clinging to someone who actually seemed capable of pulling through for me? He was a lifeboat in the tempestuous sea.

I did feel a pang of guilt when thinking of Gavin. In case there were times when I felt compelled to call him, I kept the picture of him and Sarah in my top dresser drawer, a rude reminder of the repressed anger sunken in my personal abyss. No one could deny his boyish good looks, all-American smile and athletic build. In spite of our jagged history, I still found him attractive-just no longer irresistible. Then there was Sarah, the Stepford wife every aspiring politician covets. Every time I stared at the picture, I examined her adoration for him. Her bright smile and eager eyes. That may be why I never noticed the purse clutched under her arm. Until now, that is.

The Chanel sequence purse that Gavin presented to me before our engagement party, the same one I had turned down, gleamed in the bottom of the picture next to her pale, bare arm.

Resolved, I ripped the picture, figuring I no longer required to it fend off the urge to call him.

Chapter Eighteen

LUKE MADE GOOD ON HIS PROMISE. He picked me up promptly at six o'clock in the morning in his gray Nissan Altima. Two Dunkin' Donut coffees sat steaming in his cup holders. News blared of local accidents and overnight crime. I suppose he'd been accustomed to following the news because of his job. A folded Chicago Tribune was on the dashboard.

"I thought you might want that," he said while starting the engine.

"Thanks."

"You don't say much in the morning."

"I'm far from a morning person, but this helps," I muttered between sips of coffee.

He smiled, lifting his naturally concave shaped mouth upward. It was a sight to see.

By now, the characteristics of a scenic autumn had been siphoned into Michigan's vast and ever-evolving memory bank. Winter's brisk winds were upon us. Attentive to my slight shivers, Luke cranked up the heat. Its warmth, along with the coffee, made me even more tired.

"You can rest here," he said, patting his shoulder. Since the coffee cup holders were closer to the dashboard, I scooted myself closer to him. I was surprised by how natural it felt to lay my head on his shoulder. Even his rhythmic breath morphed into my own silent lullaby. Soon enough, sleep overcame me.

After he'd parked in the airport long-term lot, he coaxed me gently to wake. Immediately self-conscious, I checked to ensure no drool had escaped from my mouth as I used his body as my resting zone. I was in the clear. I sipped the coffee for a jolt just big enough to compel me to exit the car and join Luke by the trunk for the luggage. Then, completely unexpected, I laughed.

"What's so funny? Did you spike your coffee when I wasn't looking?" he asked, amused.

"Oh, nothing much. I was just thinking it's odd that we're traveling together."

"Why's that?"

"Well, it's not like we know each other that well," I said, thinking it was quite obvious.

He shrugged. "It hasn't been much time together," he said. "But I actually think we know each other pretty well."

I thought about that for a moment, as we trekked to the airport entrance.

I guess I hadn't given him the credit he deserved. He was there at an incredibly pivotal time in my life. While the time was brief, he did see me at my saddest. My angriest. My drunkest. He lent a non-judgmental ear when I needed to vocalize my confusion. My frustration. My sorrow. And he was here, with me, for sheer companionship. Suddenly, I looked at Luke with fresh eyes. He was more than a crush.

Luke lugged my chunky leopard print suitcase and his smaller black one. I hauled my leather carry-on and purse. By the time we checked in, endured security and positioned ourselves in our seats, I began to get excited about departing familiar grounds.

Reading materials became redundant and the airplane food must have been in competition with prison squares. So I dipped into my purse for a few sheets of notepad paper. It reminded me of passing time with Natalia.

"Tick-tack-toe?" I asked with giddiness and raised eyebrows.

Luke laughed at my suggestion.

"Sure, why not. But I'm X and I get to go first," he chuckled.

"All right, you big baby,"

As we finished our game, he pondered, "Is this the kind of intellectual pastime for a serious journalist?"

"Not quite," I responded seriously. "I usually play Hang Man."

He smiled, brushing my hair out of my face. "Let's do it then."

"Okay, you can go first again,"

It took him a few minutes to make a series of small lines for his challenge, mostly because he couldn't keep his laughter contained. After unintentionally earning the head, line of a body and a hand, I solved Luke's phrase. But it wasn't without nearly cracking up with tears: I-THINK-THAT-GUY-IS-A-TERRORIST, indicating a sleeping man with a turban across the aisle.

"Stop it," I said, hitting him playfully.

I chose LET'S-GO-SHOPPING! as my phrase, which he figured out soon enough, but my mind muscles wouldn't flex for his final quiz. The full hang man's body dangled, perhaps because I was expecting something humorous. Instead, he threw me a curve with I-AM-GOING-TO-KISS-YOU. And when he did, it was sweet and soft, completely airplane appropriate yet intriguing and yearning. It had been some time since we locked lips. Too long, I thought.

Checking into the inconspicuous Berdock Hotel near Times Square took only a few minutes. Although the burgundy-and-gold décor created a certain Victorian darkness, the hotel had all the modern amenities in its compact walls. We agreed to drop off our luggage, nap and shower in our respective rooms before grabbing a late lunch and doing some shopping.

Quaint was one way to describe my room. The bathroom door nearly touched the main entryway. New York real estate, I thought.

Before I knew it, my head hit the pillow and I was in my own New York state of sleep. I rose an hour later to shower, slide on a blue knit dress and run downstairs to grab the papers I typically read online. The New York Times, The New York Post and the New York Daily News. Page Six of the Post was among my favorite guilty pleasures and it was there that I read something astonishing.

Fans of Broadway veteran Lola de Cannes will be surprised when the curtain pulls back tonight at the premiere of this season's "Legally Blonde, The Musical." The talented beauty, who has never missed a show, has fallen ill with what appears to be the stomach flu immediately before the production, according to her agent, Dwane Howzer. Midwesterner Sierra Blake, a novice to the big stage and Ms. de Cannes' understudy, will take the lead tonight and until further notice.

I set down the paper, careful to not wrinkle it, since it would be a keepsake. Sierra would get her break after all.

A pang paralyzed me for a moment. I was away from Natalia. It was like being in a body absent a heart. But when I checked in with the nursing staff, there was no news to report.

I threw on a tan fitted trench with a dark-brown belt and navy beret before tapping on Luke's door. I heard the shuffling of footsteps along the carpet. When the door opened slowly, it revealed his bare chest and black sweat pants. His eyes were sunken, hair disheveled. He clearly rose from sleep to greet me at the door.

"I'm sorry to wake you," I said sheepishly. "You must be exhausted from driving all that way from your house to pick me up." If I had been tired, he was probably on his last leg.

"No, it's fine. Just give me a minute," he said in a raspy, deep voice I hadn't heard before. "I don't want you to miss out on shopping."

I grabbed his arm, so warm and toned. It was the one with the cross tattoo. The inking of a female was in plain sight on his chest. Curiosity was eating away at me, but now wasn't the time for wagging my eat's tail.

"Go back to bed. You need rest. We'll just go to dinner and the play tonight."

When he resisted, I pulled his arm to lead him to the bed. "Sleep," I commanded.

"I'd rather spend time with you."

"Well, we can spend time together," I said to his confusion.

I removed my jacket, hat and shoes and settled down on his bed. When he raised his eyebrows, I clarified, "let's take a nap."

"How can I say no to that?" he responded.

Luke got on the bed, his chest against my back, arm around my stomach. Within two minutes he was asleep. I, on the other hand, lay wide awake, my heart thumping like a prized horse stamping around the racetrack of my chest. These feelings swirling inside me were more intense than' had imagined.

With wounds still blistering from seeing the purse Gavin gave Sarah and obviously taking her to the fundraiser as his date--while we were a couple--I turned to face Luke. Wasn't I emotionally unstable enough? Did I really need to start a relationship, or whatever this is, with someone now? My gaze rolled down to his chest, to the tattoo. Upon closer inspection, it didn't look like a woman at all. The flowing long hair belonged to girl no older than thirteen. Her eyes wide and innocent. Lips heart shaped. Cheeks slightly chunky, something that happens when girls become women and lose that last trace of what my mother referred to as "baby fat."

Then, I stared at his handsome face. I wondered, would he be able to help repair what others had so badly damaged? And, would I be willing to take a chance that he could?

The rumbling in my stomach finally overpowered the musings in my mind. I grabbed the room service menu and ordered two proper breakfast plates of eggs, pancakes, sausage and toast as well as two coffees. Since I didn't know what Luke's favorite foods are, I figured breakfast was a safe bet, especially since we missed that meal earlier today. I made a mental note to set aside money to pay for the room service, especially since he was paying for the hotel and airfare.

By the time he rose, the tray had arrived.

"Good morning sunshine," I said brightly while opening the lid. "Bon appetite."

"Could you do that every morning?" he laughed.

"Maybe in your dreams," I teased.

"Dreams can become reality." He smiled at me with such charm and confidence, as if he knew something I didn't. "But don't worry. I'd make you breakfast, too, if you were my girl."

I felt myself shift uncomfortably. "Dig in."

Eating together started off simple enough. We chatted about the flight, the hotel accommodations, the city and what we wanted to do before leaving. Then, he stared at me with his intense brown eyes.

"What became of that *situation?*"

I didn't have to ask him to clarify, I knew what he meant. One thing I didn't know was how to tell him I paid off my father's debt. He didn't know I was technically still engaged at the time and, even if he remained in the dark, I feared sounding heartless by selling something as sentimental as a ring from my would-be husband. So, option C was my best bet: explaining to him that I paid the piper without disclosing how I gathered my pennies.

Thankfully, Luke was not a reporter. He didn't bother asking. He was just relieved I was out of harm's way.

"Who's feeding your dogs while you're gone?" I asked.

"My mom. She lives nearby and doesn't mind taking them for walks or to the dog park."

"That's nice."

"She wants to meet you, by the way."

"She does?" I said, trying not to sound too surprised.

"I told her when I get you to visit, we'll go to dinner together. She's looking forward to it."

"What does she know about me?" I asked out of self-consciousness and basic, unbridled curiosity. (I'm sure either way he phrased it, I would sound like a basket case.)

He edged closer to me on the bed, brushing my hair with his fingers. "How wonderful I think you are."

"Stop, you're making me blush," I joked uneasily.

"Veronica, don't downplay my affection toward you," he spoke seriously while looking into my eyes. "I know you've had to steel yourself throughout this whole ordeal, but what I'm saying is you can be shed your armor with me."

I longed to cry, to sob in his arms, to thank him for understanding me so well. But all that would make me too vulnerable too soon. Instead, I placed my hand on his warm bare arm and kissed his soft lips. He held me tight after the kiss.

Allowing him to get ready for the evening, I went back to my room to freshen my makeup and fix my hair. Something about being with a man who understands you eases the blood in your veins. I wanted to prettify myself for him but I also was relaxed enough for him to see without lipstick, hair products, cute and coordinating clothes-basically sans the superficial facade we carry with our insecurities.

I heard him approach the door as I gave myself a once-over in the mirror. He tapped gently. A dozen red roses came to view through the peephole.

"How?" I asked.

"Right outside the hotel is a flower shop." He wore a black suit and a light-blue shirt without a tie, his dark hair gelled and just a tad of cologne. I quickly filled a paper cup with water, placed the stems in it and leaned the roses against the wall for them to soak without tipping. "We really haven't had a real date before."

"What about dinner at the hotel?" I asked, slightly embarrassed by bringing up a night of inappropriate behavior on my part.

""That didn't count," he said, shaking his head.

"It didn't? Why's that?"

"Because I didn't pick you up beforehand." He smirked.

"Aren't you a gentleman," I laughed. "So, this is a true date then?"

"Damn straight." He held out his elbow. I accepted.

The setting sun complemented an array of lights in Times Square. Passing cabs and pedestrians brought the city to life. It was like we were a part of something extraordinary, just being there, experiencing the breeze in our hair and the bustle of a thriving place. There was no stopping the unfair comparisons in my mind to Detroit. Like weighing a familiar companion to an exciting one, my hometown couldn't evoke the whirlwind of bliss New York could.

Sheer happiness placated every awakened inch of me. Walking side-by-side with Luke, with the allegra beat of street, I felt so alive. Then I remembered, shamefully, that hundreds of miles of away Natalia lay desolate on hospital sheets reeking of bleach, with her precious young life completely on hold. It wasn't fair.

Luke squeezed my hand. "Something wrong?"

"No," I assured him while forcing a smile.

We crammed into a seafood restaurant not far from the hotel. Our table was nearly unbearably close to other diners, but my shrimp linguini was delicious. Over dinner, I informed him that Sierra would be taking the stage on this opening night.

"Isn't that kind of rare? You know, that an understudy gets a chance like that?" he wondered aloud.

"I guess she just lucked out. I haven't talked to her in a while, so she doesn't know we're even using the tickets she sent." Saying that sparked a thought that I quickly brushed off.

Our bubbly blond waitress approached our table with a bottle of wine. "Would either of you care to try our house wine?"

Luke and I exchanged grins. I knew what he was thinking.

"No, thank you," I told her. This wouldn't be a repeat of last time, I reminded myself.

By the time we settled into our cushy front-row seats, my dress felt snug in the midsection. Luke asked if I was comfortable and held my hand. I fought back the urge to kiss him. The attraction was overwhelmingly intense. I secretly praised myself for skipping the wine.

As the lights went out, an announcer said "Ladies and gentlemen, the role of Elle Woods will be played tonight by Sierra Blake." An unexpected wave of pride swept through me. She was my longtime friend and, despite our strained relationship, I was still happy for her.

Any doubt that Sierra couldn't cut her teeth with the big dogs was squashed the moment she took the stage in the cotton-candy colored set among a fray of giddy sorority girls. The musical was far too girly even for me. I felt guilty making Luke endure it. He winced a bit at the continuous "Oh my God, you guys" ditzy chorus but tried not to show disdain.

Seeing Sierra as a blonde was uncanny. She had the fair skin to pull it off, though, and her slender tall frame worked well in the numerous frilly costumes her character wore. Her voice was powerful, as always, and her acting was solid, endearing and entertaining. By the end, the audience, mostly women, applauded wildly. As she bowed to the crowd, she saw me for the first time and smiled widely.

"Let's go backstage," I said.

As the crowd meandered through rows and aisles to exit, we walked the opposite way. A stagehand questioned us momentarily before checking a list and allowing us to pass. He pointed us to Sierra's dressing room. Well, the room actually belonged to Lola de Cannes, as stated on the exterior side of the door. Clad in a silk robe draped over her pink costume dress, Sierra swung the door like a tornado ripping open a trailer.

"You're here!" she cried in full dramatics.

She extended her arms to pull me in, her perfume an intoxicating, overpowering scent.

"Congratulations Broadway star."

"I didn't think you would come after... all that..."

"I couldn't miss this. I know how hard you worked to get here," I said. "Oh, I'm so rude. This is Luke. Luke this is Sierra." Sierra shot me a devilish grin.

"Pleasure to meet you," she said with sugar on her tongue and a hint of a curtsey.

"Congrats on your show. You were great," Luke said politely.

"You really think so?" She was never one to accept one compliment when she could fish for two.

She ushered us into the room that was full of costumes, flowers and makeup sprawled across a brightly lit vanity. Just as we got in, we heard coughing from the bathroom. Emerging with a sigh was a petite woman no older than twenty-five with disheveled blonde hair and a sickly pallor.

"Sierra, I think I need some more of that tea," she muttered before plopping on the small green couch near a rack of clothes.

"Lola, these are my friends Veronica and Luke," she said before pouring her a cup of hot tea from a sterling silver pot positioned above a heat mitt on her vanity.

"Nice to meet you," she said quietly while she rubbed her stomach with one hand and accepted the mug with the other.

"I'm sorry you are not feeling well," I said to the frail, petite woman. "Have you been to the doctor?"

"Poor thing is just battling a bug or something. I'm sure it will clear up on its own," Sierra interjected. "In fact, one of my roommates-I have this awful, cramped studio apartment I share with two other girls-has the same thing."

"Well, I hope you get better soon. But you should probably get it checked out, especially if it doesn't seem to be improving," Luke the Medic said.

"I would have stayed at home to rest, but I kept hoping this bug, or whatever it is, would go away and I could take the stage after all. I never miss a performance," she said before grimacing. "Well, almost never."

That same cynical thought that sneaked into my mind earlier returned.

We invited Sierra out for drinks with us. She said she had a big actors' after-party to attend. So much tension was between us. We brushed it off like the confetti she sifted from her hair. She hugged me tightly once more. Then we were on our way. It was as if I had melted into the scenery of her play. The show was over. The lights were dim. And the star had left the stage. I would have waited there for a while had Luke not emotionally carried me away.

His whisking me away was really, in my heart of hearts, what I longed for. I yearned to escape from the realities that had confronted me daily. Still, I knew it would be irresponsible to freely give my heart to someone when so much was at stake. And I was acutely aware how much desire I bore for him. It was truly frightening to confess, even to myself. So when he began to usher me into a cab to grab a drink, I thought quickly on my feet.

The first thing my fear caused me to do was mimic Lola de Cannes and her grotesque facial expressions while groping my stomach.

"I think Lola has a contagious stomach bug because I feel awful."

Luke was ever the caring medic, showing concern right away, and tried to care for me back at the hotel. But I didn't invite him in.

"I actually am going to try and rest. Thanks for dinner, though. I will see you tomorrow."

Disappointment ran across his face. I could sense he thought we were more comfortable with each other than that. He wanted me to let him in so he could care for me. As sweet as that was, I was intent on distancing myself from him-whether as a two-bit liar or not. When he lurked a little at the doorway, I did something pretty drastic. I pretended I had to run to the bathroom to vomit. It was a pathetic sham that made him go away, albeit reluctantly, but I had pulled an ace out of my pocket and played it like the table was closing. I sat on my bed when I heard his footsteps fade. I looked at the beautiful flowers he brought and scolded myself for the remainder of the night.

The next day was no less awkward. On my part, that is. I felt myself retreat from him like a ship sailing from shore. I had an urge to stay, but the current was too strong. We went through the motions of eating at a quaint, quick diner, riding in a cab to the airport, boarding and sitting next to each other. Only this time, there were no cutesy games or silly jokes. I dug my nose in a book and kept it there the entire flight home. I felt his beautiful, deep eyes on me, silently questioning what had gone awry. By the time my symptoms were too burdensome to keep up, he must have known some faking went into it. He was kind. He wasn't a fool.

He drove me back to my apartment. I rudely didn't invite him in. I told him I was exhausted and would call him later, fully aware that only one of the two was true. He smiled at me, the way only he can smile. He leaned in to hug me, so warm and strong. I closed my eyes for a second, trying not to turn to Silly Putty in his arms. Instead, I pulled away, thanked him for joining me and told him to drive safely. His smile had faded but he left without saying a word.

"Goodbye, Luke," I thought.

Chapter Nineteen

DADDINI WAS HACKING UP A STORM.

"Drink some water," I said, motioning to my unopened bottle of Aquafina.

"I'm...fine," he coughed.

"Listen, you know I'm not due back until next month, but..."

"You can't stay away, huh? Damn, kid, you got the bug bad. Let me tell you something. once its grimy little hooks set in you, there's no turning back. You're a goner for life, a scoop-chasing newsman-or woman, whatever the hell you want to call yourself."

"That is truly frightening, Daddini."

"And true, right?"

"I sure hope not."

He folded his arms. The coughing fit subsided. He took out a cigarette. We were standing outside the newsroom. The wind was fierce and it resisted his lighter's efforts.

"Damn Michigan weather. For once, I'd like to live in a place that doesn't experience four seasons in the same damn day."

You'd never know from talking to him that Daddini had one of the most extensive vocabularies at the paper. He just wasn't a showboat kind of guy.

"Anyway, I do have a slight request."

"Bring it, kiddo," he said, finally managing to muster a light.

"Is it possible to snoop around on that crooked cop case before I officially come back?"

He raised his eyebrows.

"You mean work during your leave? Who could argue with that? Certainly not me. But why?"

"I guess I think there's more to it than what we reported."

"You guess or you know?"

"Somewhere in between," I answered honestly.

Daddini was thoughtful. He took a puff and scanned the street.

"Find a way to know and come back to me with a story. I won't say anything to the Suit until you've got what you need."

"Thanks."

"Hey kiddo," Daddini called as I walked off.

"Yeah?"

He scrolled his gaze downward to his dress shirt and slacks. "What do you think of my latest duds, courtesy of my darling girls?"

"Nice. Real nice."

"Thanks. I have some good kids, even if they don't know they're shopping away their college education on their chump of a father's wardrobe," he laughed.

"They're lucky to have a dad like you," I told him earnestly.

His expression changed. It softened.

"You're a good kid, Roni."

I walked away, the wind picking up my hair and a loose tear that parted from my eye.

I steeled myself inside the car. Being a "good kid" would get me nowhere on this story. I had to be fearless, perhaps even ruthless. Maybe someone like Gale Babes, with her over-the-top image and unparalleled ego, would muster more courage than me in this situation. Maybe she'd fare better or get further. Or maybe I needed a shot of confidence, some damn self-esteem. I scolded myself that this wasn't the time to be insecure. And with that mediocre pep talk, I forged on for the facts.

Detective Sharon Ubanks was not pleased to see me. Considering the setting this time was the precinct parking garage and not the hospital coffee stand, she had less preparation for open disdain. Her unwillingness to reveal her name almost became humorous to me in the information age. While female police detectives were not rare in Detroit, they weren't exactly like tracking down a Smith or Jones in a big city.

"Detective Ubanks, remember me? I'm Veronica Maye from the Chronicle."

Her clunky footsteps stopped short. Her gaze shifted rapidly to the far corners of the garage.

"We're alone," I said, leaving my notepad in my purse because taking it out would definitely set her off.

"You won't find a Deep Throat in this parking garage so you might as well keep moving," she said, her voice stern and unrelenting.

"So you're a fan of public reporting after all," I said confidently. Someone familiar with "All the President's Men" had to be an advocate of truth.

"Don't get ahead of yourself. I just don't like scum in my precinct."

"Well then, tell me where to start." I folded my arms. For the first time, I thought she was screwing with me and I was getting really irked. I could be sitting next to Natalia now.

"It's like so many things in life, start with what doesn't add up."

If this was throwing me a bone, I'd rather play dead.

"OK. What doesn't add up is you teasing me that something's awry when the case was pretty cut and dry: Crooked cops, botched drug deal. It's Detroit, not Emerald City."

"Things are not always what they seem."

"How so?"

"Well, think about *accessibility*." It pained her to say that word.

"If you're talking about me gaining access to the scene like that, yes, I will admit that's a bit rare."

"I'm not. Your access was rare. That's not what I was referring to, though." She scrolled the garage once more for invisible eyes and ears and then lumbered away without further word.

"This probably won't be the last time I drop in on you," I called out.

"Figured that much," she mumbled back.

The Starbucks three blocks from the station was crowded with professionals from the Renaissance Center, students from Wayne State

University and the College for Creative Studies, and court employees. I would never have selected such a crowded joint had I been meeting with a more contentious source. But Virgil Thomas was a straight shooter who had nothing to hide and no one to impress (he wore crocodile shoes and tailored suits for his own enjoyment)-traits I admired most about him.

He was like a young black Dirty Harry. Joining the police force indulged the bad-ass in him that would have otherwise found an outlet in seedy behavior on the streets. And Virgil knew every nook and cranny of the part of the city that finds no affiliation with the safe confines of a Starbucks.

While knocking back his venti mocha with an extra shot of espresso, Virgil's gaze kept meeting a buff tattooed biker in the corner. Reluctantly drawing on stereotypes, I pinned him as a freed-on-bond defendant awaiting his case to begin at the nearby courthouse. Virgil would later tell me I was right.

In my two years of knowing Virgil, he had always been a simpleton, easy to read, easy to please. Before he slugged his mocha like beer at a keg party, I ordered him a second. This was an expected toll for our little meetings. But he met with me because he wanted to, not because he was using me for caffeine.

"When are you going to let me take you out, Roni?" he inquired with a trace of longing in his hazel eyes. Everybody wants something, I told myself.

"We are out, Virgil. Besides, you're too much of a lady's man for me." I smiled. He returned the expression.

"Okay, okay. You have the floor."

"You know that case I wrote about, the one with the two cops who died in that botched drug deal?"

"Perez and Michael. Yeah, I know that one."

"What can you tell me about that?"

He started on his second mocha.

"Man, ain't one person in that precinct who thinks those two were on the up and up."

"So, is that all there was to it?"

He looked at me, squinting.

"Why do you ask?"

"Just have a nagging feeling that there's more to it, that's all," I said, trying not to sound defensive.

By now, the biker was gone. This did not escape Virgil. Nothing did.

"I'm not sure you want to dig too deep on this one." He shook his head, sounding for the first time in our chat like the narcotics sergeant he is. "And, for your sake, I'm not sure I want you to dig too deep."

"You have to tell me what I'm missing. I'm not afraid."

"That's the problem. This isn't some case we're putting out there for you and the world to know about. This hits home."

And then I conjured a question I hadn't given much thought to before. "How did Perez and Michael still have access to the drug evidence room when they were on the gang unit before they died? They weren't on your squad."

"No, they weren't," he said intently. "And, to answer your question, only the chief and certain ranking department officials have open access to that room."

"What rank?"

He swallowed the last bit of his mocha.

"Captains. In all divisions. Everyone from Criminal to Road Patrol encounters drugs or drug paraphernalia."

Chapter Twenty

"INTERNAL AFFAIRS HAD BEEN INVESTIGATING MISSING EVIDENCE FROM THE DRUG STORAGE ROOM for several months before Perez and Michael's escapades became public. It started with a few baggies of pot. Then it evolved to crack, heroin and trendy drugs like Fentanyl and E. It had my undercover guys scared shitless to work with each other. Every one of them were risking their lives thinking there was a guy on the inside selling to the dealers they were trying to arrest. I even had some of them pulled because their fears were affecting their performance and I couldn't risk them getting hurt or getting others hurt. IA takes a long time to produce and we just couldn't stop our operations in the meantime. You would think it's a pretty easy thing for them to find out, right? Missing drugs, just see who has access and set up surveillance. Well, it's not that simple. There are fifteen captains with the ability to get into that room and every one of them knew an investigation was under way just about the second it started. That's why a lot of the pot, heroin and crack was snatched right before. From then on, not a bag in that room has been touched and I doubt it will be for a long time, especially if you go sniffing around like a bloodhound in rabbit season."

"Who do you think it is?"

"Whatever I say would be a sheer guess and that's not how I operate."

"Where do I go from here?"

"I think you know where to go. You just are hoping there's another way around it."

I nodded. "You got that right."

Next, Rhonda Michael slammed the door in my face.

When I reluctantly knocked again, she threatened to get her late husband's handgun and "shoot off the fingers of the whore who wrote the article about my Donell!."

Juanita Perez was less volatile. Her dark curls fell over her bony shoulders draped with a blue poncho. I thought the outfit was a bit outdated until I realized she wore it as a cloak while breast-feeding her baby.

"Mrs. Perez, I'm Veronica Maye from The Chronicle. I'm here to talk to you for a story I'm working on that may shed light on your husband's death."

"Is there such a thing as light in death? In darkness?" Her deep, dark eyes were hollow despite her loving hands cradling her child.

I thought of my mother.

"I believe so," I said.

"Maye. You wrote the article?"

"Yes, I did."

She scanned me with those tree-bark-colored eyes. "Okay. Come in."

She motioned inside her brick bungalow, where two boys around six and eight played video games on the couch. She set the baby in a port-a-crib and gestured for me to sit at the kitchen table. The teapot had been whistling.

"Do you like green tea? I have lemon and honey if you'd like."

"Honey would be fine. Thank you."

Juanita was either raised to be polite or in dire need of some adult conversation, I thought. Or she could just be curious about my angle. Regardless, I appreciated her unexpected kindness.

"What is it you want to know?" she asked quietly after waiting for me to sip the tea.

"Did your husband ever mention anything going on at work? Was there anyone there who was not following... protocol?" I chose my words carefully as not to offend her.

"You mean someone else who was stealing drugs and selling them?"

"Well..."

"You don't need to sugarcoat anything with me. Manny had a lot of good qualities but he was overcome by greed. I know that now. He wanted material things for us. Now, look at where we are. My kids don't have a father. I am without a husband. And we are struggling financially."

"Okay, I will be frank with you. I am trying to find out whether there was someone else, someone higher up in the department, who was behind these deals. Can you think of anyone like that? Did Manny ever say anything to that effect?"

She peered into the other room at her boys and baby girl to see if they were all right.

"Manny never said anything to me. He knew I would disapprove. But there was one time he was on the phone. I assumed it was with Donel!. He said something like 'we're putting ourselves on the line and he's pulling the strings. If anything ever happens, we'll be toast and he'll be living as if nothing happened.'"

"Is there anything else? Any other details you can recall overhearing?"

She shook her head.

"Well, thank you for your time, and the tea." I set the empty mug in her sink and walked past the boys on the couch.

"There is one little thing actually," she called after me.

"Yes?"

"Well, I remember it now, but it may mean nothing to you."

"Go on," I encouraged her.

"Something about going in on a uniform shop. Does that make any difference?"

I closed my eyes as if repressing the facts from registering in my disbelieving brain.

"It makes all the difference in the world," I said.

That night sleep was beyond reach. I tossed amid a sea of twisted blankets, rose to get bottled water from the fridge, read my mystery novel piecemeal, and flipped through television infomercials. Captain Bernett dreamed of a carefree retirement in which he ran a police uniform store. I had always held him in high regard, an honest cop, a man of integrity. I winced with the realization my perception of him was a brick house on a sand foundation. Had he been corrupt since the first day we met or was he like my father, devolving into something unrecognizable, a feather spiraling down the well?

With Sierra away, in more way than one, and my relationship with Luke strained, I had no bouncing board in this situation. I yearned to have my mother here, to confide in her, ask her for advice, to have her stroke my hair and listen patiently. And then I forced myself out of bed in the early morning hours, threw on some clean clothes and went to the hospital. I held Natalia's frail hand. I told her all about it. Her silence didn't alter the benediction I found from vocalizing my thoughts. Suddenly, it all seemed so clear.

It took some snooping around to find out who was working the investigation for Internal Affairs. There was Jack McNichols and Henry Foude. I knew neither of them. So I pegged the odds of them leaking information to me as microscopic. That's when I drew Daddini into the picture. His network of sources was far and wide from when he was a cops and courts reporter. As it turns out, McNichols started out in dispatch when Daddini would check the police log as a cub reporter. They would shoot the breeze and ended up staying in touch as their careers escalated. He met McNichols at The Rumbling Rock, also known as a hole-in-the-wall bar on the East Side that cops frequented on their nights off. I wasn't privy to their conversation at that time. Daddini knew McNichols would freeze up if he saw me there. When McNichols loosened up after a few, Daddini sent me a text to come in as if I had no knowledge they were there.

When I walked in, I was greeted by many longing eyes. I attributed this to the fact that it was rare for a young woman to enter this bar alone and that last call was fast approaching, so visual restraint was elusive. I didn't want to make this obvious. McNichols was no dummy and Daddini liked him as a source. The plan was simple: I sat at the other side of the bar, looking around and eyeing my cell phone, appearing to be stood up. When Daddini waved me over, I knew I was in the clear.

They were in a jovial mood, reminiscing about the past.

"Remember when Jones accidentally shot himself in the foot? That guy was the clumsiest fool I ever met," McNichols, now a jolly ghost of his skeptical self, said between sips of whisky.

"Man, I wasn't afraid to approach anyone as a reporter. I would go up to drug dealers, murderers, you name it, anybody for a quote. But I was scared shitless to go near Jones!" Daddini retorted.

He took a sip and then idly speculated, "Hey, speaking of drugs, what the hell happened with those two dirty cops?"

"What do you mean?" The old cynicism flared.

"Come on Jack. I know when there's more to a story-no offense to our Roni here," Daddini said, patting my head as if I were a compliant golden retriever who fetched the story faithfully for her affectionate master. "She broke the story about the crime, even went to the scene. Then she did some strong follows. But there's got to be something else going on. You'd be the one to know it."

His old pal and helpful tipster clammed up. Sweat sprouted from his pores. He set his empty drink on the dimly lit bar. The bartender, a man with long tresses swept back in a tight ponytail, eagerly confiscated it. Closing time approached.

"Marshall if you so much as begin to write a word--I don't care if it's on the sandpaper toilet paper in The Chronicle bathroom--before our investigation is complete, I will have our legal counsel all over your ass before the ink dries." An unpleasant cluster of spit hung on the corner of his thin mouth.

Daddini lit a cigarette.

"Hey, don't get your grandpa trunks in a knot," he shrugged. "I'm just doing my job. Do you honestly think no one else is thinking that?"

McNichols' fire was kaput. An amused snort escaped his wet lips. "You're still the same. Always looking for trouble."

"Trouble finds me, man. It just so happens I look it in the face," he said cool as ice.

"As for you," the IA cop directed at me, "Think long and hard about things before you do anything."

I nodded. Sounded like a good rule of thumb. Too bad impulsiveness is more my forte.

The early morning hours began overriding night. Daddini insisted on walking me to the car. No matter how tough I tried to be, that act never flew with him. In some ways, he reminded me of Luke. How he always saw past my facade. As I tiredly entered my Malibu, he offered me this piece of advice: "I don't know much, but one thing I can count on is that nothing's as it seems."

Chapter Twenty-One

DETECTIVE UBANKS SHOOK HER HEAD IN DISMAY WHEN SHE SAW ME SITTING ACROSS FROM HER at the Coney Island she frequented. I knew when her breaks were and that she preferred cheese fries and a gyro. It wasn't that hard to collect information from the friendly Greek owners who had opened the restaurant around the corner from The Chronicle fifty years ago.

"May I sit here?"

"The answer is no." She looked around nervously. "I will meet you in the parking lot in ten minutes. Leave now so no one sees us talking."

"Okay." I took a page from Daddini's suaveness.

She half smiled at my mellow response, relieved that further conversation wouldn't take place around prying ears.

Her pickup truck half reminded me of Jeremy's, except hers was newer, shinier and sans the sadness his truck eternally carried in my mind. A Def Leopard compact disc roared on in her player. She, with reddened cheeks, twisted the knob to stifle the sound. I smiled politely, as if to say "that's nothing to be embarrassed of."

"What do you want anyway?" I suppose she was attempting kindness by allowing me in her truck instead of standing outside in the tail-end-of-autumn winds.

"Yes, let's cut to the chase," I said sweetly so she wouldn't know I was mocking her. Who did she think she was? Like I was enjoying myself talking to her? Please. "Well, I think I know who is behind the corruption. Do you?"

"Are you asking me to tell you?" she said incredulously.

"No. I'm asking you to confirm it."

She moved forward in her seat. "Go on."

I bit the bullet, aware that withholding now would lead me nowhere.

"Captain Bernett," I spat like the words would choke me.

Her lips tightened. Her eyes stared emotionlessly at me.

"Am I right?" I asked.

Silence ensued for what seemed like hours.

"Detective Ubanks? Sharon? Am I correct?"

She pointed to the passenger door. "You better go now."

"Excuse me? That's it? You're not going to confirm it for me?" I couldn't believe my ears. All that teasing and then not a word in response.

"Go please," she said. I sighed in annoyance before heading out of the truck. "And...Maye," she called.

I looked back. "Yes?"

"Be careful," she said, as if she suddenly were a concerned aunt.

What she wouldn't confirm Virgil would only speculate at. And, after my meeting with her, I was much more gun-shy.

"Who do you think it is?" he asked me over beer at The Local Brew in the city's New Center.

"I can't really say for sure," I said. "But I am leaning toward one person in particular and it's pretty painful to think of."

"There ain't one thing positive when someone lets you down."

"So have you figured it out?"

"I have if you have," he said coyly.

'Well then, I think we both know who it is."

"I guess we do," he smiled.

That night I walked the halls of the hospital. I meandered through the cheery play area with murals of jungle animals, trees and sunrays. Weeks had passed since the accident. Natalia was sleeping through it all, a blessing in some regards but a curse in others. She was only a girl, with elementary school friends and a love of airplanes, dancing and her family. How would one explain what had happened? A daunting task when I knew the "one" in that scenario would be me.

I wondered what Luke would say. I wondered if he'd even return my call at this point. My ego, such a hideously controlling part of our nature, wouldn't let me find out.

A little hairless girl in a pink hospital gown frolicked into the play area I listlessly strolled. I smiled at her. She returned the expression. Her exhausted mother with kind eyes trailed behind, freezing the moment into her memory bank. Nothing's sadder than a sick child, I thought. And my mind naturally homed in on Natalia. I smiled again at the child and left the room before she'd see the tears falling from my eyes. I had no right to steal her small slice of joy and it would have pained me no end to do so.

My apartment felt barren. I heard the wind at my window. Scoop scattered away at the noise. The down blanket on my bed provided a haven from the chill.

My Google alert on Sierra's name notified me she was cast in a small part for a Hollywood action flick with Sean Gunner, a dashing star known for blockbusters, extreme sports and a way with ladies. This was big time for her. A lightning bolt from her recent stage debut to the silver screen.

She hadn't called to tell me. I didn't bother congratulating. Seemed as though the ball was in her court after we went to her play.

When it became clear sleep would elude me, I got in my Malibu and headed home. At least I still thought of my parents' house as home. Judging by its darkness, I figured my father wasn't there. But, as I inched my car up the driveway, I saw the side door to the garage was ajar. I pried it open to see his unlocked Jeep inside.

I stepped onto the patio to open the back door with my key. But, as I held the handle, the door swung open with almost an inaudible creak. I turned on the light.

This time, the dishes were neatly stacked on the drying shelves next to the sink. Laundry was tightly folded in piles on the couch and the rooms smelled of Windex and bleach. Impressed with my findings, I plopped down on the couch to watch TV, reminding me of time spent with my mother and Natalia. During a late-night talk show's commercial break, I heard a faint whimper. The high-pitch sound ascending. A sudden chill invaded my bones, realizing that I'd have to scope out the basement for its source. The last time I inspected that area of the house, I found myself with a gash to the head and sudden knowledge of my father's gambling addiction.

This time, I was more prepared.

Steeling myself, I walked quietly so not to give away my presence. A dim light provided the silhouette of a man on the floor. My body froze, providing an unwelcome vision of the night of the crash, the shards of glass and bloody scene that had changed my life.

Then he groaned. Cowering in the fetal position lay my father. A sad sight of a man emasculated by pain and sorrows. A gash was visible above his eye. His hands, with scraped knuckles revealing signs of a struggle, held his abdomen. He peered up at me. The concave lines of his cheeks moved when he mustered my name, "Roni." I heard it like I did a billion times: "Roni, can you pick your sister up from school?" "Roni, do you want to go in on a birthday gift for your mom?" "Roni, you did a great job on that story." Only this time my name was followed by a warning: "Roni, run!"

In a second, I glanced back at the stairs longingly. But instead I rushed to his side in a pathetic attempt to lift him to his feet. He pushed me away, showing me with his eyes the stab wound to his stomach. I gasped.

A sinister laugh permeated the room. The hairs on the back of my neck were cactus needles in a sandstorm desert.

"We could have made a deal, sweetie. You knew it was only a matter of time before your sad old man got himself in over his head again."

"I would never. Not in a million years. You make me sick," I spat back.

"Not as sick as your pops looks right now, huh?"

I thought of the near-legendary street story about him. How he poisoned his pet sharks with bleach when his club was shut down. Zambi was as predatory and cold as them, that much I knew. And this basement felt like my very own tank that he held the Clorox to.

"You need to leave. I will call the police." Even to myself, my threat sounded empty and weak.

Zambi let out a thunderous laugh.

"Police? What for? I'm just visiting a good friend who owes me some money. Why would they need to get involved?"

"Because you're caught and you're going to jail for good this time."

He stepped closer to me, his eyes so penetrating and dark. The curly black hair was under a cap yet he motioned out of habit to put it behind his ears.

"Okay. Call them," he said, and paused. "Never mind. I'll call them." Like a madman, he hollered "Police! Oh police! Come out come out wherever you are!"

Only when the other man emerged from the shadows did I realize

Zambi wasn't patronizing me. I saw his crocodile shoes first. Then the gun tucked into the side of his tailored pants.

"Virgil? What the hell are you doing here?"

"Only protecting my interest, honey," he said suavely.

"I don't understand."

"But it was only a matter of time before you did," he responded. "Sure, I threw you a curve ball by planting some information in those two dim-witted cops' heads, but you would have figured Captain Bernett always has and always will walk the straight and narrow. Then again, he's had an easier ride than me or, say, someone like good old Zambi here. So, when some of my friends around the streets heard that a young, raven-haired reporter walked right into his bar to payoff her dear dad's debt, I thought there's only one girl brazen enough to pull that off. Sure enough, Zambi told me it was you. That's some pretty valuable information for someone like me who needs to protect my assets."

"Your assets or your ass?" I said with rage-filled disdain.

He chuckled. 'Well, both now that you mention it. I couldn't have someone jeopardizing my side money or my day job, now could I?" he said.

"So you decided to have your disgusting friend here try to kill my father?"

"No, no. What kind of person do you think I am?" he asked rhetorically. "It's a small wound that he will clearly heal from. Consider it more of a message."

"The message being let a crooked cop be?"

"Exactly. Your dad deserved a lesson, too." Zambi chimed in. "I mean, do I really look like the type of man who walks around with people owing me money?"

Virgil agreed. 'We killed two birds with one stone, that's all. Actually, make that three, since we eventually would have beat your dad enough to get him to call you over here. He held out pretty good, that he did. But your intuition must have been spot on because here you are. Now be a good little girl and pledge to keep your mouth shut. The case closed a while ago. Your dad's debt is cleared."

He inched closer. His warm breath snaked around my ears.

"Agreed?" he urged confidently.

I nodded.

"All right, all right." He snapped his fingers and smiled widely.

"Now get the hell out of here," I snapped, my voice an icy stranger to even myself.

Virgil patted my moaning father on the head. "Fair enough. Let's go, man," he said to his criminal friend.

Zambi veered behind. He had his own agenda.

Before I could slide my coat off to press against my father's bleeding wound, he kicked him in the back. A holler that sent shivers down me followed. The sound was more animal than human and I cringed at the sight of its origin. Zambi smiled.

"Bobby don't forget me. We had such a memorable time after all.

"And we have some memories to make, you and me," he said, stepping toward me, so close that his chin was centimeters from my forehead. His cold fingers departed his personal space and slivered across my cheeks.

Virgil looked back from the stairs. "Come on, man. Let's go."

"You go ahead. I'm not quite done over here."

"Get away from her!" my father yelled.

"That's right, you pig. Get the hell away from me."

His grip tightened on my face and moved downward. There was no telling where it headed, but I knew from the sinister look in his eyes that no decency ran through him.

"Let's go," Virgil called. "This wasn't in the plan."

"I have my own plans," he laughed.

With all my might, I pushed him away. It was a fruitless endeavor as it only encouraged him.

When he charged at me again, I reached into my coat pocket. Like I said, I was prepared this time.

The gun from my father's glove box, the one I saw on our gambling trip, the one I plucked from his Jeep on my way into the house, fired once. It wasn't as easy or glamorous as in the movies. Then again, nothing is.

For starters, it was piercingly loud. My ears rang to the point where I could barely hear Jaws' screams. And it was harder to handle than I imagined. After all, I had never so much as picked up a gun and there I was standing before a man I just shot at close range with a weapon that felt neither sleek nor precise but clunky. Still, to his dismay, the aim was precise, even if it was a less-harmful shoulder shot.

One could call me many things: stubborn, reckless, broken, but no one ever said I made the same mistake twice. Had that weapon not been tucked in my coat pocket, I would have never trudged the same stairs to where my attacker greeted me last time.

"Take that, you cold bastard. I told you to leave."

A stunned Virgil couldn't help but let an amused chuckle escape. "Roni, you really are a bad-ass, aren't you?"

I turned the gun toward him. He intercepted the barrel's line to him with his own Glock. "I said you're a bad-ass. But don't test me. I won't be so sweet."

Zambi mustered the strength to approach me again. This time rage replaced lust. "Kill this bitch."

"Now, let's not overreact." Virgil said calmly.

"That's not overreacting. You don't want to see overreacting," he spat.

Then he reached for his own gun, positioned in his pants behind his back.

"Maybe this will be a family lesson. How 'bout that, Bobby? Didn't you lose your old lady a bit ago? How about your daughter joining her?"

I closed my eyes. I saw my mother's kind face. Her warm brown eyes, her dark hair. Her warm gentle hands caressed me. I felt the presence of God.

And then they stormed down the stairs.

"Freeze! Get your hands up now! Virgil, now!"

Zambi and Virgil dropped their guns. Captain Bernett and Detective Ubanks stood at the bottom of the stairs with their guns raised.

"Hey, it's all a misunderstanding," Virgil began. "Tell them, Roni." His threatening eyes pierced me. I didn't speak for what seemed like hours.

"Roni?" Captain Bernett interjected.

I turned to him. "It's not a misunderstanding. This is exactly how it looks."

"It's cops like you who give us a bad name," Detective Ubanks scolded Virgil. "Let's bring you to your new home. Maybe you two will be cellmates."

A familiar-looking man came down the stairs to escort the wounded Zambi and shocked Virgil out. When he saw my face it registered--he was the man eying Virgil in the Starbucks. The guy winked at me.

"He's from another department. Had to keep my eyes and ears on him," Bernett told me. "And on you, too."

"I'm sorry I ever doubted you," I told him sheepishly.

"It doesn't change anything," he smiled.

Paramedics raced my father to the hospital with me at his side. I held his hand, clung on to it actually, fearing it would turn cold. Fortunately, the warmth circulated through every finger that grasped me as his eyes pleaded for forgiveness. They voyaged on a hapless mission. I already forgave him for abandoning me, for failing me, for putting me in harm's way. My mother's radiance permeated my veins and I had no room inside me for anger. I was just...grateful. His body and soul were here on earth. We had that much to work with at least. The flaws that surfaced would be hell to deal with, but we could face them head on, together.

"I love you, Rani," he whispered in a strained voice.

"Love ya, too, dad."

And I meant it with my whole heart.

Chapter Twenty-Two

THE STORY RAN ON THE FRONT PAGE.

Barb was kind enough to let me borrow her laptop as I waited for my father to get out of surgery in Mt. Perry's Hospital North, which is right next to Natalia's Children's Hospital. I had sent Barb a text about what happened and also to check in on Natalia. Armed with her laptop and a hot cup of coffee, she rushed over sweetly to me like only she would.

Even Randall the Suit called my cell phone to personally congratulate me on such an "exclusive, in-depth piece." I thanked him politely. Daddini, never one to stay away from big news, came in to the newsroom well after his shift to edit the story.

"Glad you're OK, kiddo," he said before gloating that we beat Internal Affairs in their own investigation--and also blew the media competition out of the water.

That day, as I reluctantly couldn't bask in the glory of my career high, I sat on the uncomfortable chair outside the surgical recovery room. It didn't have my butt imprint like the one in my sister's room did. I was beginning to think I'd never rid myself of hospitals, their potent disinfectant smell and endless hours waiting to find out what was wrong or what was right.

In this case, the stab wound didn't significantly harm any organs and he was sewn back together in hours. Mt. Perry's is especially good at treating stab and bullet wounds. It seems they get quite a few of those cases.

When I was ushered in, he was resting peacefully. It was the first time since before the accident his face forgot tragedy. Morphine is pretty good at doing that.

And, at that moment, I forged past hesitation. I went to his bedside. I leaned down, like I had so many times at Natalia's side. Like I had so many times before kneeling at my mother's freshly dug grave. And, like I did next to my bed to pray for Jeremy and his family, whom I could only imagine missed him every day.

I shook the wave of anger I had been riding since the accident. Harboring ill feelings just didn't seem appropriate. At that moment, as nurses ushered by in the hallway and the IV beeped because the battery was low, I realized I did not need him to realize his mistakes, to fess up and apologize. He knew the error of his ways and I knew something even more poignant: It wasn't necessary for him to say or do anything for me to forgive him. So, with a deep breath in and out, I did. I released the hatred I had been harboring, I let go of the confusion and hurt. I was Flora's daughter, after all.

When he would wake, I would be there. A patient and loyal child who treated him eons better than he had his own little girl. His eyes were teary. It was difficult to speak. He requested ice chips and I spoon-fed them to him. He touched my hand, mouthing "thank you," and I only smiled in return.

The next few days required me to go back and forth from the hospitals. Natalia was the same sleeping child as usual while my father was walking the halls in his hospital gown and totes in no time. A police guard was outside his room for the first forty-eight hours after the crime. By the end of the second day, Zambi and Virgil were formally arraigned on a slew of charges, including attempted murder and home invasion. It was quite the high-profile case, so I guess it was not so surprising that Gale Babes had weaseled her way in, convincing Randall she was the right one for the job. He happily obliged because, even though I find her pathetic, she does make pretty good arguments. Daddini grunted at the assignment. He loathed working with her. I told him I didn't mind a dog salivating at a bone; it's in their nature and sometimes it's better to just let it be.

My first-person account, a tad out of the norm for a daily newspaper, of what happened with the cop corruption and the finality of Virgil and

Zambi being busted in my parents' basement made its way across the Internet, picked up by several major news sites. I was asked to do numerous national cable news interviews--all of which I declined. It just wasn't my style and I had more important things on my plate. Nevertheless, word travels fast. So fast that Luke was at my apartment doorstep when I went home to shower and change clothes before heading back to Natalia a couple days after the story ran.

I wanted to tell him I was sorry, that I was confused and scared when I saw him last. That I was falling in love with him. Or, rather, I already had. But when I began to talk, he just looked at me with those beautiful brown eyes and said, "I know." He held me tightly, saying only once "I love you, Roni." And this time, I wasn't afraid.

We were in bed together, just holding each other. I felt his breath on the top of my head as I rested my cheek on his bare chest. The tip of my hair brushed over the girl's mane pictured in his tattoo.

"She was a neighborhood girl who had a crush on me," he said quietly as if reading my mind. "I was about fifteen; she was ten. Like a typical boy, I thought she was a pesky little kid. A real hotshot. Never made time to talk to her or even acknowledge her presence. One day, I was walking down the street to meet my friends at the school playground to shoot hoops. I guess she tried to get my attention by riding her bike and letting go of the handlebars. I just kept walking."

I listened intently, afraid that speaking would change his mind and he'd withhold the rest of the story.

"By the time I was at the next block, I heard the tires screech. Some young guys in an Impala had their bass booming, speeding down the street. I only heard her scream when it was too late. They didn't even stop to help. I called for someone, anyone to give her CPR-or at least stop the bleeding. No one could hear me; no one was around. I'll never forget her eyes, so dark, so fearful. She finally got my attention by dying right in front of me."

A tear rolled down his temple. I held back my own.

"I vowed from that day I would never stand by as someone needed help. That's why I got into my line of work."

My palms pressed down on the side of his jaw. I kissed him slowly to let him know I meant it.

"You saved Natalia."

Chapter Twenty-Three

I SOON FOUND OUT THAT I WASN'T THE ONLY ONE MAKING NEWS.

A New York Post headline read, "Fiery Actress a Cold Killer?" That was the most sensational. Others stated something more to the effect of "Broadway Actress Accused of Killing Chicagoan."

McConner's widow had hired an attorney to find out whether police followed protocol in the case since it was opened and shut in such a short time. The legwork quickly led to Sierra. It wasn't that difficult at all. He and McConner's widow brought the story to anyone who would listen. To his credit, her father stepped up to the plate to save Sierra. Only, since he knew their relationship would put more fuel on the flames, he had another person in the department speak about the case. Sgt. Terry Bolia dismissed the hype, saying that police were well aware of what happened and did not charge her with the crime because she was a victim who had been defending herself.

Showbiz has a funny way of digesting drama. The news only made Sierra more sought-after for film roles. And once the story of Lola de Cannes broke, she was an even hotter commodity.

Turns out, Lola had saved a sample of the tea--the tea I suspected during that backstage visit was tampered with--that her understudy was serving her and found a strange concoction of herbal remedies meant to "detox" someone. That intense detoxification process usually means repeated vomiting and diarrhea. Lola, along with her expensive attorney, filed a civil suit against my old friend, claiming loss of wages and emotional and physical distress. I believe the New York Daily News headline then was "Illegally Blonde." Oddly enough, Lola dropped the case when Sierra's star began shining brightly because she didn't want to be seen publicly as her enemy.

Sierra's ruthlessness left two people in her taillights and put her in the spotlight as she always longed. We hadn't spoken since that day in New York and I wasn't sure if we ever would. Our paths veered in different directions; a lot of water had yet to flow under the bridge.

A few days before I was to return to The Chronicle, I swung by my dad's hospital room to check on his progress and pay him some company for the day. But the white sheets and light blanket were neatly tucked in and he was nowhere to be seen. I scanned the room for traces of occupancy. Perhaps he was showering or strolling the halls again. I plopped down on the bed. The stench of bleach from the sheets burned my nose. I flipped through channels without locating entertainment.

"He left this for you," a gentle voice approached from the doorway.

The nurse handed me an envelope and walked away to grant privacy. A letter with my father's writing unfolded this message:

Dearest Veronica,

There's no doubt in my mind you have your mother's strength and courage to make it through tough times. You've certainly displayed that in these past several weeks. While I, on the other hand, have been a complete disappointment to your sister, to you, your mother and myself. I wish I could rectify the situation, that I could change who I've become despite my sorrow. But I can't. I would be doing more damage to stay, with all my demons, than to go off and leave you girls in peace. My gambling problems soured every aspect of my life, but one thing I can offer is the house your mother and I paid off before she died. It's a home for your sister, the only one she's ever known. I boldly ask you for a favor--although I don't deserve to ask you anything--and that is to move out of your apartment to raise your sister in the house we were a family in. Always know I love you and her more than words can describe. And, remember what I said... that sometimes the thing your life misses *helps more than the thing which it gets.*

Sincerely,

Your Father

Behind the letter was the deed to the house. This had been in the works for some time. I didn't waste time grieving. I was all cried out anyway.

Chapter Twenty-Four

I SAT AT FRENZIE'S CAFÉ FOR HOURS, PLUGGED INTO MY COMPUTER AND SIPPING AN EMBARASSING AMOUNT OF CAFFEINE. I was doing nothing and everything at once. Pondering the strangeness, sorrow and discovery of the past couple months.

My father's letter was folded neatly in my brown slouch bag along with the latest news of the day from Gale Babes' coverage of the court case involving Virgil and Zambi. There were lots of stories out of the trial, but this one was different. No one could deliver a subpoena for my father to testify; he was like the snow flurries punctuating the season's change- declaring their presence and then drifting into oblivion. I opened the article, cut straight from the top of the front page. I beheld a picture of a woman on the stand before me. Her expression was focused, spine like steel. She was responding to the prosecutor with the two defendants in the background, intent on her every word. The caption: Chronicle reporter Veronica Maye testifies about the horrifying assault, break-in and corruption case. I could have fought against revealing my notes, my sources, my reporting, but it wouldn't have put those two behind bars for assaulting my father. I was a reporter and a witness on the stand, but more a daughter than anything else.

Reporters I've known who go overseas to cover a war are told to decompress when their assignment is done. They are supposed to go somewhere else besides home, a middle ground from the atrocities of Iraq or Afghanistan and the humdrum of daily life in the US. Some go to Europe, others the Caribbean. I felt racked through sizzling desert sand. My decompression was a coffeehouse-a midway point from the war inside the courtroom and my apartment.

I typed "coma success stories" into my Google search. When done reading testimonials of people who had come out of comas successfully, I then turned my attention to YouTube miraculous viral accounts of coma survivors walking, talking and living normal lives. That would be Natalia, I told myself. She is going to be a success story, too. "God, please answer my prayer." I whispered.

A warm hand clasped my shoulder.

I looked up in surprise. He smiled at me the way he always did.

"Hey kiddo."

"Hi Daddini."

"Private moment or do you want some company?"

I extended my hand to the seat next to me. He sat quietly.

"You know, kiddo, to say you've been through a lot in these last couple months would be the biggest understatement I could conjure. There really isn't anything to explain what's happened to you. You're a good kid. Talented as hell and smart, very smart. I've seen a lot of terrible things in the profession. People kill each other for no damn good reason. People in positions of authority elected to do good then lie and steal. And honest hard-working people lose their jobs, their homes and their pride. I can't tell you exactly why these types of things happen. All I can tell you is they do; we have proof of it in print each day. But one thing I can say-and this is what matters most-is that it's how we all cope, stand up and face another day that makes life worth living. That makes good people like you write your own history no matter what took place in the past."

He stood up, rather gruffly, as he reached for my shoulder again. I met his hand, placing mine on top of his. He smiled and walked away.

"I'm proud of you, Roni," he called back to me.

I beamed at the words.

When I jingled the apartment door, I could tell Scoop's paw steps were nearby. I patted his purring little body and gathered him into my arms. And, like a child, I hugged my buddy who seemed to understand all my hardship and woes and offered his affection to comfort me.

"Nice," I told myself. "My best friend in the world is a cat."

Phase Two of my decompressing had me take to the shower for a long hot session. I always feel emotionally and physically drained when covering a big court case. Being part of one had me feeling even worse. Luke had gone back to Chicago for work. I missed him already. We found a commonality in our bond, one of a shared desire to be together. With that newfound mutual discovery, staying away seemed harder each minute. If he were here, I'd have an actual person to hug and not one that licks his own butt, I thought. "No offense, Scoop," I told him in passing. I sunk into pillows that invited me to sleep for what seemed like hours. In reality, the phone woke me up just minutes later.

"Roni, you better get over here."

"Barb?" I said sleepily. "What's the matter? Is she OK?"

My heart thumped like a stampede.

"Stay calm and come here as quickly as you can," she advised me patiently.

"I'm on my way."

It was like I was on an airport conveyer belt that shot me past a backdrop of hospital rooms, desks and lounges. The plane was departing and I needed desperately to make it to my gate.

Barb's teary eyes stared at me from down the hall. She held out her arms, placing them on my shaky shoulders.

"Barb. Tell me she..."

"She..." she said through short, panting breaths, opposite of her patience over the phone.

"Say it!" I couldn't bear it any more. "Just tell me!"

"OK," she composed herself. "She's awake!"

"What?" I couldn't believe my ears. I shamefully had prepared myself for the worst. "She's awake?"

"Yes!"

I rushed to the room in a clumsy run. There she was, with her eyes open.

"Natalia, honey. I'm here. I'm here." I held her hand gently.

She looked around the room with uneasiness. Her eyes flickered. She attempted to talk but nothing came out. Realizing this, her eyes widened in fear and confusion.

"It's all right. It's all right. Take your time, honey. You'll be able to ask me anything and I'll be right here to answer."

Her beautiful light eyes and long locks punctuated a pale, soft face. She looked around the room again and then back at me.

"R. .. rr... oni," she mustered.

"Yes, love." Tears poured from my eyes.

"Wheer... whe... where I am?" her voice faintly asked.

"You're in the hospital. There was a car accident, but you'll be OK. You'll be better than OK. I love you so much."

"Wheer... werrr... where's mom?" she asked. "I_I wa-wa want mommy."

She tried lifting her arms, but they were frail and weak. This frustrated her to no end. She flexed her feet a bit unintentionally and I was relieved to see the movement.

"Mom?" she said again, pleading for a response.

I grasped for words. This moment had been hinged at the corner of my mind for weeks yet I was unprepared. She squinted in confusion and I started to speak. But it was too late. The strain of talking and attempting to move was too much for her long-idle body. She fell asleep.

For four hours I sat by her, waiting for her to come to. Barb brought me coffee before her shift ended and she went home to rest. When Natalia's eyes finally opened again with the same questioning stare, I knew how to respond.

"Remember how we talked about how Amelia Earhart disappeared? She went on that flight but never came back? Well, we talked about how she may have gotten lost or maybe had a plane crash. But what I really think is she flew to Heaven. She's up there right now with the angels, doing exactly what she loves, flying around the clouds and giving everyone a show.

"Well, it's sort of like that with mom. She would have loved to stay here on earth, but she had to go to Heaven. She's watching you from there and she's really proud of you. She knows you're a fighter and that you'll feel better soon. She loves you."

Natalia began to drift into sleep. "I love her, too."

I swept her hair off her face and kissed her forehead. Tears rushed down my cheeks like they did in the ambulance in the first moments she drifted off. The chair beside her bed made a screech as I pushed back toward the wall on the tile floor. Kneeling down made my shoulders level with the edge of the bed in an awkward prayer stance. Nevertheless, I clasped my hands on the bed, carefully away from her tubes, and asked God to guide us, to protect us and to help us during this difficult time and every moment thereafter.

Chapter Twenty-Five

BY NOW, SNOW BLANKETED THE GROUND AND THE CRUMPLED AUTUMN LEAVES WERE GHOSTS OF THE SEASON PRIOR.

The apartment was packed, cleaned and ready to lease to someone else. My belongings, from plates to shoes, were squeezed into a U-haul for unloading at my parents' house. It would be another few months before Natalia's release from the rehabilitation center that helped coach her mobility. She had gained enough strength to lift herself up to stand, walk and even hop a bit. Moving like a normal child her age wasn't feasible yet.

Audibly, she was phenomenal. She loved reading aloud from her schoolbooks, which I retrieved from her classrooms. Since I met with the superintendent to explain the unusual situation, he agreed to let her continue on the curriculum she left off on in order to prevent falling behind a grade. That required double the work, since she missed so much while she was in the coma. But there was little else to do between stints at the rehab center.

One of the things she found most enjoyable was going to the play area with other patients. Lively and bright, she made friends fast. I coaxed the nurses to let her go often, to make up for lost time socializing with other kids. Natalia couldn't be more in her element with her peers. I often would stand at the door to watch her blissful face as she role-played with dolls. While I stood undetected at the door one day, she selected two dolls, one small with curls and the other larger with straight black hair.

"Hi Momma," she had the little one say to the other.

"Hi, Nat," the older one said. "Let's go to the movies and then shopping today."

"OK, Momma."

"You're my favorite kid."

"I know, Momma."

I smiled to myself at the innocent exchange. The nurses and physicians told me it was healthy that she role-played to understand her emotions.

When I walked up, she greeted me with a bear hug.

"What do you have here, Nat?"

"Just dolls."

"They're pretty. What are their names?"

"This one is Natalia," she pointed to the little one. "And this one is Roni," she said of the larger one. She searched my face for approval. My presence had been detected all along. I tried to hide my surprise by just offering her a warm smile. "That's nice, Nat."

Chapter Twenty-Six

TOXICOLOGY TESTS TAKE WEEKS, MONTHS EVEN. As a journalist, covering fresh news every day, you often forget about the case by the time results come in. During that time frame, so much has already happened. So it was unexpected when I logged on to my computer one day, in my usual check on news in other cities, to see a Chicago Tribune headline saying "Coroner: State Senator's Passenger Clean of Drugs."

Below it, the story read: "Newly elected Illinois Sen. Gavin Remer's close friend died in a two-vehicle accident last fall. Despite unsubstantiated reports the pair used cocaine moments before crashing into another car in an accident that claimed a Detroit-area woman's life, police and Remer strongly denied drug use. Recently released toxicology findings show that Remer's passenger who died had used alcohol but not narcotics prior to the crash."

The article went on to offer Gavin's comments: "It is very sad that my good friend and my name were tarnished by fiction and tabloid-style rumors. I hope he can now rest in peace and righteousness without further reports of this tragic incident."

When asked for more of an explanation for the accident, he

responded: "I look forward to continuing to serve the people of my senatorial district and all of Illinois, and maintaining some privacy in my personal life with my new wife."

A picture of Gavin and Sarah was on the side of the article. It was a photo from their wedding announcement. Just below it, another file picture of Gavin was included. This one showed him with his brimming father and Harvey on the night Gavin won the election, just after Carl took the governor's office.

About two weeks later, Gavin was back in the limelight. This time, there was no hiding behind his father's coattails. Racked with sadness and anger, Jeremy's family had hired a private detective to follow Gavin around town. Apparently, they suspected the accident wasn't as innocent as he suggested and were highly suspicious of him after the drug rumors. What they found was something that shocked even me.

Their private eye wasn't some schmuck off the street. He was a recently retired police officer who savored working away from the politically charged police department hierarchy. Having his own private investigation company afforded ex-Officer Smansky, the initial investigator into Gavin's crash, license to do things he could not do as a cop, such as secretly videotape someone without a warrant authorized by a judge. It was that type of flexibility that motivated him to install hidden cameras in Gavin's regular hotel suite. The suite was situated inside the Drake Hotel, where Gavin often retreated for so-called business brunches and other work. Smansky didn't have to explain how he managed to place one tiny panoramic-view camera above the mirror by the bed and another near the medicine cabinet in the bathroom.

Sure, the footage was far from legal and would never hold up in court. But it didn't matter. By the time video of Gavin snorting large sums of cocaine - and with women who were clearly not Sarah -- hit the Internet, the damage was done. His reputation ruined, doubt-albeit unproved-of his account of the accident soared. His political career was torpedoed. One might suspect that his father, with Harvey coaching him, would maneuver around the debacle. But, like a true politician, he thought of his own survival and left his son to sink in a sea of error. Calling the situation "disappointing," Carl Remer moved on to the next task-setting his sights on becoming running mate to his party's next presidential candidate. Gavin's life was suddenly like the metal scraps and shards of glass left in his emotional rearview the night of the accident. Sarah left him soon after.

Chapter Twenty-Seven

I WAS UNPACKING IN MY PARENTS' HOUSE. It felt strange taking over the master bedroom, but it was the closest to Natalia's room and I wanted to be right by her side. Adele's voice streamed from my CD player as Scoop purred on top of the bubble wrap. Despite the cold outside, a ray of sunlight poured in from the window and embraced us with warmth.

My mother's clothes were neatly stacked on the dresser. Each sweater and pair of pants would be stowed away in rubber bins in the basement. I didn't wash them again. Her scent was in the fabric, just the way I hoped it would always remain.

From one of my boxes, I pulled out a small case. I handled it so gently you'd think it was part of a shrine. In some small way, it was. Inside lay my mother's regal-looking bracelet. I plucked it out from the case to twist it between my fingertips.

"Hey, where do you want your towels?" called the voice from the hall.

"Just in the linen closet in the hallway, please."

"Sure thing."

Luke entered the room.

"Was that your mom's?"

"Yeah."

"It's beautiful."

"I'm going to give it to Natalia when she gets out. It will replace her hospital wristband for good. I just need to get it sized."

"That's really sweet of you." He came closer, bent down and kissed my lips softly.

"I'm just a sweet kind of girl," I smiled.

"Well, I wouldn't go that far," he said as he kissed me again -- this time more passionately than before. "Oh, hey, while you're getting that sized, can you take something in for me to get fitted?"

"Well, I wouldn't go that far," he said as he kissed me again -- this time more passionately than before. "Oh, hey, while you're getting that sized, can you take something in for me to get fitted?"

"Sure." I put back the bracelet. "Just give it to me before you go back tomorrow for work."

"Yeah, I can even give it to you now if you want."

"OK. I'll take it to Harold's Jewelry down the street. They're pretty reasonable and fast."

Luke reached into his pocket and knelt in front of me. "What are you doing?" I asked.

"I need to see if this fits." He pulled out a princess-cut diamond ring. "So I need you to try it on."

"I can't."

His face fell and he started to pick himself up off the floor.

"First," I told him. "You need to ask."

A wave of relief swept over his face. He got down on one knee, holding the ring in front of his chest.

"Veronica Maye, will you marry me?"

"Yes, I will."

When he got up from the floor, he took me in his arms. The man I was meant to marry led me to the bedroom. Before he kissed me lovingly, he reached for something inside his bag on the nightstand.

"Good, now I no longer have to hold this for ransom."

"My shawl!"

Chapter Twenty-Eight

THE COP BEAT WAS THE SAME AS EVER. Grueling, exacting and adrenaline-inducing. There wasn't much I didn't see or anything I didn't hear. It was nonstop and my sources like Captain Bernett were happy to have me back. They trusted me and we had a bond in some weird way. So, it may have been surprising to him and others that I wanted off that beat. I had had enough of death. I wanted to write about life. Daddini, in typical Daddini fashion, decided to stand in the middle of the newsroom and rap about my request to move to Features.

He put the Old English "D" cap on backward and bounced around with his faux gold chain.

"It's a new day

"for 'lil Veronica Maye.

"She ain't havin' a good time

"wit crime

"and all that stuff.

"So she's off to Features to write about fluff."

"Boo!" I said as I hurled a plastic tomato at him. I bought it especially for this type of occasion. Carter laughed hysterically. Gale just had a puss on her face.

"You don't want a piece of this," he said with his best tough-guy voice.

When he returned to his desk, we all clapped. Then he took off his cap and chain, looked around the newsroom and said, "What the hell are you waiting for, people? Get back to work. We're approaching first-edition deadline!"

I thought I knew what stories were coming each and every day, but the one that came next brought optimism to even the most hardened journo. The announcement took place on live TV that night. From the thirty-minute speech, headlines were written around the world. The one at my paper stated, "President Declares War Over."

So my first Features assignment was interviewing dozens of families with loved ones fighting overseas and how they were looking forward to their return. Their accounts were heartfelt and historical. It was the most rewarding story of my short career and the best time to get into Features.

By spring, the sod planted around my mother's grave covered the uneven patches of dirt. Freshly picked petunias from her garden were placed in front of the new granite tombstone I bought. I dusted off loose grass from my purple-and-white floral skirt and beige sandals before I walked past the cemetery gates. This time, I didn't hold my breath. It seemed unnecessary to do so. Instead, I exhaled, releasing the pain and suffering I had overcome. A life without suffering was not guaranteed to me, or anyone else for that matter. A life with love, however, was granted. And, having that, I was thankful.

I drove to another cemetery in Detroit, to walk over to another grave. This one was freshly dug and surrounded by flowers. I didn't think he would appreciate those as much as what I had to give, though. I retrieved a pack of cigarettes from my purse. Along with the lighter, I placed them on top of the dirt. I submitted them and their grip on me. They had claimed his life and I refused to let them do the same to me.

I drove back to The Chronicle. Outside the building, I stood where we had stood so many times before. I thought about our conversations. I thought about his daughters and wife. I thought about his talent, vocabulary and integrity. I thought of his silly raps. And, while I pondered all the deep things he said, I saw the scraggly homeless man he had pointed out to me when I was ready to walk away from the paper for good. He was leaving the soup kitchen inside the old church across the street.

Eager to learn more, I crossed the street and entered the church. There the soup kitchen director, whose beard was as thick as his Armenian accent, greeted me.

"You want to know about the man who just left?"

"Yes. You see I was wondering about his family and the career he once had. Perhaps there's a way to encourage him to return to his normal life."

He looked at me with confusion.

"This is his normal life. That's Rod. He's a schizophrenic and he's been coming here for as long as I can remember. I opened this soup kitchen in the early eighties, so he must have been in his late teens then. He doesn't have a family or a career. You must have him confused with someone else."

"Oh, I'm sorry," I muttered sheepishly.

When I got back across the street, I leaned against the newspaper building and shook my head in amusement.

"Daddini, you scoundrel."

Conclusion

I WAS PUSHING NATALIA ON THE SWING when Luke walked into the backyard clad in his firefighter uniform. It was his third week with the Garden Falls Fire Department and that meant he had four straight days at home. Our home, the three of us, along with Luke's dogs that played and panted in the yard.

My ring glistened in the sunlight, feeling completely at ease on my finger and in its setting. It wasn't much smaller than the one Gavin gave me, but it was lighter in every sense. Luke beamed at me from across the yard. He had taken on the role of big brother to Nat and she enjoyed explaining her love of airplanes to him every chance she got. The sun hit her little face and, in turn, her face lit mine. Her laughter serenaded my heart and I could sense my mother's presence in her joy.

"Look, Momma," she called to me. It was her desire to do so and I didn't try to sway her from it. She pointed at the sky.

The looming jets roared above toward the airbase.

"Look at them soar," I said, my eyes never leaving her smiling face.

The End